Praise for Heather Clay's

LOSING CHARLOTTE

"Friction between sisters has served as a plot staple since the dawn of the novel. . . . Handled properly, it provides a near-perfect occasion for exploring the societal and familial expectations placed on young women, as Heather Clay does in her introspective first novel. . . . Clay beautifully portrays the awkward dynamic of family gatherings. . . . Bold and confident."   —*The New York Times Book Review*

"Loss is painfully inevitable, and it is harsh—Heather Clay's debut novel *Losing Charlotte* is a heart-stinging reminder of this truth. . . . These characters are so real that their struggles and their pain of not having a chance to say goodbye makes your heart ache." —*Elle*

"Explores the unnamable complexities of the grieving process, and the ways in which our understanding of those we've lost can continue to deepen even after they're gone."   —*Minneapolis Star Tribune*

"Heather Clay is a graceful and assured new writer with a great gift for character: the people in her fiction are as complex, beautiful, and real as they are in life. . . . A spellbinding first novel."
   —Lauren Groff, author of *The Monsters of Templeton*

HEATHER CLAY

LOSING CHARLOTTE

Heather Clay is a graduate of Middlebury College and
Columbia University's School of the Arts. She has pub-
lished short fiction in *The New Yorker* and written for
Parenting. She lives in New York City with her husband and their two daughters. This is her first novel.

LOSING CHARLOTTE

A Novel

HEATHER CLAY

Vintage Contemporaries
Vintage Books
A Division of Random House, Inc.
New York

FIRST VINTAGE CONTEMPORARIES EDITION, APRIL 2011

The Library of Congress has cataloged the Knopf edition as follows:
Clay, Heather.
Losing Charlotte / Heather Clay. — 1st ed.
p. cm.
1. Sisters—Fiction. 2. Loss (Psychology)—Fiction. 3. Psychological fiction.
4. Domestic fiction. I. Title.
PS3603.L3865F63 2010
813'.6—dc22   2009023439

Vintage ISBN: 978-1-4000-3171-9

Book design by Maggie Hinders

www.vintagebooks.com

Printed in the United States of America
10 9 8 7 6 5 4 3 2 1

For Nick
And gratia Jenny

LOSING
CHARLOTTE

PROLOGUE

CHARLOTTE WAS SPEAKING to her already. Not waiting there, in the dark, for Knox to crest out of sleep, but already talking, low and fast. Knox rubbed her ears, blinked, and tried to sit up. Her nightgown ticked against the sheet, making the brief flash of static that Knox thought of as "bed lightning"—Charlotte's words. Charlotte had words that Knox tried to resist, but couldn't.

She was a shape, hunched over Knox and saying I'm going now, I'm meeting Cash, go back to sleep.

Don't go, Knox thought. But what she said was: Don't tell me. I told you I don't want to know. Stop telling me.

It's not like I'm having sex with him, Charlotte said.

Shut up, Knox whispered.

He hasn't asked me. I think he's scared. He's only fifteen.

Knox's attempt to laugh quietly, incredulously, sounded like a hiss. So are *you*, she said.

Charlotte wiggled her shoulders a little. Maybe tonight's the night, she said. If I feel like it. You never know. Hold down the fort for me.

Why are you acting like this, Knox said.

Charlotte never answered questions like that. Why would she? She lifted herself off the bed, crossed the room, and let herself into the hall so quietly that Knox hated her even more, hated that her talent for stealth was just another admirable thing about her, among too many.

Wish me luck, Charlotte said, her head appearing briefly around the jamb, then dissolving into the dark again.

Good luck, Knox said, despite herself.

She waited, breathing as softly as possible so she could hear. After a minute there was just one sound, a small creak, to signal Charlotte's movement through the house. Knox felt she knew the floorboard that had made it, just as she knew everything, every bit of space that lay under their roof. She knew the roof, too, had crawled onto it from the window of her mother's dressing room twice before and sat on a loose shingle, looking out at the scarecrow cast of the metal television antennae, the spiky landscape of storm rods. And below, she knew the banisters upon which, if she squinted, she could make out fingerprints in the polish, and smudges from all the gripping and sweat and dinner grease and soap and dirt from the yard and the fields outside. It was all here, all the evidence and effluvia of a family's happiness, swimming around them. Knox could see it clearly, but all Charlotte could do was step on a creaky board on her way out, and probably not even register the sound it made.

Knox pulled the sheet taut, arranged it under her armpits, patting it around her body. She would sit, vigilant. It would be easier than sleeping, hot and anxious as she'd get trying find her way back to rest. Rest couldn't come because Charlotte had been caught once. She had made their mother believe that she'd only been on the porch for ten minutes, having gone out "to think." Knox, of course, knew otherwise, though she hadn't asked to. That night, standing at the top of the stairs, she had mentally begged her mother to ask: Get dressed, to think? Wear eyeliner, to think? But Charlotte was safe that time—safe in the way their mother struggled to keep the hope off her face, and failed. It was beaming off her like heat.

"Think, honey?" she had said. "What about? Are you all right?" She meant: School, a boy, something worse? Anything was all right if it meant that Charlotte would talk. She had taken to disappearing into silences in a way that none of them had expected. She had new breasts, still nubbly but there, under her shirt. Her hands—everything about her was long now, more real somehow, taking up more room.

Charlotte glanced at Knox from her place at the bottom of the stairs on that particular night as their mother waited. She kept her eyes on Knox and said, "No. I don't know." Knox pleaded in her head for Charlotte to make something up, to ask for help for something, however far-fetched, but Charlotte gazed through her, concentrating on a point in space beyond her head. Charlotte shifted her weight; what their mother couldn't seem to remember for long was that her sister hated questions and tended to harden under a prolonged gaze. She looked, to Knox, like she'd been tapped on the shoulder during a game of freeze tag, and was waiting only for the scream of somebody's whistle to explode back into movement and into herself.

"There's a lot on my mind," Charlotte said quietly, finally. Knox glanced away from Charlotte's narrowed eyes and at their mother, who looked as if she'd been hit.

"Is there?" their mother said, trying to smile.

Charlotte looked at the ground and nodded. Freeze, Knox thought. If she were different she might fly down the stairs and tap Charlotte back into life. But she was frozen, too. Someone had tagged them all.

Their mother closed her eyes for a moment, the way she did sometimes when she exhaled the smoke from the cigarettes, Salem Menthols, that Knox knew she regretted as soon as she reached for them, having told herself, and whoever else was around, I shouldn't have this.

"Okay," she said. "We'll talk in the morning." Charlotte turned and began to climb the stairs. Their mother followed, her footsteps thudding too loud for the late hour. They each passed Knox without speaking and went into their rooms. Knox had remained where she was until her legs began to shake from the cold and she didn't want to think of anything anymore.

Knox looked out the window beside her bed. A magnolia was there, just beyond the glass, with great bowls of blossom that smelled like lemons. Charlotte was out there, too. Maybe she had lied about meeting Cash in order to impress Knox and was walking around by herself, "thinking," or standing by the road trying to hitch into town. It was harder lately to know what Charlotte would do, even when it seemed like she was telling you. Knox lay still, and refused to shut her eyes.

BUT THEY OPENED, and she knew she had slept. The tree outside was just visible against a dull, breaking light. Everything was quiet. Knox let herself down from the bed and began to move toward Charlotte's room as if she were still dreaming. She moved onto the landing and down the hall and felt something in the stillness that told her Charlotte wasn't back in her room yet. She reached the door, opened it, took in the tumble and mess, the covers blown open and onto the floor, and saw that this was so.

I'm going, Knox thought, surprised at herself but feeling capable of something brave.

She picked her way downstairs, knowing which steps to avoid but wary of her own tread, which lacked the balance, the levity, of Charlotte's. She was less sure of how far she extended, and often bumped up against things unexpectedly. Knox concentrated hard on steadying herself, coming awake now. She reached the bottom of the stairs and slid the soles of her feet against cold boards until she stood in front of the hall closet, took out a coat of her father's, stilled the tinging hanger with a quick movement, pulled on the pair of old tennis shoes her mother gardened in, let herself out the back door.

The world was loud and busy in an instant. Knox stood on the porch in the damp air, thrilling to the sing of crickets, wind moving across the grass, the surprised nicker of the mare that stood at the fence line bordering the yard. She felt powerful in the knowledge that no one knew where she was—or thought to care. This was what Charlotte must feel on those nights she left them. Except, Knox thought, Charlotte tells me. Like babysitting; Knox was left to watch the memory of prior trouble, to watch the clock and mind the possibilities until their rightful owner returned.

Knox exhaled once, and again, more loudly, listening to her breath get lost among all the other sounds. A bird *whivvi*ed at her from a nearby tree. She stepped off the porch and began to walk.

Charlotte had told her once that she met Cash, the farm manager's son, where their driveway butted up against the road. There was a set of wooden gates and a hedge against which Cash would sit, waiting for her to come. Knox made her way down the walk, past the garage, and onto the blacktop drive, the fields around her becoming more defined with each step. On both sides of the blacktop, land rolled toward barns and toward the stands of locusts and pin oaks that jagged up beyond them. The driveway slanted down and Knox traced it rapidly, her hands opening and closing in the pockets of the coat. Charlotte would be ripped about being looked for. Another one of her words, *ripped. Pissed, freaked, chapped, fucked*—there were others. But Charlotte might surprise, too. She might smile when she saw Knox and say something beatifically kind. If she were naked, she might not scramble for Cash's jeans to hide herself with but instead open her arms to Knox, and laugh a knowing laugh when Knox lay her head against the new breasts, the shocking little flesh cones that Charlotte had shown her, lifting up the recently purchased bra that left red marks where its seams had been. She could be naked, Knox thought. They both could be. She kept moving but more slowly now, unsure of what she wanted.

When the gates came into sight she began to stamp in the loose sneakers as she walked. *Thwock. Thwock. Thwock.*

She stopped after a few paces to listen and, hearing nothing, stamped again.

Then she made for the hedge, a dense wall of boxwood that was taller than she by at least a foot. At the farthest end there was a hollowed-out place that Knox remembered as she drew closer to it. Her father complained about it sometimes: a dead cave of twigs just visible from the road. It needed to be dug up, replaced. Knox moved nearer, took a deep breath, and whispered, "Charlotte?"

Silence.

"Hey. Hello?"

She peered in, and looked away immediately. She had seen a flash of something silver: A zipper? A hook? It had been on the ground, detached from any body. Knox hummed to herself for a moment, then turned to look again. There was a bracelet, their mother's, lying in the twiggy, tamped-down grass. Nothing else. Knox knelt to pick it up, then shuffled on her knees into the hedge cave and sat cross-legged, the big coat insulating her backside and legs from the cold ground. She turned the bracelet in her hands; Charlotte must have borrowed it. Surely without asking. It was heavy, made of thick links and fastened with a turquoise beaded clasp; she never wore it, their mother, but she never threw it away, either. Other things got removed from the suede-covered jewelry box she kept on her bureau, costumey things that had outlived their outfits and uses, but not this.

The dawn grew brighter. Knox slipped the bracelet into a pocket of the coat and started to get up, wondering whether or not she should keep looking for her sister. What would Charlotte say if she were found? If Knox could find her asleep, somewhere hidden, and carry her back to bed, things might be different. The coat stuck to her skin in places, making her feel the parameters and sweat of her body as she emerged from the little cave, dragging branches against one another as she pushed out.

"Hallo," someone called. Knox stopped where she was, as if stillness could make her invisible.

"Hallo," someone called again, louder.

Knox looked up. Gary, the night watchman, stood about five feet from her, swinging the heavy flashlight he carried in one hand, and fingering the collar of his shirt with the other. He looked washed in the thin light, his clothes and face pale.

"I—," Knox began.

Gary squinted at her. He had one of those faces that a life lived at night must make. A face that made it hard to tell what a person was thinking, behind the lines and hard skin. "Better get on home," he said. "Right?"

"Um." Knox said, "I'm sorry. I was—"

"Okay," Gary said. "You get on home."

Knox felt the blood rise, flushing her neck and face. She backed up a step or two, keeping her eyes away from Gary's, then lurched into an awkward half run up the hill, heading straight for the house. She imagined Gary watching her and thought she should slow down, appear calmer—but that would mean allowing him to watch her for a longer time; she wanted nothing but to be out of his sight. She dodged the nettle piles that showed up inky in the light, like little cacti. She sucked in breath as the incline got steeper. Stride. Pant. Stride. Was he laughing, behind her? At the office parties her father held twice a year Gary usually stood, laughing, in a corner, drink in hand. It wasn't a nice laugh, wasn't meant for others to join in. She knew this. People would be surprised at what she knew about them, from watching.

Knox stumbled past the old locust with the hollow in it, the one Charlotte used to make her stick her hand in, daring her to risk squirrel bite or the spooky brush of fungus that grazed the bottom. She didn't stop moving until she reached the edge of the back step, where she bent over, hands on knees, trying to quiet herself enough to enter without making any more noise.

She let herself in and went up the stairs. She passed the door to Charlotte's room, which was still open. Bed empty.

In her room, Knox first took off her father's coat and wadded it under the bed. It smelled of dirt, of the outside. Then she remembered the bracelet. She took the coat out and shook the bracelet from its pocket, put the coat back. She got into bed with the bracelet and held its cool, small weight against her face for a while. She thought as fast as she breathed:

Oh my God.

God.

After a few minutes, her breath slowed and her hot sense of her own absurdity distilled into something else: the realization that she lay unscathed at the moment, with a story to tell if she chose to tell it. This felt close to relief and caused her to stretch out her limbs under the covers and try to forget that Gary might say something to her father, or that Charlotte still wasn't home, or that she never wanted her own Cash because it wasn't safe, and she would have to work hard, well into the future, not to let the wrong people know that this is what she preferred to the rest of night's possibilities: this clean, white bed, its canopy arcing over her like a cupped hand.

· I ·

KNOX

THE SUMMER that everything happened was the hottest summer Knox could remember. Heat pooled around them all, a soft, wet heat that nobody talked about. It was just what was.

Her students didn't talk about it, but stumbled out the side doors of the center when it was time for their breaks and stood mutely in twos and threes that didn't correspond to any friendships or alliances that Knox knew of but seemed the result of an uncharacteristic economy of movement. Stood with whomever they happened to find themselves next to, blinking, kicking occasionally at pieces of gravel, until they were called inside. On the farm, the foals stood the same way in the fields, unless they had shade or water to retreat into, in which case they drew together with their mothers into a mass of shifting rumps and bobbing necks, sometimes lowering themselves onto their sides, one by one, until the ground was piled with shapes that panted so slowly that Knox would fret about death, respiratory failure, pulmonary arrest if she watched too long, and so turn from the kitchen window of her cabin, or walk on.

Dumbstruck. Struck dumb. Knox could describe almost anything this way, on the hot days. The town and the farms that spread around it were quieter now that the July sales were over and the buyers had flown away. The land seemed to buzz like the insects did, with vibration rather than sound. Felt, not heard, its tongue thick in its mouth.

"He calls you Ugly?" Marlene said. Her mouth was half full of sandwich, so *calls* came out *callfz*. They were sitting in the lunchroom, watching the students through the large window that faced onto the courtyard of the learning center. Nine more minutes until break was over, according to the wall clock above Marlene's head.

"Well," Knox said, eyeing Brad Toffey as he stepped onto a picnic bench and seemed to ponder whether or not to jump off it, then stepped down and sat heavily on the ground, staring into the middle distance, "yeah. But it's just a nickname. I think it's funny, actually. He's always called me that."

Marlene chewed, her eyes fixed on Knox's face. Knox looked back at her and smiled, knowing that it would be long seconds before Marlene could swallow her bite and respond, that the delay was killing her. Marlene, forty-six and well into her second marriage, liked nothing more than to discuss Knox's lack of savvy when it came to "relationships"—or, more accurately, the one relationship she'd ever had. Marlene's hair was frosted and faded into overlapping patches of white, russet, and dark brown and shook a little as her mouth worked.

"Take your time," Knox said. "Wouldn't want you to choke, Mar."

"Screw you," Marlene mumbled. A fleck of mayonnaise dropped onto her chin, and she scratched it away with a manicured nail. "I don't understand it. You're not ugly. At least, not most of the time."

"It's a nickname, Mar. Not important," Knox said.

"Mmm," Marlene said, squinting at her. "I guess."

Knox shifted in her plastic chair, trying to work some feeling back into her legs and lower body. Last night, Ned Bale had proposed to her again, in his way, as they lay on a quilt at the music festival, finally cooled by the dark and the beer they had drunk while they listened to the amped-up Dobros and fiddles. Jerry Douglas was on the stage, plucking the melody for "Wildwood Flower" over a steady line of bass notes, when Ned rolled toward her and said, "We should do it, Ugly. I mean, why not?"

That was how he asked.

Knox had been watching an old man dance on a toting board near their blanket. He was wearing a T-shirt that said BADASS FROM SKELETON PASS and jerking a little mountain clog, keeping his torso rigid and still, his hands limp at his sides, his face impassive, his legs flailing quickly like a marionette's. His shorts hung so low that Knox could see the exposed jut of his pelvic bone when he kicked his foot back and slapped it with one of his hands in response to a high whoop from the second picker. The woman with him—a wife or daughter, the bloat on her face making it hard to tell which— lolled on her side in the grass beside the board, as still as the man was lively. Knox briefly wondered how far they had come for the music; Skeleton Pass was surely one of the holler towns far to the east. She knew she shouldn't be wondering anything about any-one's driving distance—she should only be reacting, plumbing for words, using them or not, moving toward Ned or moving away.

She made herself say: "I love you." Then she said: "Ned."

It was true that she loved him, she thought. And she did appre-ciate Ned asking the way he had. The impossibly vague *it*. She considered its imprecision appropriate. How could one better cap-ture the cloudy concept of "making a life together"? *It* was a fine word. *It* also allowed her to rationalize, while she kept her breaths shallow and her eyes on the dancing man, that Ned might have been talking about going somewhere for the weekend, or trying the new Indian restaurant on Vine.

"I'm just talking," Marlene said, rolling the top of her pretzel bag closed with a clip she kept in her lunch pack. "But I want you to do what's right for you. You're past thirty, and this guy's been hanging around for half your life. What the hell are you waiting for?"

"I don't know."

Marlene sighed. "Did he press you to say anything else?"

"He just said I should think about it." Knox tried, unsuccessfully, to picture something other than Ned's face just after he said this. He had been rubbing at his glasses with the corner of their picnic blanket, his eyes cast down, when his mouth flashed into a little smile. He had looked apologetic, as if he were telling the glasses to be patient, that in another moment they would be clean.

Knox concentrated on Brad Toffey as he stood and began swinging his arms in wide circles. Round, round, round, faster and faster. She allowed herself to be lulled into imagining that it didn't matter what she did, really, and wasn't this the chief beauty of her life? It traveled in concentric circles around her, like orbiting matter, and her job was to stay fixed and let that happen. Look at Marlene—did she really care what Knox's reply to anybody's proposal might be? She was zipping the pretzel bag into her lunch pack, along with her balled sandwich wrapper and empty Diet Coke can. In thirty seconds she would be smacking a Winston out of the pack she kept in her skirt pocket, offering Knox a cigarette of her own, which Knox would refuse. The information they traded with each other was immaterial compared with the fact that they were simply placed in proximity to each other in the universe and found the proximity pleasant. Marlene's husband's colon cancer scare last year could have been a heart murmur; Knox could be holding forth on the fallout of a one-night stand or the progress of a lesbian courtship right now, instead of on Ned Bale's ongoing . . . pursuit of her. The events she hauled in from the outside like lunch could be real or not real; what was important was the cadence, not the content, of the babble between them. Actually, this wasn't altogether true—Knox had risen and fallen according to the daily news of Jimmy's recovery from surgery and felt deliriously buoyant when Marlene told her the tumor was officially benign. She hoarded specific details about Marlene's life: the hell-raising, punked-out daughter on scholarship at Wake Forest, the cardinal at her kitchen window that Marlene believed was an emissary from her dead Papaw. It was just that Knox sensed she could be whoever she wanted to be, expend as much or as little effort as she chose, and their break time companionship would not oxidize with untruth or neglect. It would simply . . . remain.

"Did Brad take his medication this morning?" Marlene asked. She was peering out the window. Outside, Brad lay on his back in the bleached grass, bicycling his slender legs at the sky.

"He did," Knox said. "He's just being Brad, I guess."

"I don't know how he moves in this heat." Marlene looked at her. "You want a cigarette?"

"No thanks, Mar."

"Well. I guess I'll call everybody in," Marlene said, fiddling with the matchbook in her palm. "Unless you want to give me any more gory details."

Knox did want to. She wanted to tell Marlene about the dancer, how she had seen something magnificent in the way he pounded on the board with his slight feet, their tops corded with tendons and flashing pale, even in the darkness—and in the way he had stood between acts, looking wildly expectant, one hand pressing at the small of his thin back, two fingers of the other hand thrust between his lips. He'd blown a wolf whistle that knifed the air so cleanly, without reverberation, like a child's scream. She wanted to tell her about driving home with Ned, how they had talked and laughed together about the usual nothings, and how, once he'd parked his truck, Knox had entered his house without asking and taken the toothbrush she always used out of the bathroom cabinet and begun to brush her teeth with it when Ned came into the bathroom and put his arms around her waist and pulled her backward against him, more roughly than he might have on another night; but she didn't comment, only swallowed the bits of foam and water in her mouth and let him turn her to face him, let him pull her shirt over her head and scratch her breasts with the stubble on his cheeks and chin as he sank lower until his tongue was circling one of her nipples, then the other. How she watched him work from above for a moment, and ran her fingers through his hair, making little tents with it, until Ned pulled her onto her knees and she knelt, facing him, while he unbuttoned her shorts with such concentration that Knox wondered if he might be deliberately avoiding her gaze. How she placed her hands in his hair again and felt the smooth knobs that his skull made behind his ears, and then moved her hands onto the back of his neck and guided his head toward hers, so that they were both closer together and blurred to each other. That had seemed a kindness, to let herself be blurred.

But there was no way to tell Marlene these things. Knox pushed up from her chair now, said, "I'll call them in, you just enjoy your smoke," and leaned out the lunchroom door to yell "Time for class!" into the heat, so loudly that it startled her.

KNOX ROSE most mornings at 7:00 a.m., made coffee, and took it with her onto the porch of her cabin, careful to tie her robe tight around her because of the number of farmworkers who were always around. She had to duck a little through her front door; time had made her tall, with a tendency to pull her thin shoulders forward, so that even she was tempted to yank them back when she passed her own reflection. She was too large, really, for her house, which had been a sharecropper's cabin during the days the farm was used for hemp and tobacco, and so had to move carefully in every room but the double-height living room, crouching low when she climbed down from her sleeping loft so as not to trip herself on her own, steep staircase.

On the porch, Knox would sit for a few minutes, usually staring out at the pond that her cabin overlooked. She would sip her coffee and nod hello at the swan that blew itself across the mottled surface of the water. The swan had been a gift to her parents from a local client with a mind for the picturesque; but it had been mean from the first, even more so after its mate had stumbled, sick, into the next field two winters ago and been kicked at and trampled by a spooked horse. Knox had tried to mourn along with the survivor—swans mated for life, she knew—but it took to croaking at her in staccato bursts every time she looked at it sideways. It would scream and lift its outrageous wings for emphasis, so that all the exposed water seemed white with their reflection, and Knox had to force herself to sit calmly until the ritual was done and the swan moved away, its webs bright in the murk, scissoring.

When the last dregs of coffee had gone cold in her cup she dressed and drove the twelve miles or so into town, where she parked at the literacy center. During the school year, Knox worked with people of all ages who were learning to read; in the summers, she taught dyslexic children, many of whom commuted from other counties and boarded during the week in a small dormitory down the block. She spent the morning in tutoring sessions, rubbing the backs of T-shirts and repeating sounds:

"*Guh, guh, guh.*"

"*Huh, huh, huh.*"

Her students rubbed block letters and repeated after her, tracing a *G*, an *H*, that Marlene had covered in sandpaper, hoping to make the tactile memory of it more vivid. They tried to distract her.

"I totaled my four-wheeler so bad this weekend."

"You did?" Knox would say. "*Guh, guh, guh.*"

"Your hair looks good today, Miz Bolling."

"Thank you, Brooke. After me—*huh, huh, huh.*"

She worked through lunch, serving the potato salad family style at her assigned cafeteria table. She worked until her break time with Marlene, and then headed back into the bald fluorescence of her classroom, where she worked with the middle school and olders for the rest of the afternoon. She moved from desk to desk as the students labored through movie reviews, descriptions of their houses, whatever pieces of paragraph Knox could convince them to devote their attention to long enough to keep composing sentences, forming words. Words looked warped to them; letters misbehaved on the page. Even spoken sentences could reconstitute themselves in midair and be rendered nonsensical for the ones with auditory problems, so Knox often found herself beginning again with an explanation or command. She guided each of them toward the letter table when they needed to take a break from their compositions to reestablish the curvature and sound of one of the ABC's, make their pencils push through a letter as if for the first time.

At four o'clock or so, Knox would close the door of her classroom behind her and head home. She took the rural route home instead of the highway. This tacked an extra twenty minutes onto her drive, but she preferred to avoid the subdivisions and access roads that were lapping up against the town boundary like so much dirty water. The route she took soothed her. She drove through the corridors near the city center that delineated the older, more established neighborhoods, then past the college campus, the modest rows of houses where groups of students—she among them, once—clustered, marking their presence with mismatched porch furniture, too many cars in the stunted drives. She passed Rupp Arena, the looming Baptist church, the courthouse, and the handful of high-rises and shopping courts that made up the haphazard and dying downtown, then sped over the viaduct and into the open country that she recognized as much by feel as by sight. Knox could remember lying on the backseat of their mother's car, Charlotte beside her, and guessing where they were by the sensation of the road as it curved and dipped, and the blur of treetops she could just make out through the top of the open car window. "We're at Middlebrook Farm now," Knox would say, and Charlotte would sit up and look, say, "You're right!" her dark hair lifting in the breeze. Then she'd lie back down, cover Knox's face with her hands, count to twenty. "Now where are we, Knoxie?" How sweet it was to answer "Train tracks, coming up," without thinking, then bump over them while her sister laughed, bracing herself against the jolts the worn shocks of her mother's car couldn't quite absorb.

The road ran east to west. Knox often had to flip the sun visor down on her drive home, but in the warm weather she liked driving into the sinking light, getting dazed by it. The ripe yellow-green of the fields in late afternoon could make her almost dizzy with pleasure. She sped toward the stud division of her parents' farm, where Ned supervised the days and breeding schedules of the fourteen stallions, and on those days when she felt like it, or when she and Ned had plans for supper, she turned into that drive and walked down the pathway that ran from the farm office to the stallion barn. She might find Ned in the breeding shed, shouldering with all his weight into the side of a mounted stallion, trying to keep him on balance and unhurt until he'd had a successful cover. The grooms would be helping him, four or five men circling and supporting two tons of quivering, copulating horseflesh, calling "Whup," "Steady," "All right," for the few minutes it took. Or she might find Ned in the little room off the shed, equipped as it was with microscopes for checking sperm motility and with video machines for going over the breeding tapes made for shareholders and the owners of the mares that had been vanned in from other farms. In the anteroom, with its plastic windows that looked onto the padded ring where Danny Boy or Banjo Man had met his mare, Ned would stare at one of the two television monitors, a petri dish full of the day's sample having been slid into place on the microscope tray. Above him, on a screen, pale villi undulated against a gray ground, making Knox think each time, That is what white noise would look like, if white noise were visible.

When he wasn't supervising a breeding, Ned might be giving a tour, leading a curious couple who'd stopped in on a cross-country driving trip from stall to stall in the stallion barn, recounting the racing careers of each of his charges, his hands deep in the pockets of the loose khakis he always wore. When he took his right hand out to adjust the bill of his cap or tug on a bridle to get one of the stallions to raise his head from the feed bucket for a snapshot, one of the tourists might ask before they thought: What happened? What happened to your hand? Knox had heard this question get asked once, having left her car to idle in the drive and run up to the barn with a quick request or bit of news, she couldn't remember which. She'd hung back in the barn's entrance, her hip flush against the fieldstone that curved up toward the central cupola, and waited for Ned to come clean the way he did for the foreign exchanges down at the Rosebud when they got curious after a few beers. Three years had passed since Dynamite, now dead, possessed of a wide cruel streak unusual even in a top stallion, had bitten Ned's right index finger off at the top knuckle and spat the tip into the sawdust they used to soften the floor of the breeding shed. One of the grooms had hustled the horse back into his stall while the other two ran to her father's office for help. Her father had called 911, then thought better of waiting for an ambulance and gone for Ned with the idea of getting him in his car and driving him to the closest hospital. He'd found Ned dead quiet, standing in the middle of the shed, squeezing his right hand with his left. There was blood, but not as much blood as you might have expected, her father had said. He'd asked Ned where the piece of finger was, and Ned told him, "Here. In my pocket."

At the hospital, they'd offered to helicopter in a hand surgeon from Louisville. He could be there well within the hour, which was plenty of time. Knox's father was relieved; he put his arm around Ned's shoulders and said something like, Let's sit down here to wait. It won't be long.

But Ned just looked at him, pale, and shrugged against the pressure of her father's arm. He kept gripping at the towel that was wrapped around his closed fist, said, I don't see why I have to wait, let's get this over with now, let's do it. Her father protested, according to both of them, that Ned had to hang on until the surgeon got there. There was nothing to do but sit, and he'd find someone to give Ned some more painkillers until it was time to prep him, which would be in just a minute. The bit of finger had been taken by a nurse who had met them at the doors to the hospital—put, everyone assumed, on ice. Her father talked sense to Ned until Ned told him, in a harsh voice her father had never heard him use, I don't need it, Ben. I can live without it. And when her father had creased his eyes in a show of patience and opened his mouth, Ned had said, Get off me, Ben, I'm in too much pain.

That had done it, Ned said. His head was in her lap when he finally told her the story himself. Knox watched his face redden and his mouth twitch into his sorry, half-formed smile as he spoke of pushing her father away. Her father had promoted him to stallion manager when he was only twenty-two. He had paid for Ned's first car and cosigned for the Lexington apartment that Ned's mother still lived in.

It was the shock, Knoxie, he said. All I could think was I wanted to get home. I was embarrassed. That horse had bullied me.

I know, Knox said. She tried to imagine how Dynamite had gotten enough leverage to rip the flesh off at the knuckle. She wanted to ask about that, to pull Ned away from himself and back into a recounting of the action, the quick yank of the stallion's head. Embarrassed—she had felt embarrassed, too, when Ned grazed her cheek for the first time with the bandaged place, and she had barely been able to keep herself from jumping.

I could have waited, Ned went on, but I just yelled for them to stitch me up, and then your dad drove me home. I am one idiotic fuck, Ugly.

He was trying to laugh, which made Knox look away. You're not, she said, before shaming herself into looking back. She didn't want him to laugh just then, when he didn't mean it. It had been too late to do anything about his finger by the next morning, when her father called her, assuming that Ned had stayed over when he hadn't answered the phone at his own house. "I thought for sure he'd be with you," her father had said, forcing Knox to ask what had happened. She drove to Ned's and found him asleep on the couch, still in yesterday's clothes. When she woke him, he looked at her in fear, as if he knew that she would be angry with him for his foolishness and regret.

But what he told the nosy tourist in the barn that day, the day Knox came upon him with a group and decided to watch him from the threshold, was: "You know, my girlfriend shot it off. She hated for me to point out better-looking women." He was moving as he spoke, pulling a brass rod out of its latch and sliding a stall door smoothly open to reveal the stallion inside. His voice was sure and easy.

After a second, people began to laugh. Knox could hear release in the laughter, which lasted just a beat too long: the young man hadn't felt the need to satisfy their curiosity with something true, thank God. Knox zeroed in on a guy in maroon University of Alabama shorts and a silvery brush cut as he clasped his wife closer and nodded with exaggerated vigor into her face. She grinned up at him, nodding back. Marlene probably wouldn't appreciate the fact that Knox had found this funny. It had been all she could do at the time not to walk up to Ned and grip him in a half nelson, just to give the people their money's worth. Play the pussy whip, the ball breaker—it would be easy. She could improvise her indignation, would prefer some light fakery to the reality of Ned's need for her, his sad, sweaty head in her lap. Other women seemed to crave weakness in their men—or at least frequent displays of vulnerability. Charlotte had seemed to, for some unknown reason, in her own husband, who trailed her like a puppy, Knox thought. But Knox craved moments like these, when Ned, or her father, held people in the thrall of a joke or gesture and kept the world in love with them and their maleness. She didn't know why. In the end, she had decided to stay hidden, and made her way to the little shaded parking lot behind the farm office without letting Ned see her. She had been glad for him that day, in a way she hadn't, not really, when he had finally steeled himself to accept sympathy and free Guinness from the grooms at the Rosebud Bar.

They had dinners together, she and Ned, and the two of them and her parents, before and after the accident. Knox was pleased to see that the scrim of normality that hung over their interactions hadn't been completely pierced along with Ned's skin and bone. Ned kidded with them about suing. Her father shook his head. Knox watched them woo each other, their faces lit from below by the coals in the outdoor grill, their tongs darting forward and back, pushing corn, swordfish steaks, into the hottest places. Her father's hands looked so much like hers; and Ned's, compact and soft despite their work, their palms infused with an old knowledge of her body, were altered. On those nights, watching from her place on the back porch, Knox did have to admit that as much as she preferred normality to whatever its alternative was, it felt strange, even shocking, that something brutal could be followed by nothing other than dinner. No one howled, or ran. And yet a tiny bit of permanent damage had occurred.

WHEN KNOX OPENED the door to her cabin, the phone was ringing. She put her backpack down on a chair and moved to answer it, instinctively ducking a beam that stretched low over the entryway.

"Hey," she said, thinking it was probably Ned on the line. She hadn't seen his truck at the barn on her way home.

"It's me." Charlotte's gravelly voice. Knox's sister Charlotte was pregnant with twins—both boys—that were due at the end of September, and to Knox's ears even her sister's words sounded heavy, as if her voice too had become stooped under the barely supportable weight she was carrying. Knox did a quick mental check: they had last spoken a couple of weeks ago. Since then, Charlotte had left her a message; and hadn't she also sent an e-mail? More than one? Shit.

"Oh, hi! Sorry I haven't called," Knox said in a breathy rush. "It's been really busy here." Even to herself, who knew she *had* been busy at the center all month, with the extra tutoring sessions she'd allowed some of the parents to talk her into, this sounded like a lie.

"I thought it was summer," Charlotte said. "I've been picturing you beside a pool all this time." She inhaled at an odd point toward the end of the sentence; Knox imagined her high, curved belly; she supposed it might be difficult even to breathe by now.

"We run that learning differences program in the summertime."

"Oh—right, you've told me. Sorry."

Fifteen seconds in, and they'd both apologized for something. This was a familiar rhythm between Knox and Charlotte, or had been in the years since they'd become grown women who nevertheless remembered what it was like to hurl childish invective at each other, to love and hate each other so nakedly, and so simultaneously, that the mere existence of the other could serve as an intolerable, maddening offense. Knox had wondered whether or not the bare fact of growing up with a sister, any sister, sharing a house and a set of parents and chunks of DNA, necessitated some sort of lifetime, knee-jerk atonement. Not that there weren't actual, identifiable things to apologize for. But Knox was careful to hew to the present moment. She'd trained herself to, for her own sake as opposed to Charlotte's; it was just easier for her not to expose herself, because the role of wounded little sister was, among other things, damaging to her pride. And if pride goeth before a fall, her father used to joke with her, remembering all the times she'd stood before him with scraped knees or bruised feelings, every cell in her body concentrated upon the refusal to cry, then she'd go ahead and take the fall. Love suffused his handsome, square face as he said it. How he understood her, her magnificent dad. She'd always been helpless before him. As a child she'd dabbed his Skin Bracer aftershave behind her ears more than once before she'd left for school and spent the day moving through the halls of Lower School in the bubble of his familiar scent, moony as a lover.

"How are you feeling?" she asked Charlotte now.

"Fine, which is what's weird."

"What do you mean? What's wrong?"

"Maybe nothing, I guess. I came for my weekly check this morning, and they sent me over to the hospital. I'm lying here getting something called a nonstress test. I have this belt attached to me, and it's hooked up to a microphone, and I'm not allowed to move. Very stress*ful*, actually. Listen."

There was silence on the phone. Knox strained to hear something, and then an overpowering sound, like horses galloping in place, flooded the receiver.

"Those are heartbeats—not mine, the babies'," Charlotte said. "It's so loud in here I can't hear myself think."

"Why are you in the hospital?" Knox asked again.

"My doctor thinks my amniotic fluid is low."

"Is that a problem?" Knox felt her own heart begin to beat faster, as if it were racing the hearts of the twins toward an imaginary finish line—not because she felt afraid, exactly; Charlotte herself sounded more excited than afraid, and it was from her sister's effortful voice that Knox was taking her cues. No, it was the familiarity of this dynamic that was making her anxious: Charlotte holding the cards again, making her work for the most pertinent information. She had always relished doling out details like some smug Scheherazade, withholding context, pretending she didn't hear Knox's questions, taking her sweet time. It made Knox angry, but then Charlotte had a knack for eliciting responses inappropriate to their circumstances. Relax, Knox thought. You don't have to play.

"It's fairly normal toward the end, I guess. But if it's really low, then the babies have to come out."

"When?" In five minutes? A week?

"Maybe tonight. That's why I'm calling. Wild, huh?"

"Charlotte, is this good, or bad?" Nope—she was playing. Knox sighed. She rubbed at the shelf of bone and muscle at the top of her shoulder; she'd been wearing her most uncomfortable bra all day; its strap was digging in. It was her lot to be skinny enough that her very bones collided painfully with the material requirements of the world, though she was always trying to put on the weight to match her height, it seemed, and her ability to "eat everything in sight"—greasy cheeseburgers for lunch, doughnut after doughnut in the faculty lounge—resulted in a lot of jealous squawking from Marlene. She'd been running farther than her usual route lately, too, overdoing it; her lower back was sore. She wanted to lie down. She wanted to change her clothes.

"Sorry, I couldn't hear, what was the question?" Charlotte fairly shouted into the phone.

"I mean," Knox adjusted her voice. She'd sounded, just now, as if she were speaking to one of her students. "I mean, isn't it early for the babies to come. And are you in any kind of distress, and is this threatening, healthwise, for anybody. That's what I mean."

"Oh," Charlotte breathed out, or snorted; Knox couldn't be sure. The sound just read like so much static over the phone. "No. Everything should be okay, they tell me. The boys are cooked—

the worst-case scenario is that they won't be able to come home with us right away. It's just all moving a little fast. You can imagine."

One of the problems, Knox suspected, regarding her history with her sister, was that she *couldn't* imagine, not as fervently or with the same suspension of disbelief that Charlotte could, not ever. Knox had long accepted her lack of patience for fantasy as a kind of failure on her part, even felt apologetic about it; when, years before, Charlotte had assumed that she could pick up the mantle during a game of pretend, she'd felt shamed at the blank her mind drew when faced with what the Boxcar Children should scrounge up for lunch, or who, exactly, was chasing them as they were running for their lives. Now, when the assignment was to imagine how it felt to live in Charlotte's body, her marriage, her days, her present state of mind, Knox drew a similar blank. It wasn't that she couldn't project herself by degrees into the life Charlotte described to her when she called, just that the resulting images she came up with seemed so generic, so one-size-fits-all, that they struck Knox as applicable to faceless hordes as opposed, specifically, to Charlotte. Strangely, Charlotte was the only person who'd ever caused her to feel this shameful opacity. But that was life, she supposed; each person in it held the power to summon a different version of you.

"So it's probably good, then," she said.

"Yes. Probably." Now Charlotte was the one who sounded like she was speaking to a child.

"Okay."

"I talked to Mom and Dad," Charlotte continued. "I'm just waiting to hear whether they want to admit me tonight, and if they do, they'll probably do the C-section in the morning."

"Are Mom and Dad coming?"

"Of course they're coming. If they need to. These are their first grandchildren."

"I know—"

"I thought you might come up here with them. I don't want to assume anything, though. I know how busy you've been."

Knox tugged again at her bra strap. She could feel herself flushing. "Are you being sarcastic?" she said, the words escaping her lips even though Knox knew better than to let them.

"No. Knox. You said you'd been busy." Charlotte sighed with audible exasperation. "Right?"

"I'm sorry."

"You're getting weird. I'm in the hospital. Are you actually arguing with me right now?"

"I'm sorry, I misheard. No need to be dramatic."

"It *is* dramatic."

"Okay."

Charlotte paused. "Anyway. Talk to Mom and Dad. Let them know what you want to do. I just wanted to speak to you myself while I still had a chance." The speed and breath that had animated Charlotte's voice moments ago seemed spent. Knox swallowed, casting about in her mind for the right thing to say, the calm, conciliatory thing, but she and Charlotte had long ago stopped practicing the skills required to wrest a moment like this back. How could Knox make it not matter, conjure the lightness necessary for them to laugh it off, forget any misunderstanding had occurred? With Ned, or Marlene, or her parents, she would know without thinking.

"I will," she said. "Of course."

The words *I got proposed to for the fourth time last night* scrolled across Knox's consciousness, unbidden. There seemed to be a million reasons not to tell Charlotte something like this in order to rescue their conversation, distract Charlotte with an entertainment of some kind, and at the same time there wasn't any one in particular that she could point to. She opened her fingers and shuffled forward until the cord on her anachronistic dial phone stretched as far as it would go, then began to turn, wrapping herself up. It was strange; Knox remembered Charlotte parting the cheeks of her own ass so her sister could peer into the dark space contained there—God, they must have been bored *that* afternoon—and yet Knox felt inhibited about revealing the starkest facts of her life to her, things she might sputter to a stranger in the grocery store if she were the type to sputter. They rarely spoke about Ned, and when they did, Knox felt protective of every word, vetting it before it emerged, keeping her explanations neutral. They'd been forced by accident of birth into mutual territory, and yet emerged, Knox thought now, as if they'd been raised in separate countries.

"Good luck," Knox said. "Really. I'm just absorbing. It's taking me a moment."

Charlotte cleared her throat.

"Thanks."

"Please let me know what's happening, all right? I'll see you soon if this is really happening. I love you," Knox said.

"Love you, too."

They said their goodbyes. Knox unwound herself and put the phone receiver in its cradle. She stared at the wall in front of her, a pocket of sweat forming above her upper lip. She had hung a picture on that wall, but the wood was so old and mealy that the nail had never held, and she'd finally given up and twisted it free. She squinted, trying unsuccessfully to locate a hole in the grain. She felt emptied out, as if something had been exacted of her. Marlene would say she was jealous. She would blow smoke as she sighed, thus giving her pity, her wisdom, a visible shape. She would call Knox *hon*, a form of address so predictable that it was actually surprising. Marlene would be the perfect Marlene, puff *hon* then press her lips together, surely thinking that Knox wanted the life Charlotte had, with a worried husband and all the attention and babies and planes on the way. That was the problem, Marlene would say. Though, of course, Marlene couldn't be more wrong in that department.

FOUR CORNERS FARM, stallion division: fourteen studs, breeding shed, vet lab. Barns with beams hewed and heaved into place by Amish carpenters. Prep-house where mares-to-be-bred were given their glimpse of teaser (overweight, burr-plagued Pinto, butt of the grooms' crudest jokes) through a sliding window—to be vanned home if they bared teeth, to be declared in season and walked into the circular breeding shed if they spread their haunches a little or didn't react. Exercise track. Broodmares housed in three separate facilities, which the broodmare manager circled slowly in his truck, watching for cribbers, early foals, listening to the whinnied keening of mothers and babies once they'd been weaned from one another into separate fields. Yearling division, where the babies built muscle tone and tolerance for handling, were walked before potential buyers, before being entered for sale. Foaling barns, quarantine barns, receiving barns. Paddocks— individual ones for the hot-tempered stallions. Fields—long cleared of thistles and brush, studded with pyramids of green-black manure, pats of ancient, sun-bleached dung, striped and seamed with dried grass overturned by the mower. Trees: tall, spreading rows of them planted along existing fence lines, along the phantom fences that had been razed as the property expanded and changed. Muck pit at the back, undulating with used straw, piled house high. Fox hole. Sinkhole. Spring.

Knox had had a recurring dream since childhood, of lying down in given places on the farm, rolling on the turf until it swallowed her up, and she felt surprised, even in sleep, at her happiness in going under. She'd grown up able to squint from her bedroom window, deliberately blurring her view of a roofline that marked the presence of the one house visible on a neighboring property. She'd imagined the fences that delineated Four Corners' borders banked high as sea walls against a blank unknown that needn't be thought about or explored while the grooms shouted to one another in the fields at dusk, while viburnum and honeysuckle and forsythia and fescue grew without stopping in the gathering dark until they had twined together to make a curtain tall enough to obscure the stars. This was their Eden, where her father chose which animals were bred and born and then named them, where they'd run around naked as Eve, she and Charlotte, in and out of the pond her cabin overlooked now, their bodies festooned with silky ribbons of algae when they emerged, awed at their own outrageousness, at the fact that there was nobody around to see, that all this, the daring, too, was theirs.

She knew that any stranger might look at her now, her cabin curled up at the bottom of the hill her parents' house stood on like a child at the foot of the family bed, and make the assumption she was *that* daughter. The sad, stunted one. The one who couldn't let go. She and her parents had long handled this with frequent jokes (Maybe someday you'll get rid of me, Knox would proffer; God willing, they'd say, rolling their eyes). But she knew that her presence at the supper table and the ease with which they floated in and out of one another's days were a comfort to them— a great and necessary comfort, Knox had told herself. Though Knox was plenty proud of the world-class breeding operation her parents had built in an industry famously populated by playboys, hustlers, and dilettantes, and of the integrity with which they had obviously done it, the truth was that she was always trying to get back to something, something that seemed to reside in a past just beyond her reach, and it had more to do with what she sensed *within* the land than with what went on on its now-manicured surface. When the place had been wilder, so had they, her family— wasn't that true? If not wilder, then . . . purer. She remembered the time before the finer stallions had begun retiring off the track into her father's barn, bringing success with them with each cover, as a time before her family had been contaminated by hurt and separation. Though she'd admit it to no one, Knox had come to half believe in the magical idea that, if she dug into the fescue under her feet, past the seams of earth and limestone and shale and scattered Wyandot arrowheads she occasionally overturned even now in her vegetable garden, she'd hit a lode that contained their former selves, that predated change.

Before the farm became what it became, her father had converted four stalls in a tobacco barn. Their living room, still unrenovated, was furnished in winter with the wrought-iron chairs that lived on their porch in summer. He'd started from scratch, at twenty-seven years old, and there was something eternally romantic for Knox in the vision of her parents, of all of them, at this nascent stage, her dad playing sappy country songs on his guitar for them in the evenings after dinner, painting the rooms of their house himself one by one, lucky break after lucky break, cupping her mother's butt with his hands when he kissed her in the kitchen.

Of course, the business was evolving, the sport struggling to hold an audience. Her parents were getting older. Nature itself seemed at times to have withdrawn its promise to support the little universe that sustained them. It was already years ago that some alchemy of the cherry trees in early flower and the leavings of an invasion of tent caterpillars had frozen an unfathomable number of area foals in the womb; Four Corners alone had suffered forty or so stillbirths the first season of the MRLS epidemic, and some mares had died, too, in the bargain. That mystery had been defined as a syndrome, given its own name, and the cherry trees had all been cut down, but the sun shone hotter than ever this summer; the snowless winter had been too short; many claimed the foals were born faster and weaker each year; Ned kept wanting to marry her. At thirty-one, Knox was getting old, too, really, she knew it—climbing up to that crow's nest beyond which the only real choice was to look around at the view and climb back down again, into actual middle age. She could hold fast against certain encroachments, but others—time, fate, the weather—felt too vast for her to combat, and, on her worst days, she didn't know how much longer she could hold out. The view out the bedroom window of her cabin was different from the view she'd had as a girl, dominated not by a magnolia but by a half-dead catalpa—trash trees, her father called them, but this one flowered into glory every May despite the insult. Instead of squinting as she used to, she performed an act of imagination that excised all evidence of impermanence from her thoughts, until she'd made all her fears about the end of the world disappear, just like the roofline of her neighbor's house all those years ago. Ned would call it stubbornness. Knox thought of it as survival, and, though her safe choices were plain for anyone to see, she felt she carried a hot secret when she engaged in this willfully naïve thinking, and that at her core lay something defiant—not safe, but radical, even dangerous. To put things in her Bible-studying mother's terms: if Eve had been able to live as if she'd never tasted the forbidden fruit, innocent in her actions if no longer in her mind or in the eyes of God, wouldn't that have been noble? The way a child could be seen as noble when, desiring to hide, he stood in place and plastered his hands over his eyes, defying all natural law by placing faith in the totality of his own perspective.

Try explaining that to somebody like Marlene. Knox would sound crazy. Hell, maybe she was.

KNOX HAD SOME PARENT REPORTS to finish. She could either stand in place like an imbecile, the phone still in her hand, or get to them while she had a chance, considering she might not even be in the state tomorrow. There was nothing she could do, for the moment, and she already had plans to join her parents for dinner. In the meanwhile, she ached for some distraction from the whirl in her head.

She crossed the yard, passing too close to the edge of the pond and causing the swan to unfold its neck from across the length of its back, where it rested during sleep.

Kwaa, kwaa! Kwa kwa ka!

"Quiet, bird," Knox said, noting the theatrical sternness in her voice. She occasionally caught herself playing to an imagined audience, throwing language into the air as if the burnt land was the back of a packed theater. She skirted the bank and began to walk up the road that led to the Parrish Barn, where a computer was housed in the observation room. She didn't have a computer in her cabin but was welcome to walk in the direction of her parents' house, up the other slope of the shallow cleft she lived in; there was one in her father's study. Still, Knox liked the Parrish Barn, a quarantine barn for sick and barren mares, virtually deserted in the early evenings, and she longed for silence at the moment.

She grazed her fingers along a middle rail as she moved up the fence line; her fingertips were blackened with dried paint when she lifted them away. During the few summers she'd been encouraged to accompany Charlotte to sleepaway camp, she had remembered the feel of fences the way the older girls claimed to remember the skin, hair, faces, bodies of boys they had left behind in hometowns. Knox could lie in a faraway bed and know exactly how it would feel to rest her palm against the polished wood of a stall door. Or to wrap it around a milkweed stalk and yank, the sinew of the plant cutting against her as she pulled. She felt blacktop pebble her knees when she knelt on the dock to practice her sailing knots and straw prick her feet when she waded barefoot in the cold grass toward the mess hall; and she could never leave trees alone, would pluck leaves and work them between her fingers like the tiny, petrified blobs of black that she snapped off the edges of the boards now as she walked and fidgeted with, let fall.

She hadn't spoken much during those few summer weeks away in the mountains of North Carolina, not even to the boys from the brother camp who'd sought her out at the dances, looking to impress Charlotte by doling out attentions to her little sister—they called her Legs, and Red, referring to her tall, skinny figure, her strawberry-blond hair and lashes. Knox hadn't minded the special notice she received; she'd just never known what to say. She was unable to bat back the nicknames, keep the jokes in play. This had happened, too, with the girls. The sophisticated girls from places like Dallas and Atlanta who, in their faded board shorts and boyfriends' borrowed oxfords, seemed all the more eager, at first, to know her. Knox knew she wasn't beautiful. She also knew that this wasn't supposed to matter, but it did. Even the compliments her father gave her at this age, in an obvious effort to shore her up, were damning: he told her she was *striking*, exhorted her to wait until she *grew into herself* and then *wow*. It was Charlotte, for the time being, who made her exotic. Charlotte with her haunting face and bedroom hair and baritone voice and contraband cigarettes, the knockout body, her way of floating among the assembled at breakfast as if she didn't even notice where she was. Charlotte with the magic; she'd always had it. A pimply twelve-year-old sidled up to Knox at the punch table and told her he would "drink your sister's bathwater, if I could" in a voice so thick with desire it scared her. Her fellow campers were attracted to any knowledge about Charlotte that they could gain; and though Knox stood to benefit from their curiosity, she had vacillated quietly, fatally, between lame attempts to foster the girls' interest and annoyance at their hunger for information. They wanted stories, gossip, anything. They wanted Knox to hate Charlotte, or to be her closest confidante, to be her equal, her opposite, her superior. But it had been difficult to follow the script, or to be vivid enough in whatever part she might play—the rival, the source, the enigma—had she ever managed to decide on just one.

"Your sister is the most . . . ," one or another of them would say. When she couldn't come up with the proper word, she might shortcut right to: "You know?" Knox knew. She kept herself from asking: Did you mean to say *favored*? *Enviable*? *Overrated*? Exactness seemed important. But of course she never did anything but smile and cock her head, waiting to be dismissed from the conversation.

Thank God that part of her life was over.

The Parrish Barn was cool inside and fairly empty, most of the horses having been turned into the fields for the night. Knox made her way past stall doors labeled with white cards: HEAR THE MUSIC, NO FOAL; SWEET CANDY, NO FOAL; PRIMA DONNA, DROPPED FILLY. Prima Donna had miscarried, then. Knox looked closer; the mare stood at the back of her stall, her muzzle pressed against a barred window. She looked all right, though still heavy and swollen about the middle. Her ankles were bandaged, and a persistent fly worried her withers, causing the skin on them to wrinkle and twitch.

"You rest, honey," Knox said. "That's right."

The mare stamped once in the straw. Knox watched her, willing the mare to turn around that she might convey . . . something. Pity? Understanding? After a minute she gave up and let herself into the observation room.

The air was close, stung with medicinal smells, stale food and coffee odors, the sharp dust, straw, and manure from outside.

There was a littered desk, a thirdhand couch, a large window onto the adjoining stall, through which a vet or groom could keep an eye on whatever mare most needed to be watched. Knox sat at the desk, turned on the computer, and logged into her e-mail account, organizing a few battered Styrofoam cups into a stack as she waited for the connection to fire.

Three new messages flashed up: one from Marlene, one from herself (a file of unfinished reports she'd sent from the center to the farm address earlier that day), and one from Ned. Knox cleared her throat. She would start in on the reports and ignore everything else for now. She clicked on her file, opened the letter she'd begun to compose to Brad Toffey's parents. She had decided on addressing the report to "Mr. and Mrs. Toffey," though she had only ever met Brad's mother, Dorothea, and had heard from Marlene that she and her husband were having problems—Dorothea herself had apparently called Mr. Toffey a honking bastard when Marlene had asked if he should be included on Brad's school pickup form. "There's good Toffeys and bad Toffeys," Marlene had said. "I know just about everyone in that clan." Marlene had tried to tell Dorothea to let the center know if there were family issues it needed to be aware of. But unless Brad's behavior at the center changed drastically, bad Toffeys weren't really anyone's business.

She spent the better part of the next hour explaining to the Toffeys, plural, how their son had progressed during his summer school term. He had begun composing stories of his own (the protagonists were always named Brad and possessed of superhuman powers), whereas back in May he had been nervous even to dictate to her, fearful he would sound stupid. She emphasized everything she could think to about Brad's accomplishments, knowing that Mrs. Toffey had a hard time, that she tended to wrap her fingers around Brad's pale, hairless forearm if he got recalcitrant in the carpool line, drag him toward the passenger door, tell him not to "be so damned hyper." Knox tried to ease Brad out of that grip with her praise and made a mental note to put his rough drawing—

of a Laker dunking a basketball, "BT" emblazoned on his uniform—on the front cover of the mimeographed journal her class would publish at the end of the summer.

She moved on to another report, finished that and two more before she thought to open Marlene's e-mail, take a tiny break before getting to the final two reports she had to finish. She swiveled round once while the message opened, dizzying herself with a small rush of speed and air and messy scenery before stilling the chair and herself with her feet, read:

> *You know, I thought about it, and you are ugly. Can't believe I didn't see it before. Love, Mar*

Knox laughed out loud. From the other side of the barn, the mare snorted in response.

"Hey," came a voice behind her. Knox turned in the chair and saw Ned standing in the doorway.

"Oh—"

"What's so funny?" Ned let the screen door catch on its loose spring and bounce against his back, where it rested. His glasses were smudged and glinted pink in the sunset light from the window when he cocked his head.

She smiled. "Nothing. Marlene's a shit. You surprised me."

"Didn't mean to."

Knox stretched her arms up and tilted her head back. She twisted her hands at the wrists, like a ballerina, a sorceress, and took a deep breath. Ned stayed where he was in the doorway. Knox held the breath, stretched farther, then exhaled, mildly taken aback that Ned wasn't reading her movements as an invitation to move closer. She laced her fingers together and lowered them to her lap.

"Well hi," she said. "Charlotte thinks she's having the babies tomorrow."

"I was just up at your parents'. They got a call from Bruce, said she's going to have the surgery tonight."

"What?"

"Yeah. You should go up to the house."

Knox blinked. "But I just talked to her," she said. "It's supposed to be tomorrow."

Ned rubbed at his chin with the back of his hand. "Well, I guess they were able to schedule it earlier. I think they want to get 'em out. You should go on up."

Knox gripped the arms of the swivel chair as if to push herself out of it, then paused. There was something so still in Ned's face, though now he smiled slightly at her.

"I shouldn't be worried, right?" she said.

"No. Your mom's running around like you all just won the lottery. Everything's fine."

"Mm." The light was fading even as they spoke, and Ned's dun-colored work clothes seemed suddenly indistinct from the outlines of the screen door, the dusty barn aisle behind him. Knox bit her lip, attempting to ground herself against a kind of creeping vertigo, wake herself up. The room was oppressively hot. She wanted to move out of it and outside, just as she, impossibly, wanted to finish the reports she'd been working on, sit alone at the desk, walk down the hill to the cabin when she was finished, get a run in before the last light, warm up some dinner. She worked to quell a strange, unsummoned annoyance at the notion that her routine had been so fatally interrupted.

"Could you give me a ride? Or—" She saw a reticence tighten Ned's mouth at the request, a balk that made her want to back right off, as much as it confused her. "I could walk. I'll walk up there."

"Could you? One of the stallions nicked his foreleg; the groom wants me to go have a look. I'll try to stop by after and see what's happening."

"Okay." So she was being asked to be careful with him. Perhaps that was it. Last night hadn't drifted into the ether—nor, she realized, should she have expected it to. Not so quickly. Well, if he needed a bit of distance, she could give him that, was happy to, even under these circumstances. It was a step toward the status quo; the quicker she made it the quicker ease between them would be restored.

"So I'll see you later," she said. She hoped she sounded generous, sincere. Still, she felt surprised when Ned turned as she spoke, hooking his blunted finger into the screen door's handle.

"Sounds good," he said. He pushed the door open, walked through it. The soft treads of his boots made very little sound against the concrete; after two or three steps Knox felt unsure of where he was. It was only when she heard his truck's engine turn over that she knew for certain he was out of the barn.

Knox sank back in the chair, faintly hurt, her feeling of disorientation growing stronger. She swiveled back around and glanced at the computer screen. She knew she should be rising into action, and yet remained where she was for a moment, then another. She clicked the report file closed, and, before she could think about it, clicked onto an e-mail attachment that Charlotte had sent her months before.

The computer sputtered and hummed. The screen went blank for a moment, became a square shape that began to define itself by faint degrees as Knox watched. Two knobs, like the fat heads of fiddlehead ferns that grew by the pond, showed themselves inside the shape, grew brighter. Glowing type appeared at the bottom of the square. It read: *Charlotte Bolling Tavert. Frat. M M. New York Presbyterian Hospital. Digital Lab.*

It was an early sonogram of babies. The picture came a bit further into focus, then stopped refining itself. Knox stared. She brushed a strand of damp hair from the side of her face and tried not to be angry at herself for feeling so little every time—only a sensation of waiting for something in the image to become animated, for a tiny foot to kick through the frame at her, forcing her to duck. She could see the head-heavy, concave shape of one body curled in on itself; the other knob looked like a belly, or maybe a backside.

"Little aliens," Knox mouthed at the screen.

Knox heard only the rustling of straw as the mare shifted her stance. She pictured the mare's heavy bay head at the stall window, gazing out, wanting space, the light reflected in her wet eyes, threads of snot quivering in the soft caves of her nostrils as she breathed. She realized she did feel something. To see the twins like this was to imagine their pleasure at being suspended in the fluid and heat of her sister's body, ultimately protected, and hadn't she wanted, admit it, to be in exactly that place at points in her early life, to crawl inside her sister and rest, letting Charlotte be her mouth, eyes, ears, bed, blanket? Was she jealous, of all things? She didn't want children of her own. She and Ned didn't speak about this, but he knew, just as she knew that everyone, including Ned, assumed a woman could be talked into motherhood eventually. Well.

Knox picked out an unseeing eye, a black bead that looked to her like a caper. It had all transpired so quickly. Charlotte had become a person with babies inside her, before Knox had even had a chance to get used to the weird enthusiasm with which she'd become a wife. She was spinning beyond Knox once again, uncatchable as mist.

"Damn you," Knox said to the screen, shocking herself. The words in her mouth sounded comical, strange enough to move her. She reached to shut the computer down, resolved to let Marlene finish the last reports if that became necessary. She rose from the chair, the material of her skirt gripping its cracked leather surface for a moment before nudging itself free. She walked out of the room, past the mare, down the barn aisle, and into the rosy evening.

It wasn't until she found herself outside that she remembered the unopened e-mail message from Ned. As she made her way toward the fence line, long grass whipping at her bare legs, she briefly wondered whether or not it contained something that he thought she'd read, or if he had been annoyed or disappointed when he realized, as he must have, that she hadn't looked at it yet. Well, she thought, maybe that was what had been wrong with him.

There wasn't time to worry about it now. If Charlotte was about to be operated on, her parents would be packing for New York; she would be faced with whether or not to join them.

Knox stopped against the fence, gripped a middle plank with both hands, and held on. It was still warm with the day's heat. She stood still for a moment, suddenly more scared than displeased by the momentum she felt. She wanted nothing more than to remain here, curled against the post like a weed.

She turned just as Ned's truck appeared in the distance. It was coming from the back of the farm, where the shop was, and heading silently away from her, up the far hill. At the top of it Ned stopped and turned right, moved down the access road that would bring him to the entrance to the stallion division, where he'd speak into a security squawk box and drive through a pair of painted metal gates. Knox watched his pickup get smaller and less distinct. The only word in her mind was: wait. She raised a hand and raked it through her hair before she remembered the fence-black on her fingertips. Friction had a way of turning the paint to a dust so fine it could be inhaled as an irritant; she closed her eyes, trying not to breathe.

BRUCE

BRUCE TAVERT HAD LEARNED early that mothers can leave. In fact, if he'd been asked to identify a major theme in his life—and there was a party game to this effect, he thought—then that particular theme might have been it. Mothers can leave. Can and do.

Two events in his childhood taught him as much. The first occurred when he was eleven, a fifth grader at the Bancroft School in Manhattan.

His best friend, Toby Van Wyck, lived in a suburb just north of the city. Toby commuted in with his father, the two of them rising early, breakfasting together, then taking the thirty-five-minute train ride to Grand Central. On the train, Mr. Van Wyck skimmed the *Times* and the *Journal*, while Toby listened to tapes on his Walkman (Squeeze, the Hooters, New Order, old Who) and penned designs and characters onto the outside of his plastic organizer, which he would show to Bruce once he arrived at school, having taken the subway from Forty-second Street to the Upper East Side with his father. Toby's mother usually drove in to pick him up at the end of the school day, his baby sister strapped into her car seat in the back. Some days, his mother took the train in, and left Lisa with the au pair.

One day, Toby's mother didn't come at all. Bruce stood with Toby in the school lobby, fingering the Hacky Sack that he kept in the pants pocket of his uniform. It had been at least an hour since the headmistress had called Toby's father at work in an effort to find Mrs. Van Wyck after she saw Toby and Bruce together at the end of pickup, sitting against a wall with their knees drawn up to their chests, their backpacks pressed like carapaces behind them. Bruce's mother was out front, reading her newspaper in the sun, waiting in case Toby needed to come home with them for the rest of the afternoon. Now, Bruce flipped the sack onto the back of his hand, where it rested.

"Sure you don't want to play?"

Toby looked at him. Bruce noticed red points on his cheeks that made it look like he had a fever. "Yeah," Toby said. "Okay."

They turned to face each other. Bruce dropped the sack onto his right ankle, angling his foot just so for a light, easy catch. He popped it to Toby, who caught it, sailed it into the air, turned a 180, and caught it again on the bottom of his shoe before lofting it back to Bruce. They had been hacking like this for a few minutes when Toby stopped a toss from Bruce with a listless motion and began to dribble the sack on his toe, watching it as it bounced up and down, collapsing flat when it landed and thrusting itself slightly taller, looser, in the moments in between. They could hear the soft *thunk* of it against Toby's sneaker in the emptied-out lobby. Toby said, "I think my mom's with her boyfriend."

Bruce kept his face still. He knew to do that much. He wished he had the sack himself so he could concentrate on it instead of on Toby's foot. His heart was beating with sudden excitement and sorrow. Divorced mothers had boyfriends. Toby's mom was married.

"Dude," he said finally. "She has a boyfriend?"

"He's a dick," Toby said. "My dad's met him."

Because breathing seemed like it might hold the power to hurt, to offend, Bruce held his breath. He folded his hands in on each other, making fists, and scratched at layers of palmy sweat with his fingernails. He was glad when Toby kicked the sack over, though he hesitated to do anything but hold it still in the hollow of his ankle and stare at it, as Toby had.

"Have you?" he said finally.

"Met him? No. But I know he's a dick. He builds houses in my town," Toby said. "I guess he built one on our street."

It looked like Toby was going to cry, which caused Bruce's excitement to constrict and go colder inside his chest. Just then the headmistress came out of her office and told them that Mr. Van Wyck had agreed to pick Toby up at Bruce's apartment at six o'clock. They were free to leave.

"Yes!" Bruce said, exhaling held air with the word, listening as it went more whispery than he'd meant it to. He pocketed the sack and followed Toby out into the too-bright sunshine.

He and Toby didn't speak about the boyfriend for the rest of the afternoon. They did what they sometimes did on weekends: hung out behind the doorman's podium in Bruce's building, watching the live footage of people going up and down in the elevators and passing by outside. They hooted when someone picked his nose or, better, grabbed or scratched anywhere near the vicinity of his balls. They made a few crank calls from the extension in Bruce's room. They hacked in the living room, the largest space in the apartment, and yelled monosyllabic answers to the questions Bruce's mother called from the kitchen, where she was making dinner. The questions went like this: Tob, would you like to spend the weekend with us? And: Bruce, wouldn't that be great? Bruce could tell that his mother was trying to make the best of the situation, so that Toby wouldn't feel worse. He was grateful for his mother's good manners. He was grateful and, under the circumstances, vaguely ashamed that she loved his father. Toby's mother never called. At six o'clock sharp, Mr. Van Wyck buzzed from downstairs. No, he crackled over the intercom, thanks, but he couldn't come up for a drink. He and Toby had better get on home.

Toby said goodbye. Bruce held the door out for him, handling the knob carefully, as if it could break up, an eggshell in his hand.

At dinner Bruce brought it up. He took a breath and said, "Toby thinks his mom . . ."

"What?" said his mother, peering at him.

Bruce felt the same mix of excitement and dread that he'd felt in the school lobby when Toby had told him. He almost laughed, for some reason. "Has a boyfriend," he said.

From the way his mother looked quickly at his father, Bruce knew that it could be true.

"Well," his mother said. "Maybe Toby's confused. Do you think that could be?"

"I don't know," Bruce said.

"Did he talk to you about it very much?"

"Not really."

"Here's the thing," his mother said, turning her unused spoon over on the tablecloth. "Sometimes things go on in families that are tough to understand, and all we can do is be there for our friends."

Bruce looked at his father. His father was nodding. Bruce nodded, too.

LATER HE LAY in his bed, thinking of Mrs. Van Wyck with a man who was not Toby's father. In his mind the man asked her to undress, and Mrs. Van Wyck just smiled and stood where he imagined her standing, behind the butcher-block island in Toby's kitchen, her hands encased in the oven mitts that were worn and burnt in places, with metallic thread shining through. In front of her, resting on the island, was a cookie sheet with rows of warm rolls arranged and rising and browning upon it, the kind of rolls that came out of the refrigerator in a cardboard tube, which Mrs. Van Wyck always let Bruce twist open until it popped thrillingly and gooed cold, colorless dough. She let him do this on those nights when he had come to sleep over, come in anticipation of Tang and Stouffer's spinach soufflé and Kraft macaroni and cheese—and the kind of rolls that Bruce's mother would never have allowed at her table, choosing instead to serve stale seven grain, or toasted pita, or nothing at all. The rolls bloomed between Mrs. Van Wyck and the boyfriend, who approached her, unzipping his pants. He was faceless. Bruce let himself stroke the smooth tip of his penis as he thought of this. Just for a couple of seconds—a light, electric touch. The next morning, he allowed himself to forget that he'd done it.

THAT WINTER, Toby's mother went missing for good. She had become prone to skipping appointments and relying on the au pair for long stretches during the afternoons; but when she wasn't home by dinnertime one January evening, Mr. Van Wyck waited until almost midnight and then called the police. Two days after the call—days during which Bruce remembered wondering why Toby wasn't in school—an investigation was begun. After a couple of weeks it yielded only this: Mrs. Van Wyck's unlocked bottle-green Volvo wagon, found in the long-term lot at Kennedy, the keys still in the ignition.

Everyone talked. There was nothing else to do. Bruce's mother said that the talk went on for even longer than it otherwise might have, because the Van Wycks had money. There were a couple of news cameras outside of school at 3:00 p.m. every day for a week. The papers ran pictures of the car and interviews with the few neighbors and acquaintances who were willing to go on record with their suspicions about the boyfriend, whose name was Viri Minetti. He was a man of violence, several of them said. He had walked out on jobs, had threatened to sue certain clients when they'd tried to replace him with another contractor. He had been overheard screaming at Sis Van Wyck on the back patio of the Van Wyck house, on a late autumn afternoon, screaming unprintable things, things only a lover could scream. It wasn't difficult to imagine: the residents of nearby houses creeping toward their windows, pulling curtains aside an inch, and seeing only the barren Van Wyck yard, the leaves at the bottom of the drained pool, the small frost-repellent tarps stretched neatly over the shrubbery. Perhaps they saw Sis's legs stretched out on the divan that protruded from underneath the patio awning, her feet, in their beige Pappagallo flats, flexed against Viri's rage. She called that area of the house, with its adjacent changing rooms and warm shed full of floats, towels, and skimmers, "the swimmery," which had made Bruce's mother laugh the first time she'd heard it. "Manischewitz," she'd said, half to herself, on the train ride home from Toby's swimming party the previous summer, "I'm glad we live in the city."

"Why?" Bruce had asked her. At that age he had still loved to hear his mother expound on her convictions, make the little speeches that grew more passionate as they wore on until they consisted mainly of the fake swearwords she concocted for use in front of children, the words that could still break his heart when he remembered them.

She'd only muttered distractedly: "Poor Sis. Swimmery. That's some Stepford stuff, sweetie. Some real grade-A bullpie."

Bruce had nodded, knowing—a little—what she meant. She meant the way everything matched, the tight smile on Toby's mother's face when Toby had made a production of farting in the pool, the way she'd bitten her lip when some of the other mothers, who hadn't seen the way the dining room table was set with flowers and trays of sandwiches, had begged off lunch and left early.

"But she's decent hearted, of course," his mother said. "Just fitting into that kind of stupid . . . that paradigm. I told you I knew her a little at Barnard. She had some fun then, you know? She lived on my hall. Obsessed with Lennon. I remember that. God."

Bruce had nodded again, unsure of *paradigm*'s definition but somehow not wanting to mar her reverie by asking, and they had slouched into New York, pausing at each local stop to pick up gropey couples, dazed from the sun and underdressed for the air-conditioning inside the passenger cars, and solitary old men, and vivid coveys of teenagers who yelled and cackled to one another as they swept down the aisle in search of seats. Bruce's eyes and throat were dry from the chlorine, and when the motion and tiredness overtook him and his head lowered itself onto her shoulder, she reached around and clutched him close to her chest, which smelled like Jergens lotion and coffee and the fact that she'd been sweating, some, under the Van Wycks' canvas outdoor umbrella.

When his mother talked about the disappearance, it was obvious, though she didn't say it, that she knew Mrs. Van Wyck was dead. Think about it, she would say to Bruce's father, less careful about excluding Bruce from their conversations than she had been during those first days, Sis would never. You're telling me she'd just get in her car and drive to JFK and vanish on her own, leave those kids! Jesus! Once, Bruce's father had asked—only after putting his arms around his wife—was Sis, could there be any drugs involved? Could she have been disoriented in some way? And Bruce's mother had just smiled at him patiently as if he were a sleepy, petulant child, and called for Bruce to get ready for bed using the voice she used when she argued, even though Bruce was right there in the room with them, pretending to watch TV.

Though no body had been found and no charges had been pressed against Viri Minetti (the Volvo was found to be clean of any prints, hair, clothing fibers, anything that might implicate his involvement, and the day that Mrs. Van Wyck went missing was the day that witnesses assured police they had seen him on site in Larchmont, miles away, inspecting his crew's progress on a restaurant renovation right on Main Street), Bruce could tell that the most terrible thing had happened, was done with already. He thought his mother was right, but he couldn't feel it, not really. He looked forward to the day that Toby would come back to school, thought that the sight of his friend might make him feel something real. He practiced what he would say, the brief and unembarrassing comfort speeches he would make as he and Toby walked to classes together, avoiding the eyes of the other boys. Toby would glance at Bruce in gratitude for being his protector, for teaching the others by his example to be cool, to look out for the one who was marked by something so bad that it would always be as bad as it was right now. But Toby was taking a long time. Three weeks since the cameras had first shown up and he still wasn't back. Bruce's mother, who had been leaving periodic messages for Mr. Van Wyck and gotten no response, agreed that Bruce could call Toby at home after gaining his assurances that he would keep it quick, not ask Toby a lot of questions, not sound overly tragic, not talk about trivial things like sports or video games. She hovered in the doorway to his room as he dialed.

A woman answered, and for a confused moment Bruce was wild with the possibility that Mrs. Van Wyck had been found. He opened his mouth and looked at his mother, who was staring over his head out the window of his room, her hands visibly outlined in the pockets of her tight jeans, her lips pursed and twisted in what looked like concentration. He was about to say, Hey!—to drop the receiver in his hurry—when the woman said, "Hello?" again in a voice that sounded nothing like Mrs. Van Wyck's. He was a fool. A stupid idiot. He breathed in through his nose, turned away from his mother to face the wall, said, "Is Toby around?"

"Who's calling please?" the woman asked. The speed and efficiency of her response made Bruce wonder how many calls Toby had received since his mother—what was the word for it? Got lost? Pretty positively died? Charlie or Jeb could have been calling Toby all along, laying their claim to his loyalty, gratitude, news. Bruce forced himself to stay on the line and wait for the friend who, he realized now, might already feel betrayed by him for some reason he wasn't experienced enough to guess. The staticky blast of his own breathing made him think of crank calls, how all it took was breathing to make somebody—an older girl from Spence who babysat in Bruce's building, Mrs. Sulemain from Science Lab, whose number he and Toby had filched from the faculty directory—nervous and jumpy. Breathing, just by itself, could make someone snap, Stop calling me (1) whoever you are, (2) you fucking prick, (3) please (the responses varied from crank to crank, Mrs. Sulemain's always being the filthiest and most pee inducing), and then hang up. The soft rhythm of his own exhalations sounded amplified now, like someone—or something—was getting him back. His ear felt hot and itchy. His heart beat the same way it had that day when Toby had told him about the boyfriend. The dick. The killer.

"Hey," Toby said, suddenly there.

"Hey!"

"What's going on?"

"Oh, nothing. You know, school."

"Yeah?"

Bruce thought to himself: So this is how it's supposed to be. Moving fast. Like everything's normal, but even faster. Okay.

"So—when do you think you'll come back?" Bruce said. He wondered if his mother was willing him to turn back around, so she could give him a *go easy* look from where she stood. He stayed where he was, fingering the corkboard that covered the wall by his bed. He found that he didn't care what she wanted him to say. She didn't know what this was like.

"Oh—I'm . . . don't know. I guess probably next week."

Toby's voice sounded different, but not too different. Just a little soft and scratchy, as if he had just woken up. "That's good," Bruce said, "because the coach said you could totally play in the tournament, even though you missed some practice."

"Yeah, he called me."

"Cool."

There was a pause. Bruce could hear voices and canned laughter in the background. Television sounds. Toby, unlike Bruce, was allowed to have a TV in his room.

"You watching *Jeannie*?"

"No. *Dukes*."

"Jeannie's hotter than Daisy." Bruce usually sang this, but today he just said it plain.

"Nuh-uh." It was a routine they had. Next, Bruce was supposed to yell "Boingg!" the way Jeannie did when she crossed her arms and tossed her ponytail to perform a trick, and Toby was supposed to laugh in response, *kuh-chee, kuh-chee, kuh-chee*, like a leering Roscoe.

Bruce took a breath. He yelled, *"Boingg!"*

He listened. There was nothing, except for the background laughter and what sounded like a sniff from Toby.

"Kuh-chee, kuh-chee," he tried, taking Toby's part. He knew his mother was watching him, could feel her look on his back, but he

had to keep moving fast. It was clear that if he didn't leap over the quiet places both he and Toby would fall into them, be left clawing at air, plunging down. He was a superhero, straddling canyons. He was Road Runner, clicking his feet together, powering on. *Meep meep.*

"Yeah," Toby said, "ha."

"Mrs. Sulemain got arrested," Bruce said without taking a breath. "She stole something from the school. I don't know what it was."

Toby stayed quiet for a moment. "No way," he murmured. Bruce couldn't tell if he sounded awed or merely dazed, polite.

"I think she stole money from another teacher's desk," he went on. "She had to go to jail. They put her in handcuffs and everything."

"Wow," Toby said. Bruce's mother crossed the room and sat down beside him on the bed.

"People are saying she does drugs. They made her crazy."

"Like, cocaine?"

"I guess," Bruce said. "She needed money to buy more of it, whatever it was."

"Is she still going to teach lab?" Toby was warming up to this, Bruce could tell.

"I don't know," he said. "I don't know any more than what I just told you."

"Bruce—," his mother said. Bruce tried to ignore her. He was dancing now.

"But I do know," Bruce said, "that that's the biggest thing that's happened since you left. Soolster arrested, dude. Going to the pokey."

"Jail," Toby whispered. "Geez. Are you kidding?"

"She cried when the police came," Bruce said. "Seriously."

Bruce's mother lunged across him and grabbed the phone.

"Toby," she said. "This is Brenda, Bruce's mom." She glanced sideways at Bruce. "How are you doing, honey?" She kept her eyes on Bruce as she listened, said "Mm-mm" in a softer voice.

"Ask him if he'll be back on Monday," Bruce said. His throat felt dry.

"We're thinking of you, Tob," his mother said. She pressed two fingers into the place between her eyebrows and put her other hand up between her and Bruce, as if to block him from view. "You call us if you need us. Okay. Bye."

She hung up the phone. They sat together on Bruce's bed. Traffic noise drifted up from the street below.

"Quite the performance," his mother said, finally.

Bruce shrugged his shoulders.

"Don't do that."

"What."

"Shrug at me. You know what I'm talking about."

"No, I don't."

Bruce couldn't help himself. When his mother was unhappy with him, he got trapped in the body of a hater, was left pounding on soundproof glass while that guy, embarrassed, venomous, spoke words for him, gestured for him.

"Do you honestly think that you're helping him by doing that? By making up something ridiculous?"

"What."

His mother made a face, imitating him. "Whuhht," she drawled in a deep, dopey monotone. Then, remembering herself, she said, "I think you're a smart guy, bud, and a nice guy—too nice and smart to take up and slander Mrs. Subbylane or whatever her name is with some horse-ass story just to make Toby feel better— I mean *pokey*, what is that?—when he won't feel better by being told a lie, because his world . . ." and here she blew air through her lips and rubbed her eyes, and because she was upset and the venomous version of himself had bodysnatched him and addled him and sealed him into the glass interior pod, Bruce made fun of her.

He snickered: "Sulemain. Not Subbylane," like Subbylane was the funniest thing he had ever heard in his entire life. Then he said, pumping his voice full of scorn, "How do you even know that's not the truth? And I just forgot to tell you?"

His mother didn't look at him. Eight stories down, a horn sounded, and the gears of an accelerating truck ground together and sighed, ground together and sighed.

"I guess it's lucky that you don't totally get this," she said. She picked something, some hair or fleck, off the back of his shirt—delicately, as if he might scald—before lifting herself off his bed and letting herself out of his room. Blinking, Bruce listened to her pad down the hallway. I do too get it, he said to her in his mind. I *do*.

SIX YEARS AGO, at the Colony Club, Bruce saw Jebbie Jackman at a wedding—the same wedding at which he and his wife met, though she remembered Jebbie only vaguely when they talked about that night. "The white-dinner-jacket guy? Really drunk?" she would ask, and Bruce would have to answer yes, though it pained him, somehow, to answer at all. Jeb, who had also gone to Bancroft and had left at some point (Bruce thought seventh grade) before clubs and girls and nights logged in diners, sucking back eggs and butter-soaked toast and glass after glass of water in an attempt to blunt the throat burning that afternoons full of bong hits in someone's parent-free apartment had given rise to—Jeb had been part of a group, when they were still young enough to sport bowl cuts and hairless bodies without shame, that had included Bruce, and Toby, and Charlie Potts. The four of them had built a makeshift half-pipe together in the backyard of Jebbie's country house, skated it until Toby had legendarily sailed over its side doing a twisty move and sprained both of his wrists. They had competed for top Atari scores and traded in cards and candy and comics and tapes and the occasional *Playboy*—trafficked in all the usual areas of boy commerce, worn Stan Smiths with their uniforms to school. Jeb had been there, that fifth-grade year, was the eleven-year-old equivalent of a friend to Toby, just as Bruce had been—and he had been there at the Colony Club, thus weaving himself and Toby and Charlotte together in Bruce's mind whenever he thought of that night.

He'd felt old, and changed, and uncomfortably reminded, when he'd recognized Jeb right away. They had exchanged hellos, reaching around the backs of their dinner partners to slap hands and shake; after dinner was finished and most of the guests were on the dance floor pretending to boogie to the stale band, they were able to draw their chairs together. They rested their elbows among flung napkins, plates of partly eaten cake, flickering votives, loose petals turning to parchment. Jeb was drinking Scotch out of a champagne flute. The bar had run out of highballs.

"What's keeping you busy these days, Bruce Tavert? Keeping you going?" Jeb's eyes, shadowed within the fleshy contours of his face, scanned the ballroom. Bruce noticed sweat along his hairline.

"Um," Bruce said, trying not to laugh at the way the question was phrased, the bleary-retiree formulation of it. "Man, I wouldn't want to bore you." But, to avoid ending the conversation before it had started, he had gone ahead and bored, with a description of his job, the fact that his offices were moving downtown, hoping to shore up more interesting business, start managing funds for design companies, artists, SoHo types.

"Rich ones," Jeb said. His expression didn't change.

"Mm," Bruce said. He had pushed for the office move, partly because he hated describing himself as a money manager. It sounded narrow and . . . expected, somehow, though he couldn't think who would be expecting it. Still, the idea of working in loft space, which he pictured as perpetually washed in ethereal white-blue light, and of afternoon meetings over cappuccinos and protein smoothies, with people other than representatives from state teachers' associations and suits from utility companies (an area he specialized in particularly) felt like hope, like absolution. He was restless, to tell the truth. On good days, he managed to be glad of this restlessness. At least it meant that he was alive. On bad days, he wondered how, at thirty-one, life had come to feel so circumscribed so quickly, consisting as it largely did of bed, shower, subway, office, conferences at the Midtown Hilton, trips to the second-floor vending machine. He didn't say this, though he considered trying to.

"Check out that waitress," Jeb said. "I'd fuck her."

Bruce brushed at a flake of pastry that was clinging to his tux pants. From the onion tart, he thought. He said: "Oh."

Jeb drained the rest of the Scotch from his glass. He looked at Bruce. "Sorry," he said. "I'm pretty pissed. Did I offend you?"

"No. That's okay. You didn't."

"I'm an asshole. I can tell I offended you."

"She is pretty," Bruce offered stupidly, though he hadn't really looked. "So how are you, Jeb? What's going on with you?"

Jeb grinned into his empty glass. "Shit, Tavert, how long has it been since we've seen each other?"

"Well, not since around the time you guys moved away. Maybe sixteen years, something like that. We were kids."

"Yeah. Well I guarantee you I've been a loaf since then. I guarantee you that."

"Well—" Bruce realized he had no response. What would do, a reflexive I'll bet you haven't? I'll bet you're just being hard on yourself? Anything that came to mind sounded trivial and false. And yet, he wanted to say something bright, something useless.

"Shitty band," Bruce said.

Jeb looked at him. "Hey," he said, "I heard your mother died."

Bruce inhaled audibly. It had been years and he still did that.

"Yeah. She did," he said.

"I'm sorry."

"Thanks."

"I really, really liked your mom."

"Thanks, Jeb."

Jeb picked up a fawn-colored petal from the table and rubbed it between his fingers. Bruce watched as it was crushed into a tiny ball that darkened with its own moisture and the condensation from Jeb's glass. Jeb rolled it onto the white cloth with the tip of his index finger; it left a threading, sluglike trail. He brought his fingertips up to his face and smelled them, then offered his hand to Bruce.

"Rose," he said. "Smells like perfume."

Bruce smiled.

"Your dad doing okay?" Jeb asked.

"Yep," Bruce said, relieved that Jeb hadn't found it necessary or been bombed enough to get into the long-ago whats and hows of his mother's cancer (pancreatic) and length of treatment (nine and a half months). The details sounded too banal, too common, and he hated being asked about them. Unlike his father, who could still assume a grim expression, his eyes trained on the middle distance, and recite the events and progression of his wife's illness as if they formed a litany, an epic poem, whose final lines he would only remember if he could speak it whole, start at the beginning and let rhythm and chronology guide him toward the elusive end. *In the Vale of Tawasentha, / In the green and silent valley* . . . He had moved out to the Springs, where he lived in a rented bungalow on a friend's property and spent his days in a yurt he had erected himself, overlooking the rocky bay. Inside the yurt he typed at a manuscript that Bruce had never seen any part of and knew nothing about; he worked on his "art projects," which were mostly red circles painted on board, painted as large as the turning circumference of his father's body allowed. "It's just what I feel like doing," he told Bruce. "Making these circles. The world is too big to learn anything new. So I stand inside and draw a line around myself, over and over."

"Wasn't he a teacher," Jeb asked.

"Adjunct mathematics professor. Up at Columbia. But he retired."

"Ah."

They drifted into silence. Bruce wanted a drink, thought of asking Jeb to go to the bar with him. But he feared that they would get separated if they moved from where they sat. It seemed the two of them should remain together until he found something real to love about his old classmate. That was it. It felt important, right now, to love something about Jeb Jackman. He signaled the waitress, who was stacking dessert plates at a nearby table. She frowned at him, then mouthed over the medium din of the electric bass, the wailing backup singers, "I'll be right there."

"Shit, brother, you've got the right idea," Jeb said. "That girl is not to be believed."

"Yeah, well. I'm just thirsty."

"Sure," said Jeb. He laughed once, an aggressive "pah" that

laced the inside corners of his lips with spittle, though the expression in his eyes remained grave. The girl made her way over to them.

"You wanted something," she said to Bruce. It was a statement, not a question, and from the slight nasal inflection in her voice, the bemusement that played across her mouth, the way she stood over him, taller than he had realized, her shoulders set in a languid slope that seemed to curve down through her hips, he knew to regret calling her over. She didn't match her surroundings, or the task of fetching drinks. She looked, truly, like she belonged in a bed, or stretched out by someone's fire, blinking sleepily. Her hair was pulled back into two messy pigtails, and a silver and turquoise bracelet circled her arm just above the elbow. Bruce willed away the desire that began to snake through his body—desire that felt tainted and foolish because Jeb had claimed it first, because he couldn't imagine it ever being returned, because he sat in a tuxedo, implicated in the mindless party that jumped all around them.

"That's okay," Bruce said, sounding more forceful than he'd meant to. "I changed my mind."

"He wants a Dewar's and water for himself and one for me," Jeb said. "Christ, you're a work of art."

The girl ignored him.

"I just work for the caterer," she said to Bruce. "So you'll have to go to the bar yourself. Sorry." She shifted her posture; Bruce perceived a mild bovine cast, a heaviness, in her lower body that only seemed to underscore her . . . grace. Grace was what it was.

"No problem," Bruce said. "I'm sorry we bothered you."

"We'll pay you," Jeb said. "I'll pay you whatever you want."

"You didn't really bother me," she said. "We're about to set up coffee over there, if you're interested in that. Maybe your friend could use some."

"Okay."

"Hello. Over *here*. What color underwear are you wearing?" Jeb said.

The girl kept her eyes trained on Bruce, and smiled. She took her time with the smile, letting it spread over her face in degrees.

Bruce felt himself smiling back. She knows, he thought. She knows what kind of effect she has. She likes it. Well, good for her.

"Bye," she said, and walked away. Her walk was heavy but sure. Bruce noticed that her long feet, in their flat, lace-up shoes, toed in a bit.

"That's all right, baby," Jeb said. "Your ass is a little too full figure for my taste anyway, now that I've seen it up close."

Bruce sighed. "She can't hear you."

Jeb said nothing. He picked up a cloth napkin and wiped at his forehead with it, letting his eyes close.

They watched the dancers for a few minutes. Bruce drummed his fingers on the tablecloth through the whole of "Proud Mary." As he watched the waitress setting out mugs next to a huge silver urn at the other end of the ballroom, he realized that a small happiness was taking hold somewhere within his chest, maybe his rib cage. It was opening, like a tiny flower.

"I'm sorry," Jeb said during a pause between songs. "I drink too much."

Bruce looked at him. It seemed unbelievable that he had forgotten Jeb's presence for even a second.

"Champagne and Scotch—plus a couple beers before the ceremony. Bad combination. The champagne at these things always gets me."

"Yes," Bruce said.

Jeb watched him. His lashes, almost transparently blond, seemed to reflect light. The sheen of sweat on his face tinted his skin a pale, lambent green, and Bruce could see the pocks in his complexion up close, as if they'd been magnified. He fought to hold Jeb's gaze.

"Do you ever talk to Toby Van Wyck?" Bruce asked suddenly.

"Naw," Jeb said. "I lost touch with him."

Bruce nodded.

"I do think about him, though," Jeb said.

"Me too."

"He still in Florida?"

"No idea."

"I remember all that happening," Jeb said. He leaned forward. "I remember the memorial service. We had those rubber bands that we were playing with and nobody minded."

"Yeah."

"They found her, you probably heard that. I'm sure you heard that."

"I did."

"Incredible," Jeb said.

Stories, shared, could inspire love, Bruce thought after. Jeb Jackman, prematurely middle-aged, doughy, pickled, he was all right.

(When Bruce first told Charlotte Toby's story, the parts he knew, he kept details to a minimum, and refused to fuel her pity with too many observations of his own, because by that time he knew that her pity, while extravagant at times, could be fleeting, that she could be distracted from it. The facts he included were as stark as he could make them: Toby's mom had gone missing, there had been publicity, his father had remarried quickly, Toby had moved to Naples with his father and stepmother, though they occasionally returned to the Westchester house in the summers, and in Bruce's junior year of high school Mrs. Van Wyck's remains had been found. She had been buried at the edge of an abandoned car lot on Long Island, unearthed when the lot was cleared to make way for a senior-living condominium development. The forensics people who identified her had confirmed that she had died from blows to the head and chest, and the police had charged Viri Minetti after all, based on some evidence linked to the body that Bruce couldn't quite remember. Confirmed, forensics, unearthed, blows. Newspeak was the language he had learned it in, and he doubted there was any other language to use that was any more comprehensible, so he stuck with it. Holy, Charlotte would say, her eyes filling so automatically with tears that Bruce thought her acting for a moment, then despised himself for the thought just as quickly as he'd had it, nodded, and looked back at her, half proud that something he described could move her so. Holy.)

Bruce reached—awkwardly, his elbow bent to avoid dipping his cuff into the flame of one of the candles—for Jeb's hand, shook it again. He didn't feel surprised when Jeb tightened his fingers around his—a firm handshake would be rote to him and didn't necessarily signal particular regard. Then the moment was over, and they both let go and faced forward again. Bruce rested his chin on his palm. He had never said anything to Toby about Mrs. Van Wyck, the disappearing into nothing. This was a pain that surfaced, from time to time. But what he would have said if he had known how—this he was never sure of.

Bruce's fingertips curled around the lower part of his face and brushed against his top lip. He thought that they smelled strangely sweet.

"Good to see you," he said to Jeb. "Really good."

"Right back at you," Jeb said.

They watched the girl together, until one or the other of them excused himself to make a trip to the bar.

AT THE END of that night, Bruce approached the waitress. He told himself that he meant to apologize to her, in case she'd felt harassed. He came upon her standing at the bottom of a back staircase, outside the kitchen. She was talking to a man and a woman, who were leaning into each other, passing a cigarette back and forth. The waitress had one elbow hooked around the newel post of the banister and held a mug of something steaming in her other hand. She stood with her back to him. She laughed at whatever the man had said—a low, gravelly laugh that she was too ready with. He felt he knew that this wasn't her real laugh, though he had no idea what her real laugh would sound like.

"Hi," he said. He tried to step out of the shadow he was standing in, so as not to appear to be lurking.

The man and the woman looked at him, then gestured to the waitress, who turned almost completely around to face him.

"Yeah?" she said. Her tone wasn't as friendly, somehow, as Bruce had expected it to be.

"I, uh, I'm sorry if you were offended before. I wanted to say something before I left."

"Offended before what?"

"Well, when the guy I was talking to came on to you like that."
Bruce grimaced. This had been a bad idea.

"Umm," the waitress said, remembering. She swung forward a
bit from the post, letting herself dangle, letting whatever she was
drinking rock toward the edge of her cup. The man and woman
watched her. Bruce could tell from their expressions that they
were waiting for her to make them laugh. "You mean your golfing
buddy with the panty fetish?"

"I guess—"

"This guy was classic," she said, turning to her friends. "You
know, the kind who doesn't even seem to be into it? Like he's pos-
ing as a pig, but he barely has the energy? Sad, really."

The other woman nodded, looking appreciative. The man said,
"What did he do?"

The waitress looked at Bruce. Her eyes were cold. But just as
Bruce was about to retreat and let her role-play Jebbie's indiscre-
tions without him, something in her face softened. She's decided
to be kind, Bruce thought. Interesting, that she had to decide that.

"It doesn't matter," she said. "You're nice to apologize."

At this, the man and the woman did laugh.

"Scamper," the waitress said to them. "You have work to do."
Then, to Bruce: "You're not my type. That's why they're laughing
at me."

Bruce hoped that his smile looked convincing. He had a sense of
wanting to cheer this person for the way she fascinated him, for
the lightness she had sparked in his chest, and a sense of wanting to walk quickly away from her. Watching her from some safe
distance—that would be ideal. And yet he stayed where he was, the
smile creasing his face.

"I'm Charlotte," she said to him. "Would you like some tea?"
She held her mug out to him. "Loving cup. It's green tea, I think."

"No, thanks."

"I don't drink anymore, so . . ." She raised the mug to her lips
and slurped from it, her eyes popping at him as she did so, punctu-
ating her sentence.

"I'm Bruce."

"Hold on—" She turned away from him and stuck her head through the swinging door that led into the kitchen, yelled something Bruce couldn't quite understand. Bruce found himself staring at the place her black T-shirt gapped open over the waistband of her skirt, at the crescent of white flesh that was revealed as she stretched away from him. "Sorry," she said. "I thought I heard somebody calling me."

"Well," Bruce said. "I should go."

"No. Okay. It was nice meeting you."

She looked at him. "Hey, do you want to come hear some music with me?" she said. The question had a plaintive quality that seemed to belie other things about her.

"Now?" Bruce smiled.

"It's a friend's band. They're playing on the Lower East Side. Where do you live?"

"Lower West."

"Close enough," Charlotte said. "Great. I'll just get my stuff and we'll go."

INCREDIBLY, they shared a cab downtown. Bruce slumped against the seat leather, Charlotte having given the driver directions to a club, shouting them through the Plexiglas safety shield. He could hardly believe his luck as they sped down Fifth Avenue, the lights of the city bleeding past their windows, reaching into the darkness inside the car just far enough to touch the edges of their clothes and faces before bouncing and sliding away. The spiky ends of Charlotte's hair went red, then white, before she caught his eye and he looked away from her.

"You've been kidnapped," she said.

"I know," he answered.

She laughed. Bruce knew that she was making fun of him, at the nonchalance he tried to affect, but he felt himself not caring. He was too glad to be in motion, to let this girl carry him where she wanted to go. Charlotte. The Flatiron District blazed before them, and they veered left. The cabbie's cell phone rang. He raised it to his ear, began jabbering angrily in . . . Urdu? Bruce looked: the name on the medallion was Jinkha Birywani. Bless you, Jinkha, Bruce thought. Keep driving. Drive us to wherever it is from whence you came. I would like to see the sun rise over the wet streets of Delhi.

Jinkha hung a hard left, a hard right. They moved into the East Village. They had to slow down for the bar goers who leaped from curbs and crossed Ninth Street in pairs, holding hands as they walked or ran in front of the cab. One skinny-looking girl slapped the hood as she moved past it, the sleeve of her sweater so long it obscured her hand and furled upward like a ribbon before coming down again. She wore a leather choker and mouthed something at Jinkha through the windshield. At a stoplight, Charlotte rolled down her window, laid her head against the seat, and turned away from him. He watched air brush against her hair and clothes as the cab started moving again and taunted himself with the impossibility of reaching out to touch the hollow place where her throat met her collarbone. He liked it that she didn't need to speak, felt proud that he didn't seem to, either.

They reached Avenue A, at which point Jinkha screamed into his phone, snapped it shut, hit the brakes, and turned around in his seat.

"Kitty cat?" he barked. From behind the shield he sounded as if he were speaking to them from under a layer of water. Bruce stared at him. He wanted nothing but to keep moving through space. He had no idea how to respond to the bit of nonsense that had just emerged from Jinkha's mouth.

"This is it," Charlotte said. "Thanks." She produced a worn change purse from her coat pocket, unzipped it, and began to fumble inside it. She held it close to her face, trying to see its contents by the light of the neon sign outside.

"Oh," Bruce said. "The Kitty Kat Lounge."

Charlotte turned to him. "I don't have any cash. I can't believe it. I'm so sorry."

"Oh," said Bruce. "No. This is mine." He reached for his wallet, glad for the chance to feel necessary.

"You're going to think I used you for cab fare," she said, half frowning, half smiling, as she opened the car door, bathing them in harsh yellow light.

"Never," Bruce said, pushing ones at Jinkha through a metal slot. He felt good. He felt great—more naturally himself on this block, with this girl, than he felt in his own life, at his office, with his friends, walking west on Bank Street toward his apartment. Why was that? He wouldn't question it. He would only take Charlotte's hand, let himself be lifted onto the curb and through a door. A waifish guy working the club entrance nodded at Charlotte and waved them both past his change table. They pushed through a velvet curtain, into the dark. Into people, smoke, hard music, sweat, ammoniacal wafts of alcohol, and the beery grit under everyone's feet. Charlotte led him to a chest-high table by the stage, told him to wait there. She disappeared back into the crowd. Bruce stood against the wall, watching the redhead on the stage twist at the hem of her baby-doll dress as she bleated lyrics into a standing mike, then turned away from it dramatically, as if it had hurt her feelings. She did this over and over, then began to jump in place while the lead guitarist built up chords one by one. At last the chorus exploded, and the redhead launched into a spooky dance, her arms rising above her head. Bruce thought of wings.

Charlotte reappeared, holding a beer in one hand and what looked like a glass of water in the other. She set both on the table.

"There's the drink you wanted from me earlier," she said. Then: "You're carrying this off rather well." She grinned, gesturing at him.

Bruce looked down. He had forgotten he was wearing a tuxedo.

"Did you need me to pay for the beer? I thought you didn't have money," he said, looking up.

"No. I used to work here. The only possible perk that could come from that is free beers for the rest of my life."

"Well, thanks."

"Don't thank me. You deserve it."

"Why," Bruce asked. He immediately wished he could push the word, with its desperate sound, back into his mouth.

Charlotte looked at him. She looked at him for so long that he doubted she would answer at all. "I'm not sure," she said finally. "But there's some reason."

"Mmm," Bruce said, hoping he sounded skeptical. Amused. He tapped against the side of his beer bottle in time with the drum-beat from the stage. He felt that anything might be possible, as long as he watched the redheaded singer and didn't do what he wanted to do now, which was put his arms around this girl, this waitress, and weep with relief.

He found out that she had come from Kentucky, had worked her way north, to New York, via one boarding school and two colleges—one of which was too small to contain her and the other from which she graduated only after cobbling together credits from her sporadically attended classes, a summer volunteering for a relief organization in Portugal (Bruce, lamely: "They need relief, in Portugal?"), and the plays and student films that she had been able to characterize as independent projects and apply toward a drama major. He found out that she had worked as an actress, an assistant to a floral designer, a bartender, an assistant to a photographer, and, now, as an assistant to a caterer (a friend of hers)—which sometimes required waitressing at events. He found out that she had one sister, one brother (both younger), two parents, many past boyfriends, no current ones. She lived on East Seventeenth. She voted Democratic. She had been bulimic briefly, a long time ago. Her favorite writer was Flaubert. Favorite movie, *Delicatessen*. She could be self-aggrandizing when she talked—but, Bruce thought, adorably so. Understandably so. She was twenty-eight years old. She had once been photographed kissing Susan Sarandon in a bar, on a bet. She had been flown to Brazil by a phil-anthropist, on the pretense of being hired to videotape a round-table on the environment. The philanthropist had wanted her in his bed, reserved only one room, of course, of course. There were other stories. She did drink—eventually had a beer herself—she just didn't like to. It was implied that she had to be with someone she trusted in order to drink. After the beer, and the next, Bruce thought he could hear something of Kentucky in her voice, in the way it started to slide wetly along the vowels.

At three o'clock in the morning they found themselves in the Duane Reade on Charlotte's corner, rifling through a two-dollar bin full of health and beauty supplies. Charlotte, who had insisted, laughing, that she would need vitamin B to stave off the next morning's hangover (she had trusted him, after all), had gotten distracted by the bin on her way to the checkout counter and was now enlisting Bruce's opinion of press-on nails, rouge colors, false eyelashes, rash ointments. They leaned over the bin, and a woman moved toward them. Her head was wreathed in white shocks of hair that floated around her face as if independent from it, held near it by tenuous magnetic force rather than skin and follicles. She was stooped and overly, messily lipsticked. She said, "Fuck fuck fuck, hold on, hold on, fuck, you fuck," to an apparition she perceived somewhere beyond Bruce's head. She made as if to rush it, then, just as she drew abreast of Charlotte, turned to her and, stepping hesitantly past, said, "Excuse me, honey," her eyes as lucid and kind as they were clouded with hostile confusion the moment she turned away from Charlotte and snapped "Fuck you goddamn fuck" again, at nothing, and moved away.

Bruce saw it. He saw that Charlotte was charmed. In a dangerous, dangerous world (in which people succumbed, despaired, got lost) she would sneak through, untouched. No—she wouldn't have to sneak. People let her through. The universe let her through. It excused itself and stepped aside, afraid to muss her as she stood, her eyes popping at him in mirth and wonder, wrapped up in a glowing corona of Duane Reade twenty-four-hour fluorescence.

He would bide his time for as long as he could. Then, an eternal six months later, he would ask her to marry him.

BRUCE AND KNOX

WE WERE SNOTS, he would say to Charlotte later when he talked of his friends, his childhood. Little preppy shits. *Were?* Charlotte might say, and grin. She liked to lord what she saw as Bruce's WASP privilege over him, ignoring the fact that her own family was rich, that for several years running he had attended school on scholarship, that his mother was Jewish and required him to purchase things like Stan Smiths himself, due to her refusal to kowtow to the great American marketing machine. It was as if Charlotte were a sharecropper's daughter and he a Yankee titan, a regular Rockefeller, when she got in one of her moods. "You picked a fine time to leave me, Lucille," she'd sing loudly at him when he tried to defend himself, looking straight in his eyes, aware that he didn't know the words. "Four hungry children and a crop in the field." So you know some corny country music, he'd say, quelling the impulse to ask her not to stop, for there was something knowing and hard in the back of her singing voice that wasn't a joke, that he wanted to keep hearing. You've got that over me. Big deal.

They fought.

They recovered, again and again.

They moved in together.

Bruce insisted on paying for a moving truck to gather her from her East Side studio and bring her to his place, though she told him she would have preferred to let friends help her load into cabs, a borrowed car or two, to caravan her crosstown the way she had promised them they could. It's not a funeral cortege, Bruce had said. Oh, but it is, Charlotte replied, pulling at the short hairs that curled at the nape of his neck. She pulled at his hair until it hurt, though he wouldn't say so. It's the beginning of the end, she said.

On the long-ago day Charlotte had moved in, he'd stood in the living room, looking out toward the street. There were fresh flowers on top of the sideboard he had inherited from his mother. Dahlias from the corner deli. It was September. The bathrooms were clean, lit. There was a wet washcloth folded over the kitchen faucet, its sides hanging down and dripping patternlessly into the shiny well of sink. All the windows were open.

He thought that he might hear the moving truck before he saw it. It would have to turn a corner somewhere nearby; his was a one-way street. The truck's mammoth groan might reach him as it turned. Sound could carry like that on a Saturday, in this neighborhood.

Bruce checked his watch, considered getting himself another glass of water. He was wearing jeans and a freshly laundered shirt. His hair was wet and combed. Below his windows, he watched a black teenage boy surrounded by dogs making his way toward the river. The boy held fistfuls of leash ends in his hands and walked slowly; dogs wove back and forth around him, moving forward in a mass. Bruce counted: one, two, three, five—eight dogs in all. The street was cobbled here; the kid moved right down the center of it. Something few people knew, that he wasn't even sure if his father remembered, was that his mother had lived for a time on this same street—might have even lived on this block—after college, back when she was part of that population, the good-girl intelligentsia, that worked for lawyers and architects and literary agents, lunched alone over black coffee at Schrafft's, lived in pairs, iced liters of pinot grigio in the shower before dinner parties. Bruce's mother used to tell him about it, her face animated with a kind of darting, weary pleasure underneath the scowl she wore when she talked about the indulgence her life had been before she settled down to the true work of raising him. I was Brenda Shapiro, she would say. I painted my fire escape blood orange. I used to sit out there on weekends, doing God knows what. Reading to pigeons, or something. Oh, honey, I was shameless. I was a mother-bleeping cliché.

When Bruce moved back to New York after her death, after school and the few other places that he'd tried on for size before drifting, bewildered, back to the only city he knew, his father gave him the option of moving into their old apartment; it hadn't sold yet, the furniture was still in it. Bruce could sleep far uptown in the twin bed of his childhood if he wanted to, boil things in the glazed, damaged pots that his parents had received as wedding presents. He could spread out, alone, in any room; Bruce's father was already living in the Springs by then. No thanks, Dad, Bruce told him, though he had no sense of what else he would do. I'll find something.

He had crashed on a friend's floor, then met a woman of indeterminate age at a party and stayed with her while he spent his days going to open houses all over Manhattan, with no criteria to narrow his search other than a vague feeling that he would know where he was supposed to live when he saw it, based on an impression, on some distinguishing feature: hand-built bookshelves, a bike rack in the vestibule, a bit of graffiti on an outside wall that he would have no choice but to read as significant. He would spend his whole inheritance, plus the little he had saved in his own bank account, on the rooms where he now lived, stacked three over three, like the layers of a cake. The front door of the building opened into a brief entry hall that disappeared up a carpeted staircase. To its left was a numbered door that opened to reveal the first floor of the house, the bottom layer, which was empty when he'd moved in except for stacks and stacks of newspapers, short and tall stacks, leaning at angles, striated yellow, white, gray, like hacked-out cross sections of earth—stacks in the living room fireplace, on the deep windowsills, the kitchen that overlooked a dried-up back garden. The upper floor had once been a separate apartment; the Realtor had told him the previous owner had occupied both at once, without ever taking the time to integrate them. Bruce often wondered about the man who had lived in this place, his life divided onto two floors. The upstairs door was still numbered; the place where the guy had slept was at a different address than the place where he had made himself breakfast. He must have run up and down the house staircase twenty times a day, or maybe preferred to camp for periods of time in one or another of his apartments, to effect that kind of temporary vacation from his life.

Bruce didn't feel young. The last time he had seen his father, his father had taken him drinking, something they had never done together. They had sat in a hotel bar on Fifty-ninth; his father had sipped at a beer and, in his way, urged Bruce to get drunk. Bruce accepted the first shot of whiskey out of politeness, or maybe fear: his father was too giddy, the bar too expensive. Bruce had just returned from a trip to Asia, having accepted the invitation of a classmate who had moved to Hong Kong to work for the AP—he answered each of his father's questions about the boat they had taken into China, the terrifying airport landing, the floodlit racetrack in Happy Valley. Another round, his father would call, just as Bruce had reached the middle of an answer or explanation, and Bruce would have to shake his head no at the waitress, or let her set another shot in front of him and leave it brimming there, untouched. His father's nails were bitten down; it took Bruce moments to remember that they had always been that way, that his pants had always been stained here and there with ink marks. He both loved and dreaded his father for trying to give him the gift of blankness that night, to narrow his focus to a set of empty glasses, a bed to tumble into gratefully at the end of the night. Though his father wasn't a drinker himself, Bruce knew that these were the things he wanted for both of them: strong physical sensations, and escape. The things that he had not had to think to rely on when mathematics and his wife were still wholly alive to him.

Thank you, he kept saying to his father, for the drinks; he was forever saying thank you, had been since he was a kid; the impulse toward gratitude for even the smallest, most self-serving gestures was somewhere drifting among the viscous platelets of his blood.

He heard a truck rumbling, far down the street. He smiled automatically. He felt the sweat begin to heat and slick his armpits, and thought of holding the shirt away from his body with his fingers, so he wouldn't wet it before Charlotte arrived. It still surprised him that she provoked a vanity he hadn't known in himself. He prepared himself for her, worried over what she might think, threw out his oldest, torn boxers and bought new pairs, joined a regular pickup game at the gym, carried himself taller in those moments before he caught sight of her—then forgot himself so completely during their times together that when he glimpsed himself again, in the mirror over a restaurant's bathroom sink or in the bits of misshapen glass that Charlotte had pasted to the wall above the bureau opposite her bed, he felt like laughing over his earlier nervousness. Here he was, the wine consumed, his pressed clothes removed from him, his hair wild, the skin on his face rougher, his eyes clearer, and he looked fine. Better than before, if he cared to make a judgment—which, at those times, he didn't.

"Hey hey!" A shout, from below. Bruce looked down and Charlotte was there. She wore a printed silk dress that he had never seen before, buttoned carelessly over a T-shirt, sneakers on her feet.

"Hi," he shouted back, leaning out the open window. He knelt on the sill, which Charlotte had already turned into a makeshift window seat over the course of her weekends at his place. There were a few tapestry pillows strewn on it now, a brass ashtray which Bruce had cleaned the butts out of this morning, rinsed, dried, put back in its place.

"*That's* what you wear to move in?" He spoke at a lower volume, now that his head hung over the street, just above her.

Charlotte laughed, looked down at herself, yanked at the waistband of the dress. "I know," she said. "I'd packed everything else. This happened to be on top of the Goodwill pile."

Bruce smiled. He tried to stop smiling, but he couldn't.

Charlotte smiled back, drawing her brows together. "Why am I nervous," she said, loud enough for Bruce to think of neighbors, listening over their morning tea. "Why am I standing in the street like this?"

"Hold on," Bruce said, in a quieter voice than she had used. "I'm coming down."

"I have two hot Israeli movers, by the way." Charlotte could never let him go; she extended conversations a subject or two beyond their natural conclusion—often nodded, then kept talking, after the word *goodbye*. "They let me drive."

"They did? Where are they?"

"I don't know," Charlotte said, looking around. "I imagine they're tight on my tail. I asked them to let me out at the corner. I lost confidence once we hit all these little streets—the progress felt so . . . slow."

"Stay," Bruce said. "Hold on."

He hit his head on the window casing on the way back in and kneed the ashtray aside in an attempt to raise himself from the window seat. He opened the door, flipped the deadbolt shut, and let it bounce on its hinges as he ran down the stairs. The possibility of framed photographs of people from Charlotte's life on the mantel, the bedroom walls, excited him. He had lain in his bed until late last night, awake (after she had called to wish him good night and complain about having left so much work until the last minute—which she always did, he was learning—to complain again that she didn't need a moving truck, she didn't have enough real furniture to warrant it), and imagined her clothes in his closets. He imagined her coats, the long gray tweed he had seen, and the celery-colored poncho, and a rain slicker, if she owned one, perfuming the darkness of the closet by the front door, hanging among his own coats. He wished they were hanging there already, believed for the few moments just before sleep that they might be, so that, if he had the energy, he could get up and close himself in with them, finger their empty sleeves, explore the little piles of detritus in their pockets: the squares of cellophane, pennies, tokens, crumbs, broken matches, bits of gravel.

Out on the street, the air was cooler. Bruce felt a flick of relief that he had remained relatively unmussed until this moment: his head wasn't bleeding from the place where he'd knocked it, his shirt wasn't soaked through, not yet. He remembered the building door a couple of beats before it closed and locked behind him, and whirled around to hold it open with the palm of his hand. He kicked off one of his shoes, used it to prop the door, and hopped on one foot down the cold brownstone steps to Charlotte. He opened his arms to her.

"Welcome to your house," he said.

She leaned into him. "Thank you," she mumbled into his shirt.

Bruce wanted to hold her here forever, his nose in her hair.

"I almost had a nervous breakdown this morning," she said, still mumbling.

"Oh," Bruce said. He blinked. He didn't exactly want to hear about it, not now. "Let's sit here on the steps," he said. "You really drove?"

Charlotte wiped at her nose with the sleeve of her T-shirt. She looked at him, then moved to sit down beside him. "Just for a few blocks," she said. She began to smile again. "It was great. I sat between them at first, they were letting me downshift, and I screwed it up, you could hear my stuff sliding around in the back and the thing almost stalled, but then I begged them to just let me try driving, so they did. The steering wheel on those trucks is gigantic. It's up to my chin."

Bruce laughed. He knew that this would become one of Charlotte's stories, the one she might tell next, when they found themselves among new friends around someone's kitchen island, or drinking on a roof. The Israelis might become skinny Russians; a hand might be placed on her bare knee; the wheel might become so big that all three of them had to turn it together; the truck might jump onto a curb. He had learned early not to question the evolving details of Charlotte's tales in front of others, though exactitude was somewhere in his nature, and it took willpower not to mind a little.

"I didn't get to bed until four," Charlotte said. She reached for the cuff of his shirt, began to tug the small button at his wrist.

"You were packing until that late?" Bruce asked. He touched her back. He felt a tiny thrill; perhaps she'd brought everything, perhaps she possessed more than he'd realized. He wanted all of her objects in his house, even the useless ones.

"Well, I really finished up this morning. But I was on the phone for hours last night," she said. She withdrew her hand from his cuff and placed it over her face. "I am so tired, love."

"Why?" Bruce said. What he'd really meant to ask was: Who? Who were you talking to?

He didn't have to ask. "I feel like I called everyone I know. I called my sister, but she didn't answer the phone. I'm sure she knew it was me. Then I called Stephen. Remind me never to call him again in the middle of the night. Not that I plan to."

Charlotte scratched at the gritty swath of step between them with her fingernails. Bruce resisted an impulse to cover her hand with his, to still it. Stephen was one of the old boyfriends. An actor whom Bruce had met. He had met so many people already. The caterer Charlotte staffed for, Helen from Trinidad, her temporary coworkers, the waves of friends that seemed to shift by the week, according to both Charlotte's ideas about them and certain of their given characteristics: stamina, thick skin, ego, drama. From what Bruce had observed, it was important either to possess an exaggerated surplus of these qualities or not to have them at all if you expected Charlotte to keep choosing you, talk about you at parties, cook you supper, call you in the middle of the night. He wasn't sure yet whether he was blessed or doomed because of where he fell.

"You know that I used to go out with him, right? God, I hate that phrase: *go out.*"

"Of course. You told me all about that."

Bruce reached down and began to rub his exposed foot. It was cold out here. He needed patience when Charlotte forgot things, forgot bits of conversation they'd had, things they had confided in each other.

"I did tell you. I remember. Well, it doesn't matter," Charlotte said.

Bruce nodded, tucked his foot behind the opposite knee to warm it.

He and Charlotte had bumped into Stephen in a restaurant on Sixth Avenue not too long after they'd met; Stephen had joined them for coffee. Bruce had known right away that Stephen and Charlotte had been together; right away he had despised Stephen's gnomish upper body, the way he hunched over the marble table and accepted everything offered him, from their invitation to sit to the hard bread in the basket to the coins that Bruce pushed toward him once the bill was paid, protesting that someone deserved to pocket the extra change. When Charlotte made a trip to the bathroom Stephen had picked up her coffee cup and dipped his finger into the sediment that coated the bottom, said something to the effect that Bruce had his blessing, that Charlotte was special, a friend, good luck, he hoped they would all have a chance to "spend time together" in the "future."

"Sure," Bruce had said, for lack of any better response. He made no attempt to correct Stephen's impression that he and Charlotte had any kind of assured future—or past, for that matter; he himself wasn't even completely convinced that she was seeing him exclusively. He felt surprised at any gallant show from a man who, only minutes before, had described a theater director he and Charlotte knew as a "hideous cunt," sending Charlotte into fits of laughter. Stephen shrugged; he fixed the chipped surface of the table with a look that struck Bruce as defiant. Bruce watched him. His hair was gray and almost shaved at the temples; his face was thin, all angles.

"I don't know," Stephen said. "I honestly wasn't sure if you were her new boy when I first walked in. She's never been with anyone like you before. But it makes sense. She deserves someone who will balance her, the way you seem to. Do you mind my saying that?"

Bruce shook his head. Had Stephen been watching them from some hidden place before he'd walked by their table? Had he deduced all this in thirty minutes? He tried to remain wary. He reminded himself that Stephen's observations were shallow, nothing to base hope on, and shook his head again, as if coming awake. He shifted in his chair.

"My initial reaction—she's admitted to herself that she isn't a very good actor, for example. That takes courage. She's one of those who's too much herself to really disappear into a part, you know?"

Bruce said nothing.

"To gravitate toward what's good for you, or to what you're good *at*, takes real maturity. I admire it, is what I'm saying. God knows I'm not there yet," Stephen said. "She's paranoid about relationships. But clearly, she's safe with you."

Bruce felt a sudden thrill: if this went much further he thought he had license to be rude. Under the table, he tapped at his knee. "You seem pretty comfortable speaking for her," he said.

Stephen smiled at him. There were narrow gaps between several of his front teeth; he had the bright gums and teeth of a child. "I mean, I think she grew up on a fucking horse farm! Do you know what I mean? She is not from New York! I don't think she should end up with an actor. She'd come to her senses eventually, and then have to wreck her life."

Stephen placed his index finger in his mouth and sucked on it. He winced.

"Where are you from?" Bruce asked. His voice was quiet, angry. He didn't know why this was the question he chose; he had many. He supposed it was the only question whose answer didn't threaten him, or Charlotte, in some way. He wished there was some water left in his glass.

Stephen looked at him.

"Kansas," he said.

Bruce choked. "You're kidding."

"For some reason, I don't dislike you," Stephen said. "So I'm going to be honest with you. I am from Topeka. I am absolutely serious."

Bruce wrapped his hand around the back of his neck and looked at Stephen. He felt a laugh rising, a delirious laugh that, given a choice, he would have preferred to repress. But I dislike *you*, he thought. He held the laugh in for as long as he could. Then it erupted from him in a hard wheeze. He was still settling by the time Charlotte returned to the table and had some difficulty catching his breath. Stephen was laughing, too. He had muttered, through his laughter, something about what an asshole he could be, something both proud and apologetic. Charlotte stood over Bruce and watched him as he tired himself and finally stilled. He could see that she was irritated.

"Talking about me?" she asked them both, smiling.

"No," Stephen said. "Actually, talking about me."

"We should go," Bruce said, looking up at her. He felt sorry that Charlotte looked uncomfortable, sorry for his part in it. He thought she deserved a graceful exit.

"If you're ready," Charlotte said. She seemed to relax. "Stephen, it was—interesting to see you."

Stephen laughed and rose to kiss her.

Outside, she had said, "He hates me," but before Bruce could console her she had sighed and changed the subject.

Bruce had thought of Stephen since—thought of him at those moments when he felt unsure of his place, of whether Charlotte was moving through him, the way he'd watched her move in only a short time through other phases, through friends, proclivities, even colors ("that's *my* favorite color"), the diaphanous shirt and skirt she wore together for days at a time before discarding them. He didn't know. Perhaps everything that Stephen said—it was hard to remember, later, exactly what he had said, or whether he had been directly insulting—had been true. What Bruce did think set him apart was this: though he wondered about Charlotte's focus on him, whether she truly loved him or whether she sought him as Stephen had thought—for balance, as a kind of antidote for something—there was no possibility that would kill him. He could allow for Charlotte to be attracted to him for a few less-than-flattering reasons, as long as she remained attracted, as long as there were other reasons, too. Maybe he was the first to allow her such a thing. As Bruce looked at Charlotte now, he realized something else: he was able to let himself be comforted by the suspicion that she didn't fully understand, either, why she was here. Her lips were chapped. Her hair was loose, hanging over her eyes. Premeditation like the kind Stephen had alluded to, the making of logical choices, seemed ridiculous in this flat light, at this hour on a Saturday morning.

"What did you talk about?" Bruce said. He couldn't stop himself. "Or was it private. I understand if it was, even though the guy is unquestionably a jerk."

Charlotte raised her eyes to him. She smiled, looking relieved. "You're right," she said. "No, I'll tell you everything."

Bruce looked toward the river. The guy with the dogs was making his way back already. At this distance the pack was no more than a dark, shape-shifting blob at his feet, backlit against the stripe of highway, the pale suggestion of water.

"It was dumb," Charlotte said. "I got worried. I wanted to know what I had done before to end things. I got this idea it had been my fault."

Bruce nodded. Charlotte kept looking at him; some heat seemed to be rising under her skin, coloring her neck, the tips of her ears. Bruce wanted to close her eyes and draw her to him, just sit with her until the truck pulled up. But he didn't stop her. He supposed too that, as much as he craved all her history—and he did—some part of him drew the line at reassuring her about a conversation with an ex-lover.

"He just said that we didn't care enough about each other, and that we hadn't given each other enough *room*, whatever that means." She looked down at the step, and frowned.

"Well," Bruce said. He had room for her. He'd realized it from the first night; he had the perfect space, had left it open and unpainted just for her. I've been so ready for you, he thought, for the thousandth time. It was time to move inside; his foot was freezing. He needed motion. He looked down the street. Dog-boy was moving closer. He wondered if the Israelis were lost.

"I don't want to go through that with you," Charlotte said.

Bruce turned to her. The color had reached her cheekbones; she was looking at him as if he could change something with what he said next. What he said was: "Okay." He stopped himself from saying: So don't.

Charlotte inhaled. Her face changed. She smiled at him. "Sorry," she said. "You look cold. Do you want to go inside and wait? We don't have to talk about this." She reached her hand toward him.

"It's all right," Bruce said. "I don't mind talking. Let's just do it upstairs. They can buzz us when they get here."

She nodded and reached her arms around him. Bruce let her hold him still, even though he was ready to move for the door. She arched her neck back, exposing her throat to him. He bent down and kissed it, then kissed up her jawline, up to the bare lobe of her ear, which he bit lightly.

"Okay," Charlotte said, laughing. "Upstairs is a good idea."

Bruce released himself from her arms, moved up the steps, and held the door open. When Charlotte moved past him, he looked down the street one more time, in the opposite direction of the dog walker, nearly flush with the building now. He saw a yellow truck far down the block. A man hung partly out of the driver's side window, as if trolling for street numbers.

"Coming?" Charlotte called from inside, where she stood outside his apartment door.

"Yes," Bruce called. There would be time. The movers would find the building, ring the bell. He hopped up the stairs toward his shoe, toward Charlotte, and let the glass outer door close behind him. As he pushed into his spotless living room behind her he thought of what she'd said, that she'd tell him everything. He swallowed. Everything was what he wanted.

. . .

KNOX LET THE HEELS of her sandals knock against the cabinet below the kitchen counter in her parents' house, over and over, until her mother walked over to where she sat on the counter, placed one of her hands on each of Knox's knees, and told her that unless she stopped that right now she could expect something terrible to happen to her, and soon.

Knox smiled down. She placed her hands over her mother's, felt their heat, the slick of lotion on her skin, the slight ropiness of vein. She felt the chill of the gold cameo on her mother's right ring finger. Her mother's hands, their nails manicured to deep pink ovals, were like her: slightly but perfectly built. Built so that their small parts mesmerized with their vividness, somehow, enough to create an illusion of size.

"Sorry, Mama," Knox said. "I didn't realize I was driving you crazy."

Her mother cowbit her knee with her thumb and forefinger. She made a face, nodded once. Knox waited until she had walked away to press against the cabinet with her heel, quietly this time, feeling the weight of the shelves and pots as she pushed them back inch by inch. She held her foot in place. She had entered the house roiling, somehow—expecting to feel helpless and overwhelmed in the face of having to follow her parents and their fragmented conversation from room to room, having to piece together what was to happen next by herself, based on half-answered questions and distracted movement. She had worried that she might fly apart in the middle of all that strangeness, in the house that she loved for its steady rhythms, for its dinner on time, its ritual half-hour naps at six o'clock, its wry, affectionate, glancing talk. On opening the door into the mudroom and hearing the voices in the kitchen, she had stood in place for a few moments, fighting a queasiness in her lower abdomen, waiting for it to pass. Then she had stepped into the gleam and clutter of the kitchen and found a calm suspension that surprised her. Her parents stood near the stove and smiled at her when she entered. Her brother Robbie sat slumped in the club chair in the far corner, leafing through the pages of a magazine. Oh, Knox thought, all right. This is something I can do. She said, Can you believe it. She asked what was happening. She reentered herself, felt the light blouse and skirt she'd changed into hanging on her body, defining its shape. She took the slice of tomato her father offered her and popped it into her mouth. Yum, she said. It was still warm from the garden and flooded her mouth with sweetness.

We're having pasta, her father had said. We're waiting to see if we can charter a plane tonight, but there'll be time to eat. We talked to Charlotte; she's fine. Excited. They're going to wheel her in in an hour.

Now her brother said, "Guess who's the sexiest man alive?"

"Don't know," Knox said. She wondered if she should pour herself a drink.

Robbie flipped a page of his magazine. It made a snapping sound. He narrowed his eyes, not answering. "How come they don't do an issue for the sexiest woman alive? Or do they," he said.

"What is he talking about," her mother said. She dipped two fingers into the pot on the stove with a practiced quickness; Knox thought of a gull dipping its beak to snap a fish, rising in a white flash. Her mother blew on a piece of spaghetti, then raised it to Knox's mouth for her to nibble.

"Tell me if this is ready," she said.

"I think it is," Knox said, tasting. She swung her foot forward, letting the cabinet door release its tension and fall back into place.

"I like it really al dente," Robbie said. "Is it al dente?" He scratched at the place where his sternum lay under the thin, over-washed cotton of his Mr. Bubble T-shirt. Since he'd entered his Virginia college last fall he had collected a whole closetful of T-shirts that doubled as advertisements for American household products; Knox had seen Tide, Mello Yello, Tony the Tiger, and the Jolly Green Giant all march across his bony chest over the course of the summer. She looked at him. He was a boy in places and a man in places lately. Though the center of him remained reedy and slender, the work he had put in at the foaling barn and as a hot walker at the July sale showed in his arms, which had gone toned, darker from the sun, coarse with golden hair. Knox had been there on a few late afternoons when he stood on the diving board of their parents' pool, patchy with sweat and complaining that he smelled worse than all the stalls he'd mucked combined, and jumped without taking even his shoes off. He'd swim a couple of lengths and then emerge, heavy and streaming, looking like both the little brother Knox had always known and the person—handsomer than Knox might have predicted—that he had almost become.

"What's al dente again," her father said. "Is that the underdone one?"

"It's the perfectly done one, my darling," her mother answered from inside the steam that billowed from the colander as she shook it over the sink. Her tongue touched the inside corner of her mouth with effort. "You all can go ahead and sit down. Robbie, fill the water glasses if you don't mind," she said, her face reddening from the heat.

"Knox can do it," Robbie said, even as he heaved himself up and made his way over to the cupboard.

"I didn't ask her," her mother said, turning to give Knox a look that was amused, incredulous.

"Poor Rob," Knox said. "Works all day and slaves all night. I don't know how he manages."

"Barely. I barely manage. Would you like one ice cube or two, princess?" Robbie said as he opened the door to the ice maker. The exposed well of ice breathed a whitish smoke into the air that climbed up the middle of Robbie's body and made him look cold, suddenly unprotected. Knox fought an impulse to cross the room and hug him at the waist, rub at his limbs until they were warm again.

They were waiting for the charter service to call back, and for the next update from Bruce. Her mother had already packed some things in a duffel that sat, looking deflated, at the bottom of the back stairs—packed like a wild woman, her father said, packed for both of us in under five minutes. Charlotte was at thirty-five weeks, early but out of the woods, and the babies were healthy, just ready to come, due to the low fluid.

"Gross," Robbie had said, from his place in the corner. Knox coughed, partly in laughter, partly to blunt the edge of her brother's obnoxiousness. Rude was still a function of age for Robbie, rather than a full-fledged personality feature. Knox could tell that it would fall away from him—that it probably already had when he was with people other than family. She could relate; only in this kitchen was she the type to sit on counters, more prone to watch than to offer help with dinner. As a guest in other houses she itched to take over the stirring of sauces, would rather chop than entertain the hosts with talk as they worked. Work was both an offering and an excuse to become more invisible. And yet here she felt compelled toward neither of those possibilities. She sat, in the midst of things, until she was asked to do something, anything, else.

"This is serious, babe," her mother said to Robbie, though Knox could see that she kept humming, choosing to be more excited than worried, within her current. If she were alone, Knox thought, she might be smiling to herself.

They sat down at the table.

"We might be able to jump on a commercial flight if there's no jet available," her father said, rocking back a little in his chair.

"Let's just wait and see," her mother said. She reached for Knox's plate, set it beside the serving bowl, and began tonging helpings of pasta onto it.

"I could call Delta and see if there's space on the night flight."

"We'll know more once the charter company calls back," her mother said. She ground pepper from the mill over Knox's plate: *crack, crack, crack*. Her mouth looked too set, suddenly. Too concentrated. Stop, Knox thought to herself, I don't want any more.

"I don't like that much pepper," Knox said, and immediately flushed. She had sounded, absolutely, like a child. Her mother glanced at her.

"Okay," she said. "I'll take this one."

"Your mother is the only one who really likes things spicy," her father said. "But she forgets."

"I do," her mother said. "I forget that you all are total philistines about food."

Knox breathed. She filled with a wanting: to get up from her place and circle the table, put her arms around her mother, her lovely mother, for letting slights pass unremarked on. Around her father, so dependably *there* under the blue cotton of his shirt, under the sheen the overhead light cast on the curve of scalp where his hair had thinned, for his assumption that she would accompany them on tonight's trip, his strong kindness, his readiness to make things okay. Around Robbie, who sat chewing at a hunk of bread that he had already fished from the basket, his constant hunger hanging off him like a logo, the bones of his smooth jaw popping audibly as if to egg him on. These moments came. It was hard for her body to know how to contain them when they did come. They felt like a breaking. It had occurred to her before that this was all she needed, that any other kind of love existed for people who didn't have this.

"How were the kids today, Knoxie," her mother asked. "I need to talk about something else, otherwise I get too nervous."

"They were good," Knox said, determined to convey what she felt through her voice, through her talk. She sat up straighter. "Some of them are improving so much. I want to bring a group of them out to the farm before summer school's over. Let them roam around a little bit."

"Ned could show them around the stallion complex," her mother said. "That's an idea."

"Or they could come to the foaling barn," Robbie said. "We could use a little excitement over there. All we do is stand around and sweat and translate dirty jokes from Spanish into English."

"That's nice," her father said. Knox laughed, though she noticed that her father regarded Robbie with a grim expression for half a beat before he looked at Knox and smiled. She knew that

Robbie could push the apathetic student act far enough to worry her father, who had made a bid for a small part of the farm acreage—acreage that now spread for two miles on either side of the road—the week after he graduated from college. "I think you should bring them out," he said. "Call over to the office and have them set it up."

"I can just tell Ned," Knox said.

"I asked him to stay for dinner, but he said he couldn't," her mother said.

"I know," Knox said. She made a note to call him later, if only to register herself in his thoughts. She would call his machine, become a voice that played through the rooms of his house as he walked through them later, his boots weighing on the old boards.

"The sexiest man alive is the star of a popular television show. He's from Ohio," Robbie said.

"Who," Knox said.

"You can't give up, you have to guess who it is."

"Maybe we should go over our options," her father said. "We should decide what the plan is, don't you think?"

Knox's mother got up from the table and went to the refrigerator. She opened the door, bent forward at the waist, reached in, pushed several cartons and bottles to one side, then the other. "Would anyone like butter with their bread," she asked.

"I would," Knox said, though she didn't usually take butter. It was easy to abandon whatever preferences she had when her parents cooked for her—or to forget, temporarily, exactly what those preferences were. During breakfasts at this table, to which she came as often as not on weekend mornings, she drank cup after cup of coffee simply because it was on offer, and left feeling heavy and unmoored at once, as if she might float out of the top of her head if it weren't so leaden. She walked home, nodding like a narcoleptic, and crawled into bed, wondering why she hadn't refused something—that last piece of bacon, the cluster of grapes that her father had clipped for her with a pair of kitchen shears. Now she slathered butter on a piece of crust, and listened.

"Do we all fly up tonight, or do just Mom and I go, or what," her father was saying. "That's what I'm going to need to know. If this was a month from now, I'm guessing we would descend on Charlotte in shifts, but since we're all together—"

"Can I say something?" her mother said.

"Yes. Of course."

"I just think it's a lot for the two of them, with the whole family all at once. We should wait and see what Bruce and Charlotte want us to do."

"So," her father said. "Min, it never hurts to go over the possibilities. Whether or not the kids—"

"Let's just say that whoever wants to go can get packed, and we'll wait for the charter company to call," her mother said. "We don't know what's going to happen. They might not even want *me* up there tonight."

"That's ridiculous, honey."

"It's not," her mother said. Her voice rose on the *not*. Knox noticed that the redness she'd seen in her mother's face as she stood over the sink had either returned or never dissipated. Then, more quietly, she said, "Sorry. I just don't want them to be overwhelmed."

"I don't have to go," Robbie said. "I can come up next week, or before school starts."

Knox thought she saw gratitude flash in her mother's eyes. She wondered if her mother imagined having Charlotte all to herself, if she feared any possibility other than that.

"I don't have to go either," Knox said. The sound of her voice surprised her. "But I'd like to. Charlotte and I talked about it this afternoon."

Her mother looked at her.

"You talked to Charlotte?" she said.

"Yes."

"What did she say?" The innocence in her mother's expression—the braced, expectant quality of it—made Knox momentarily wish she hadn't spoken.

"That she wasn't sure what was happening next. She told me it would be good if I came, actually."

"She did?"

Knox nodded.

After a few seconds, her mother smiled in her direction. "Of course she wants you there. I think everyone should do whatever they feel they need to do," she said.

"Okay."

"As long as the center can spare you right now."

"Okay," Knox said. She felt exhausted. She buttered another piece of bread, then put it back down on her plate.

"Dinner was delicious," her father said.

"Back to the subject," Robbie said.

"What?" Knox said.

"The sexiest man alive takes baths with a Vietnamese pot-bellied pig."

"I'll mull that bit of fascinating crap over."

Robbie rolled his eyes and stuck his tongue out at her. Her mother covered her smile with her hand. "Jesus, tough crowd tonight," Robbie said, just before the phone rang.

CHARLOTTE HAD LAID a wooden shelf across two stacks of bricks in front of the kitchen window. She had bought a small pot of basil, a pot of rosemary, a mint plant, an African violet in bright foil, and arranged them in a row on the shelf. She had bought a grapefruit-sized water mister, filled it at the tap, and placed it on the shelf beside the African violet. She had stood back and admired what she had done. She had placed one hand at the small of her back. Bruce had watched her from the hall. The sun was white in the kitchen and fell across her in a dazzling shard. He imagined it warm on her skin. That night Charlotte had twisted leaves from the basil plant, chopped them into a mossy pulp, made tomato and basil omelets for their dinner. He praised them extravagantly, appealing to the domestic pride that flowered from her in these tiny bursts.

Charlotte had stood on the bench in their living room, in the midst of a party she had given to mark some minor occasion—

Cinco de Mayo, or Bastille Day, or the Derby that ran each year just an hour from her parents' house, about which Charlotte seemed to know little other than that the rest of her family was always in attendance, sometimes with a horse running, and that more juleps needed to be made, please: more. The mint on the shelf in the kitchen was brown by then; papery leaves lay scattered on streaks of dirt. A new pot of mint was bought, ice, sugar syrup, bourbon by the handle. Charlotte stood on the bench and her friends cheered. The television blared in the background. She danced to the music someone had put on: some Spanish guitar, or Piaf, or "Fulsom Prison Blues." The song would be a detail that got lost. Bruce would remember, though, Charlotte lifting her shirt until her breasts were exposed. He would remember that the television was louder than the music, that it was possible to keep track of the race from across the room. "They're all in line . . . wait, number five, San Dee Dee is getting set, all right, the jock has got the colt calmed, and they're—" From his place on the window seat Bruce could see the pale blue veins that stretched from the aureoles of Charlotte's tits when they appeared from under the raised hem of her blouse, though he was too far away to make out the goose-pimply texture of the skin just around her nipples. Her skin looked whiter from a distance. Charlotte caught his eye and beckoned to him in an exaggerated burlesque. Her—their—friends turned toward him, laughing. So he was expected to join her? Bruce glanced around, smiling. He was a little drunk. He shook his head. He had made the mistake of inviting a couple of guys from work, had invited Jeb Jackman to be kind; there was Jeb, whom he didn't even know, by the doorway, with his fat tongue hanging out. Bruce shook his head. He waved his hand at Charlotte, as if to say, *Go on, honey, enjoy yourself. Go on.* A bell rang on the television; the gates crashed open.

Charlotte had leafed with him through the pages of photographs from their wedding. They had been sitting at the table in the back garden; the sky above them was overcast. An event photographer recommended by Charlotte's boss at the time had taken the pictures, had arranged them into a leather album with a silver-embossed image of a tree on its cover. The photographer, the hiring of her, had been one of their primary expenses, along with the fee to rent out the restaurant for an afternoon, the small price exacted by the justice of the peace. Charlotte herself had bought carrot sticks, potato chips, pretzels, cheese, and shaken them onto glass dishes that were arranged around the restaurant's one small room, with its wall of windows that overlooked the same stretch of river Bruce could see from their front steps, its yellow walls, its scattering of distressed folk art. Her parents had paid for the liquor. The restaurant was just down the block from their apartment; Charlotte had used their street as an aisle, negotiating the cobblestones in her heels and borrowed dress. Her sister preceded her down the street; her parents came after. Charlotte had looked so serious, serious in a way that made Bruce momentarily want to go to her, or to yell out something funny, something that he might expect her to yell herself if her face weren't so drawn, so still. Something like: *Hurry up! Bike messenger behind you, watch your back!* The dress emphasized the fact that Charlotte's body had grown fuller, more lush, since he had met her. She moved toward him. There was no music, only the hush at their end of the street, the collective hush of the waiters, who stood in their white shirts near the restaurant entrance, watching, and a knot of friends and family, the few of Charlotte's parents' crowd who had made the trip up to New York and stood, dressed impeccably in silks and gabardines, with broad smiles on their faces. Across the street, a couple with a stroller stopped to look. They shaded their eyes from the sun, joggled their baby back and forth to keep her quiet. Bruce could hear a bird, distant passing cars. His father stood beside him; Charlotte's brother stood just beyond. Afternoon light flashed in the windows of the brownstones, flashed in a quick pattern that Bruce couldn't connect with any object or movement in the weather. The play of light showed up in some of the photographs; in this one, here, Bruce could see it, a nova sparking just behind the head of Knox, whose bare, freckled shoulders were thrust back, as if she'd been conscious her picture was being taken and assumed her most elegant pose. For an instant that day Bruce had thought of the flashes as music. His head had been all over the place; he had felt guilty at moments for missing his new wife, for wanting to be alone with her, away from these people for whom she obviously felt she had to perform. He had felt guilty for thinking that dignity didn't become her—and another thing he had seen was that Charlotte's sister had felt the same way. She had stared at Charlotte at the reception, as if trying to locate the sister she recognized under that bridal patina.

Look at this one, Charlotte said. Look at us.

It was a picture of the two of them, kissing by the restaurant bar. There was a grainy quality to it; the photographer had obviously swept a bit out of focus in order to turn quickly and capture the moment before it ended. What Bruce noticed about the picture was his hand, the way it sat on the back of Charlotte's neck, gathering her head to his, tangling in the gloss of her hair. It looked to him like a brute hand, too strong and clumsy in its gesture, too insistent. His eyes were open, too, as if he'd surprised even himself with the pressure of his ardor. Charlotte's eyes were closed. She looked pliable, acquiescent. Like a movie bride, disappearing into her joy.

It's nice, Charlotte said.

It was a nice picture. Bruce agreed. But there was something about it that shamed him, too, that left him exposed. He wanted her to turn the page. When she didn't, and kept looking, he glanced around and commented on the new bricks they would need to order for the patio, come next summer.

THEY LANDED at Teterboro. Just Knox, her mother, her father; they had left Robbie at the back door, waving, the magazine still in his hand. Knox had a moment of regret walking away from him, away from the house; how appealing it would be to sink into the couch in the den beside Robbie, to watch, as he cruised the movie channels with the remote control whose intricacies only he fully understood, opening windows on the television screen that revealed other shows in progress, small worlds enclosed in boxes over the actors' shoulders that reminded Knox of the thought bubbles in cartoons. There would be salty chips, and beer, and warm lamplight, and no need for talk, where Robbie was. But Knox had chosen. Of course she had chosen the flight, which had been smooth until right at the descent, during which Knox allowed herself to feel heroic for an indulgent moment—to imagine, as the interior of the small plane rattled and the digital altimeter over her mother's head subtracted from itself, that she was rushing to Charlotte's side in her time of need. That she was that kind of sister: the Jane Austen kind.

Now that they were inside the small terminal, waiting for the car her father had ordered to take them into the city, Knox's mother looked at her and said, "Do you think we should call the hospital?"

"How soon will we be there?"

Her mother smiled and rolled her eyes. "I know," she said. It was the face she made when she reached for a second helping of pie, or took one of the cigarettes that Robbie had offered her on his first weekend home, having invited her onto the back porch and baited her with a declared desire for "Mom time." "But could you call again? Here's Bruce's cell number." She handed Knox a piece of cream-colored paper that Knox recognized as having come from a pad she kept on her desk in the library.

Knox took the cell phone her mother handed her and dialed the number on the piece of paper. After nine rings, she was prompted by a mechanical voice to leave a message.

"He's not answering," Knox called across the terminal lobby. "Should I leave a message?"

Knox's mother blinked. "I guess so. Go ahead."

Knox kept her eyes on her mother as she spoke into the phone: "Bruce. Hi. We just landed. We'll call you again in a few minutes. Or we'll see you first. Hope everything is going well." She licked her lips, which felt dry. Her mother looked girlish, sitting prim on a huge piece of modular furniture by the window. Knox sometimes thought that, as her mother aged, she could see her returning to who she had been physically as a child—to the soft smoothness, the eager glow, that children worked so hard to shed. She sat down beside her mother.

"You're going to be good," Knox said. "A grand grandmother." She sounded effortful, saccharine, to herself, and wondered if she should pretend to be teasing. She turned her mouth up at the corners.

But her mother didn't look up and began rummaging for something at the bottom of her purse.

"Thanks, darling," she said. She put her free hand on Knox's leg. "I'm really glad you came."

Knox's father strode in through a pair of automatic doors, which *chirr*ed closed behind him.

"Car's out front," he said. Warm air from outside seemed to swirl invisibly in. Knox thought that her father looked imposing, sure. He walked with his hands in his pockets, his shoulders pushed a bit forward, the way her own tended to be. "There's a phone in it. I just called the hospital and they told me that Charlotte's still in the operating room."

Her mother stood up. "Okay." There was a lack of breath in her voice, as if she'd failed to inhale before speaking.

Knox rose; she picked up the backpack she had stuffed with a few things from the cabin, lifted it onto her shoulder. The three of them walked together toward the glass doors. Knox noticed how shiny the floor was underneath their feet, under the finely made leather shoes that her father wore. The doors parted for them, and they were out in the hot, close night. Bugs jumped under the lights of the canopy above them. A black car sat idling in the drive, its rear doors open.

"It's all happening as we speak," her father said. He squeezed Knox's shoulder as he guided her into the backseat of the car. "So we'll just get there as fast as we can."

Knox's mother went around the other side of the car and scooted into the middle of the seat. She clutched her purse against her lap. Knox's father got in next to her mother and closed the door.

"Okay," he said to the driver. Knox saw him take her mother's hand as they pulled away from the canopy. Inside the car it was plush and cozy. Knox thought quickly, guiltily, of Marlene. She would gripe at Knox for leaving her on no notice, but Knox thought she would understand. A couple of days. This is where she needed to be. A cesarean, a new reality that was hitting her in increments, shaping itself around her. She would make something up if Marlene asked her about the expense of flying to New York, something about getting a good fare on Delta at the last minute. There was no need for Marlene to know that Knox's life at the reading center was different from the one she had grown up with, the one she could return to now, made a child again on nights like this. Marlene had never, not once, been on a plane.

"Remind me to call Marlene," Knox said. A light drizzle started up outside. They moved onto the highway. The brake lights from other cars fuzzed in the sudden wet on Knox's pane, flaring like bright thistles. Somewhere, just ahead of them, were the lights of New York.

"Okay," her father said.

The hospital abutted the East River; there was a long porte cochere, a circular drive leading up to it. It was raining hard by the time they got there. Knox opened her door and knew to push out of the car as quickly as she could, so that her mother wouldn't suffer any brief frustration at being hemmed in. But when she stood, she realized that her mother had climbed out after her father, and that the two of them were jogging toward the entrance. One of her father's arms was raised against the weather, as if he could elbow it out of their way. Knox hiked her backpack over her head and walked after them. Here was another set of glass doors, a reception station that her parents seemed to know to bypass. A hall, a huge elevator, onto which an expressionless person, in plain clothes, rolled a waist-high machine of some kind. One floor up, and the person rolled out, getting hitched in the gap for a moment before Knox helped him by forcing the machine a bit from behind. On four, Knox's father touched the small of her back, and they emerged into a hallway. At the far side of it, chairs of differing sizes were grouped among what looked to Knox like tall cages, built of cheap, untreated wood. As she passed them, Knox saw that the cages housed a number of stuffed animals: a straggly lion, a hanging macaw, a kind of ape holding a synthetic yellow banana. There were children's drawings on the wall, drawings that, compared with the ones at the center, struck Knox as being so studiously naïve that they might have actually been made by adults.

At the end of the hallway, her parents approached a white desk. This area seemed to Knox to emit the color white; the only variations being the pink overshirt worn by the short-haired woman who was busying herself above an open file cabinet. The woman did not look up at her parents' approach, but smiled at them when her mother said, "Excuse me?" Knox never thought of her mother's voice—or her own, for that matter, not since boarding school—as being accented, but in the odd quiet of the hallway, she could hear a distinct lilt that she wondered if the woman noticed.

"Can I help you?" the woman asked.

"We're here to see Charlotte Bolling. Charlotte Tavert," her father said.

"Oh hi," the woman said, extending her hand toward her father to shake, then shaking her mother's hand in turn. She shook with energy; Knox could see the tendons and muscles shift in her slim arm as she moved it. This is a woman with a regular squash game, Knox thought. She allowed herself to imagine the woman's life, her virginal stint at Yale Med School, cradling heavy books in her arms as she walked across a quad, her Dorothy Hamill hair gleaming in the sun. She remembered, as if remembering a taste, how to make Charlotte laugh. It rushed back to her. She would say something about the nurse. Charlotte would snicker and say something like Yes, she's a walking seventies hair commercial. The kind of joke they used to have together, when Knox was a kid.

The woman nodded at Knox, who brushed a drop of rain from the side of her face.

"You're Charlotte's family," she said, stating the fact with self-satisfaction, as if she had invented Knox and her parents herself. "Why don't you wait here, and I'll go check. If she's in the recovery room, you might be able to go down and sneak a peek at her."

"That would be great. Thanks," Knox said. She felt a need to reassert her presence, her age. To hear her own voice.

"Can you tell us anything? Is everyone all right?" her mother said.

"Are you the doctor," her father said.

The woman smiled again. "Intern," she said. "As far as I know, everything's gone smoothly. You know things started to move quickly once your daughter got here. We thought at first that she'd be in triage for much longer. I'll go check. I'll send Dr. Boyd up if I can."

"Thank you," her father said. "Thanks very much."

The woman pushed the file drawer closed and moved down the hall, away from the direction Knox and her parents had come in. The shoes she was wearing made loud squishing sounds on the linoleum that Knox could still hear once she'd turned the corner.

"Would you guys like something? I could go see if there's a vending machine," Knox said.

"No, but get yourself something to drink," her mother said. "Absolutely. We'll be here."

"All right," Knox said.

She left her pack on the floor by her father's feet and walked back toward the wooden cages. There was a public phone hanging on the wall there. It was mounted low over the chairs, so low that Knox had to kneel on one of the smallest chairs—a red one obviously meant for a preschooler—in order to dial comfortably. Marlene picked up on the first ring.

"You expecting a call?" Knox said.

"Well, hello," Marlene said. Her voice was so full of warmth that Knox felt first surprised, then shamed. She wished for a moment that she could just be calling to say hi, that she phoned Marlene at home more often, for reasons that weren't related to students or scheduling.

"What're you doing," she said.

"Oh, Jimmy's got the football on. I'm sitting here bored out of my mind. I feel like the season's closing in on me. Seems like it starts in June now and just never ends."

"Guess where I am," Knox said.

"Where."

"New York. My sister's having the babies." Knox swallowed. She felt suddenly, terribly, far away from her life.

"Oh! Oh hon, that's wonderful. That's wonderful! But—it's a little early, isn't it? I guess twins usually are. Is everything okay?"

"Yep, looks like it. But Mar, I'm sorry, I won't be back for a couple of days," Knox said. "I just wasn't thinking and I got on a plane to come up here. So I wanted to ask you to cover for me if it's all right. The reports I've been working on, I got through *T* so there're only a couple left, I've been doing them alphabetically—"

"What is wrong with you?" Marlene said. "Just enjoy yourself, I know what to do. What kind of person apologizes for being with family at a time like this?"

"A responsible educator like me, I guess," Knox said.

"Oh, is that what you are."

"It takes one to know one, so maybe you wouldn't understand."

"What I understand is that being around babies is a good thing for you right now. I'm ready to become a godmother. Lord, I thought you were calling to tell me you'd run off with Ned. Maybe I'm disappointed."

"I'm sorry. I'll call you, Mar. Thanks a lot."

"Don't thank me. God. Be with your family. I'm going to combine the classes until you get back."

"Thanks."

"Okay, hon."

Knox hung up the phone. She bent at the waist and reached toward her feet in an attempt to stretch her legs. Her nose grazed her skirt just above her knees; she inhaled the familiar smell of her detergent and briefly missed the swan, reminded of its body at rest, piled onto itself. She felt suddenly irritated with Ned. Why did he have to put her in a position to disappoint him, when things between them worked well as they were? She exhaled and reached a bit farther, extending the tips of her fingers as far as they would go. She would call him later, and hopefully the sameness she depended on would be restored. She kept longing out of her mind and thought of diving, of falling off the tip of a board in a tight pike, unfurling the length of her body to straight, slipping into water that way.

BRUCE HAD STOOD outside the window of the thrift shop at St. Luke's Church. He had pretended to eye the plaid windbreakers, battered lamp shades, beaded and misshapen evening bags (why did a church thrift shop, geared to the poor, look so crowded with sequined *purses*, he wondered) that hung on the other side of the glass.

Behind him, Hudson Street pumped with traffic. To his left stood the iron gate that marked the entrance to the church garden. If he moved through the gate and took the path that wound around behind the church and into the small garden, where a few benches were arranged under the trees, he would find his wife. She was back there. He had watched her disappear down the path. If he let himself go to her, he might find her sitting on the one swath of grass that was unspoiled by trash or the scrubby groundcover that squirrels and rats scratched in, making the leaves above them shake as they moved. He knew the place; they had sat together with the newspaper and sandwiches there, before. She might be sitting on the grass, or lying down on it, her dress drawn up to the tops of her thighs. The backs of her legs would be crosshatched in red when she stood, and she would shake out her dress and put her hands at the center of her back, look around. He could picture this easily, the bits of grass that would go flying when she shook out her dress, the way the cotton of it would have gone thinner in the heat, would cling to her differently. He stood where he was. He walked through the gate.

Bruce saw Charlotte before she saw him. She was standing near the door to the rectory, a metal door that opened onto the garden from the back of the church. She was speaking to a woman. The woman held on to the hand of a little girl; the girl dragged against the force of the woman's grasp, leaning away from her as if she were walking into a windstorm. Her body hung at an angle to the grass. If the woman lets go, that kid will fall, Bruce thought. He moved toward his wife. It crossed his mind that if the girl slipped from her mother's hand, he could reach her in time to catch her body and prevent her from possible injury, and that Charlotte would see.

"Sure," he heard Charlotte say, laughing. "Go ahead."

The girl straightened suddenly, and reached toward Charlotte's belly. She touched it with her hand slightly cupped, like she was trying to deliver an extra puff of air to Charlotte's skin, or measure all that was contained under the slope of her dress. Bruce felt a rush of pride that made him almost hostile toward the girl, toward the tentative awe in her touch. That's right, he thought. You wish you could have her, but you can't. Sorry.

Charlotte looked up at him. He had almost reached her, was stepping over the edge of the lawn now. Bruce saw that the smile on Charlotte's face didn't die, but remained where it was.

"Oh," she said.

The woman looked up at him, too. "Bruce," she called to him.

He froze. He looked more closely at the woman. Was he supposed to know who she was? He waited for her to become familiar, ticking off the seconds as he searched her face.

"You remember Iris," Charlotte said.

"I, um," Bruce said. "Hello."

The woman laughed. "I'm not even sure we've actually met. We're neighbors of yours."

"Well, hi," Bruce said. "Sorry I didn't recognize you."

"This is Nora," the woman said. She gestured at the little girl.

"Hi," Nora said, scowling at him.

Bruce felt the sun's heat on the top of his head. The weight of it reminded him of the child's game, the one that consisted of one person widening his fingers over the crown of another person's head, insinuating the spread of a yolk. He felt better, now that he could see Charlotte, but he still wished the woman and her child would go away.

"Bruce has been following me," Charlotte said.

She smiled up at him. Her expression was so sweet that Bruce forgot not to smile back, despite the fact that she meant to embarrass him in front of this stranger.

"Mm?" Iris said.

"He gets worried about me in the big bad city," Charlotte said. "Don't you," she said to Bruce.

Bruce smiled at Iris. Looking into Iris's face, which held an open friendliness in its heart shape, in the freckled darkness around the eyes that made Bruce think suddenly that she was old to be the mother of such a young girl, he thought it might be easier to simply confess everything. If Charlotte was bent on talking about this, he might as well be allowed to speak from his own point of view. "I told her that it makes me nervous for her to take the subway by herself. You know, at this point. I've seen how people won't give up their seats. It's just—"

"I get exhausted taking the subway myself," Iris said. "It can feel like a battle."

"Yes," Bruce continued, encouraged. He kept his eyes on Iris's, which were catlike, flecked with tiny shards of yellow and green. "Exactly. I asked Charlotte to take a cab uptown if she had to go, and then she walked out the door, and I had this feeling that she hadn't listened to anything I'd said."

"You followed me to the Christopher Street stop," Charlotte said. "And don't talk about me like I'm not here. I'm right here."

"I did follow her. I mean you," he said, turning to Charlotte. "I did. And I was right. You were going down the steps into the subway."

"He practically jumped behind a trash can when I turned around," Charlotte said. "Oh my God. You should have seen yourself."

She started to laugh then. When Iris started laughing too,

Charlotte bent forward a little, her knees bending to support her. Nora looked from Iris to Charlotte and back again.

Charlotte straightened. She stopped laughing and looked at him, her hand rising to shield her eyes from the sun.

"You shouldn't do that," she said.

"New York can be a tough place," Iris said.

"I'm sorry," Bruce said. Charlotte was right, but his voice was more defiant than apologetic.

"Don't do it anymore."

"You two are cute," Iris said. "If my husband had worried about me for one second, who knows, we might still be married."

Nora began to tug on Iris's arm again. "Mmah," she whined.

"You followed me here, too," Charlotte said. "How else would you know I was here?" She looked into Bruce's eyes. Bruce could see something dissolving in her face, some hope leaking in. She likes for me to be stronger than I am, Bruce thought. That is the only way.

"I didn't follow you," Bruce said. "I came to find you. There's a difference."

This morning, by the kiosk outside the Christopher Street subway entrance, Charlotte had told him she needed to be alone, then walked slowly toward the corner, turned it, and moved out of sight. He had waited for her, back at the apartment. Hour after hour went by. He straightened up, wiped the coffee cup rings off the glass-topped table with a paper towel, sat down on the couch. The air conditioner chugged through its cycle, quieted, then whirred on again. Ice crystals formed on its filter. There was only the sound of the air conditioner and Charlotte's words: I need to be alone. By the time he moved to unlock the door and walk out to find her, he was shaking. She had left her cell phone on the hall table, the one that he'd provided her with for these final months and weeks. The keys jangled a little before he slid them into his pocket, before he let himself onto the street like any husband, on any Sunday. He made himself walk like any husband. Maybe he would bump into his wife while he was out getting some fresh air. He tried to think like that.

Now Charlotte looked at him.

"He came to find me," she said. "Nora, what do you think of that? Should I trust this man?"

"No!" Nora said.

Charlotte laughed.

"Let's all get out of the sun," Iris said. "Bruce, it was nice to meet you officially."

"Thanks," Bruce said. "You too." He put his hand on Charlotte's bare shoulder. He smiled like any husband, which was exactly what he was. He touched Charlotte lightly, in case she decided to move away, but when she leaned into him, he spread his fingers, and kept his hand in place.

KNOX COULD see Bruce standing by the desk, wearing loose green scrubs over his clothes. He held what looked to be a shower cap in his hand. As she moved up the hallway she noticed shower-cap coverings pulled over his shoes, too—their bright seams disappearing into the cuffs of his pants. He stood in profile to her, and when she drew closer he launched into a little soft shoe, his hands stretched out with their palms up, his back foot touching the floor, propelling his front foot forward. His mouth formed an O over the loosened surgical mask that hung below his chin like an air-sickness bag. A white minstrel, Knox thought. Al Jolson meets . . . but the only rhyme she could think of right away was "Nels Oleson," the shopkeeper from *Little House on the Prairie*. She started to laugh. That could be a joke for Charlotte, if she could ever explain it. But it would be enough to tell her that Bruce had been dancing, that he was reaching for their mother's arm now, attempting to co-opt her into a graceless do-si-do.

"Bruce," Knox said, and she was happy for him as he shuffled toward her, her mother's hand still in his, and bent to kiss her on the side of her head.

"They're about to move her into the recovery room, darling," her mother said. She was flushed, her eyes shining. "It's already done, they're getting the babies cleaned up."

"They need to be incubated," Bruce said. He was slightly breathless from his dance. "They say Ethan's lungs want some help to clear, but they're formed, and both of them are looking great. They're just about four pounds each." He dropped her mother's hand and brought his fingers to his rough cheek as if to remind himself that it was still there. "Sorry you missed it. But it was a little scary, I admit."

"We're going to go see them," her mother said. Though she was obviously speaking to Knox, she kept her eyes on Bruce. It was the first time Knox could remember any of them seeing Bruce like this: larger, more dashing, somehow, within his rapture. Her mother looked wooed.

"Maybe Charlotte first, if they'll let us in," Bruce said. "They've been stitching her up for a while, and I don't want to leave her for too long."

"Ethan," Knox said. She watched Bruce, too. Alongside her gladness for him she noted the murk in her mind, the same darting loneliness she'd felt during her call to Marlene. It hung in her, at half depth, like a bit of sediment or a fish adrift. She would have to swim past it on her way up to the surface, to the present—where a sharper, more reactive version of herself waited. Ethan was Bruce's father's name—she was nearly sure of that. She pictured Mr. Tavert in the baggy brown suit he'd worn to the wedding, lying trapped under glass, his lungs wanting help to clear. What kind of help? A tube with a tiny bellows at the end of it, for a nurse to luff open and closed as if she were standing in front of a hearth, her cocktail melting and forgotten on the mantel.

"Ethan and Ben," Bruce said.

Knox looked at her father, whose face darkened visibly with emotion. Without deciding to, she moved to stand close beside him.

"Isn't that great, Knoxie," her mother said.

"It sure is," her father said. "It really, really is."

"Ethan and Ben," Knox said.

Bruce watched the ground. Knox thought he might be humbling himself with his body, as animals do when they feel dominated. He might be reining in an excess of pride, or trying to.

"I hope that's all right with you, Ben," Bruce said. "We were going to ask you next week, but—"

"It's fantastic," her father said.

"Gosh," Knox said, rising, with effort, into the moment. "Wow."

Dr. Boyd took them to Charlotte. He talked as he moved down a hallway, past several open doors that Knox tried not to look into. So many doors, some leading into dark rooms, some into rooms that looked almost coldly bright and crowded with people. He was talking mainly to Knox's mother, who hung at his side, making it clear with her posture that if he were to pause in his speech he would be forced to resume it again, to answer questions she had at the ready. Bruce and Knox's father walked together, behind Knox. Dr. Boyd, with his gin-blossom nose, his pocked cheeks, his blunt, bluish hair, said that Charlotte had done well, the twins would be groggy from the anesthesia but most probably unaffected, their breathing was being watched, particularly that of the first one out—that would be Ethan, Knox thought; how arbitrarily he had become the oldest!—the perinatologist had been called, Charlotte was being given something called oxytocin to help her uterus contract. "We're watching that," Dr. Boyd said. He spoke with an energy that felt close to glee, Knox thought.

He reached for a metal door handle, pulled it like a trigger, ushered them through one of the closed doors. The room wasn't small or large; it was sectioned into areas by curtains that could be drawn shut. Charlotte's bed was at the far end of it, closest to the window. She looked up at them when the door opened, and smiled as they moved toward her, past the only other occupied bed in the room. Knox couldn't help glancing at the sleeping woman in the near bed as she passed by. The woman's mouth was slack; her massive head listed to one side. Knox felt a twinge of pity for her without knowing why.

"Well, look who's here," Charlotte stage-whispered. "Come here, you guys."

Knox had forgotten. She had forgotten again just how Charlotte was, was struck by all the ways Charlotte's outlines, so bright now, matched and didn't match the duller ones in her memory. Charlotte's forehead and cheeks were high with color, as if she'd been slapped or had ducked in from the cold. Her head was propped up on some kind of ergonomic pillow, the rest of her prone; a fuzzy strand of hair clung to her left temple. She was beautiful. Wearing earrings of glass, etched-glass triangles, a fact that surprised Knox, until she told herself, Of course she is wearing earrings, it wasn't as if any small vanity would be thrashed off, lost in the linens, incompatible with birth, with this room. A sheet stretched from below Charlotte's breasts to a hanging point beyond the foot of the bed; the intern Knox recognized from the reception desk was reaching under the sheet, kneading at some part of Charlotte's swollen lower body that none of them could see.

They ranged around her like she was fire. There was a slight smell of shit in the air. Knox's father moved to touch Charlotte's face, push the hair to one side; then he backed up again to make room for Bruce, who slipped into the space by the bed.

"Kid," her father said, soft. "This is nice going."

"Have you seen them yet?" Charlotte asked. She was grinning.

"Not yet," her mother said, "but—"

"They're . . . you're not going to believe it," Charlotte said. Her voice, even as it rose over the words being exchanged between Dr. Boyd and the intern and nurse, still carried the friction of a whisper in it. "You are not going to believe."

"Oh, honey, and they're both going to be fine," her mother said. She craned upward, smiling, in her navy travel pantsuit and printed scarf, so Charlotte could see her better.

"Yes," Charlotte said. "I know they are. I—" She looked up at Bruce. "My heart's still beating fast. It's beating really fast."

"Let's keep this short," Dr. Boyd said from the other side of the bed. He peered into the clear bag that hung on an IV stand next to him. "We're still waiting for the medication to kick in."

"They're massaging my uterus, Knoxie," Charlotte said. "Isn't that lovely?"

Knox wanted to lie down on the bed beside her sister and learn all the new fat and blood that had crept into Charlotte in the four months since she had last seen her, trace the borders of this puffy, blurred body and learn it by heart. "Nothing like a good uterus massage," Knox said. "I prefer mine first thing in the morning."

Charlotte laughed once, in a kind of cry. She held Knox's eyes with hers.

"With your napalm," she said. "Knox. Do you like the names?"

"I love them. I honestly do."

"Not too original," she said. She glanced at their father, but only for half a beat, before her eyes found Knox's face again. "But I thought they were good."

"Food names are trendy now, I think," Knox said. She felt the room divide like a sea, leaving only her, only Charlotte, in the deep seam between the waters. "I see it at the reading center. We have a Sage. But Ethan and Ben are perfect."

"Food names," Charlotte said, thinking. Sweat stippled her upper lip. The skin on her neck was pink, blotched.

"It's a choice," Knox said.

Charlotte snickered. "Oh," she said. "Don't—it hurts." She looked at Dr. Boyd and said, "Can I keep my sister with me?"

Knox thought then that she would have to be extracted from the room with an oversized cane, like a vaudeville entertainer who had worn out her welcome onstage. She wouldn't be able to stop performing tricks for Charlotte, half-demented as she suddenly felt with relief, with love.

"My heart," Charlotte said, and Knox, with her own so giddy and full, thought, I know.

"It's like I'm on too much speed," Charlotte said, looking up again at Bruce.

Not that the lady's ever been on speed, folks. Bah-dum pum.

"Let's give her some privacy now," Dr. Boyd said, in such a way that Knox expected him to follow them out of the room. Her father nodded and guided her mother through the door. Knox watched them go, then turned back toward Charlotte.

"Bye," she said, inflecting it like a question.

Charlotte blinked, smiled, closed her eyes.

"She's tired," Bruce said.

Yes. Knox covered her disappointment with an expression that she hoped conveyed good humor, understanding. She took a breath, made her feet move. Dr. Boyd stayed where he was, as did Bruce. She closed the door behind her.

In the hall, her parents were waiting. Her father rubbed circles into her mother's back.

"You have to remember this is major surgery," her father said.

"That's right," her mother said.

"We'll have more time with her in a minute," her father said.

Knox ran her fingers through her hair. She either wanted to have her back rubbed, too, or she wanted to walk, walk anywhere, until it was time to be let back into Charlotte's room. She allowed herself to experience one moment of bittersweet shame that her parents still felt the need to comfort her, at her age, when she found herself on the wrong side of a closed door, with Charlotte inside.

"We'll go see the twins now," her mother said. "Let's go ahead and do that."

"Yes!" her father said, and Knox smiled and nodded. Her father leaned back into Charlotte's room to ask whether this was a good time to look in on the babies.

A nurse was dispatched to lead them to the neonatal intensive-care unit, one floor up. She was older than the squash-playing Dorothy Hamill, less wholesome looking; in the elevator she examined her fingernails. Knox could tell that the nurse fought for a moment to remember where she was when her parents breached the silence and began to ask their questions; it was clear from her face that she had been thinking of her lover, of the hamburger-noodle casserole in her freezer, of her own sister or her own babies. Well, Knox thought, she has a life.

"How long will each of them have to be in this unit?" her mother asked. "What does that depend on?"

"Mostly weight," the nurse said, not unkindly. She raised her eyes from her fingers and watched the tinted panel above the elevator door, waiting for the number of their floor to flash. "And whatever special problems or needs they might have."

"But they're fine," her mother said. "We were told that they're perfect, just premature."

"That's great," the nurse said. She crossed her arms over her stomach, wrapped her hands around her elbows, which were left exposed by the short-sleeved tunic that she wore. Knox could see her fingers exploring the rough skin of her elbows, her upper arms; she was probably reminding herself to exfoliate during her next shower. "Preemies always have to be watched. They're still developing, but I'm sure yours are fine at this point, neurologically. This wasn't one of mine, so I don't know the details."

Knox's mother looked up at her father. Her jaw looked set; the skin on her neck seemed to tighten.

"Mina," her father said.

"If you don't know any details," her mother said, inserting a breathy laugh between phrases, "then it's probably best not to scare us."

"Sorry," the nurse said. "Well, here we are."

A plucked note sounded, and the elevator doors opened. The three of them followed the nurse around a corner and stopped in front of a small window. Knox realized that she had been imagining a wall of glass, an endless movie nursery, now that she stood jostling for space and peering into a room gnarled with equipment.

"I'll just let them know who you are," the nurse said. "You're not allowed in here right now. The NICU's very restricted, even if you're family." She pronounced it "knee-cue."

"That's all right," her mother said. "Thank you."

The nurse entered the room and spoke quickly to a woman in vivid, multicolored scrubs—the baby scrubs, Knox thought, the whimsical nursery scrubs, Ned would find that funny—before letting herself out again. Inside the room, the woman walked toward one incubator, its sides transparent, and pointed to it. She waited beside the machine, though it was too far from the window for them to see much of anything, then moved closer to the window and pointed to another.

"They're called Isolettes, those beds they sleep in," the nurse said. She positioned herself against a nearby wall, there not being enough room for her at the window. Knox wondered how long the nurse would remain with them, if she was charged to watch them the way a retail assistant was assigned to shadow potential shop- lifters. Inside the room, the scrubbed woman's eyes were crinkled above her mask. Knox looked in through the plastic sides of the Isolette she pointed to now; whichever twin was inside lay laven- der on white cloth, mewling silently, like a newborn cat. He lay on his stomach, his face turned toward them, eyes shut. He was naked except for a tiny striped cap on his head. Tubes snaked out from under him, and from taped places on both of his feet. As they watched, the woman reached in through a flap in the Isolette, gently turned him faceup with both of her hands, taking several long seconds. She arranged the tubes, two of which Knox could now see were taped to his chest, one of which disappeared into the chapped skin above his bandaged navel. The woman then reached for another tube and wiggled the tip of it into his mouth. The baby closed his lips, which looked like nothing but dabs of pink wet, around it. She reached behind the Isolette, produced a pair of dark blue eyeshades, and placed them over his eyes, then went to the other side of the room, flipped a switch. The light above the baby brightened.

"Oh," her mother said.

"Oh my God," Knox said.

"So . . . incredible, look," her mother said.

They looked. They looked. A full minute went by.

"He's a potato," her father said finally. "Look at him."

"How can he . . . do you think he's Ethan?" her mother said.

"Those sunglasses," Knox said.

"The light is for jaundice," the nurse said.

"He's like a snowbird in Boca," her father said.

Her mother started to giggle. She wiped at her eyes.

"They should be next to each other, though," Knox said. "I think they should be closer together."

"Sweet," the nurse said, glancing in. "Do you have any more questions."

Her mother stopped laughing. "How are they possibly going to be okay?" she said. "Ben?"

"They will," her father said. He kept his eyes on the glass. From Knox's angle, it looked as if he was gazing into his own reflection. "They don't say they are going to be all right unless it's true. Bruce said tube feedings and time to grow were all they needed."

"Oh," Knox said. She felt sure she spoke, though she had the sensation that she might just be experiencing a loud, pressing thought. She didn't recognize anything about the baby, except that it was unquestionably human, albeit a kind of human that she had never seen before. The antipathy she had felt for the sonogram images Charlotte sent her evaporated in the warm breath that fogged the inch of window just in front of her mouth; what was left wasn't quite love, not yet. More like—curiosity. Mystery. Hilarity. Shock.

The baby body seemed to pant. The little patch of its skin that passed for a chest moving up and down, up and down.

THE GATES crashed open; the bell sounded. Bruce had never known such happiness, or such fear. He thought he had, but he hadn't. He laughed at the pattern he'd held in life, the pattern of being warned about what was upcoming and thinking the warning was all he needed. In fourth-grade science class he had listened while the dyspeptic Mr. Towne explained about bodies, men and women, the moods and ravages of puberty, and thought: Well, now I know. Those troubles are left for everyone else, the ones who haven't been warned. It was arrogance, of course. Just because something had been described to him didn't substitute for experience; this was a simple idea, but he kept forgetting it. He crashed into his own morphing self, his dropped voice and thrumming teenage blood with a kind of shock. He forgot, until his mother's death reminded him, that he hadn't experienced death yet. Each rite of passage was, for Bruce, a loss of innocence, and the babies were no different. He had seen them, mottled and bloody, lifted one after the other from Charlotte's womb. He had heard their Apgar scores stated in the firm tone the nurses here had, watched them fret under the cleaning cloths and be bundled into those plastic boxes and wheeled away. They were all right. He had read books, pored over the literature Charlotte brought home, befriended men with their own warnings and descriptions, but nothing had prepared him for the unsteadiness he still felt in his feet as he stood beside Charlotte's recovery bed, holding her hand, waiting for the doctor to return to the room. Boyd had just left, but a nurse had called him back. Routine, she said. All he could think was that there were two of them: perfect. Ethan and Ben.

"Come with me," the squash-playing intern said. "She's gone back into the OR."

Yes.

Coming.

It must have been three-quarters of an hour since they'd begun cooing through the window. Knox thought she could have remained there through the night. The endless, lost time that Charlotte's room had evoked—the room, she could see now, that had held her sister's spark but also a lesser redolence of waiting, of the uselessness that hospitals necessitated for families, the television noise, the pilgrimages to the cafeteria, the standing by as the patient dresses herself methodically in stale clothes for her overdue release—was distilled, outside the NICU, into what felt like no time at all. They had learned that the nearest baby was Ben. The nurse had said goodbye and left them. Knox looked up when she departed, then turned back to the window. She stared at tiny Ben's tiny parts: his locked fists, his bent legs, the nub of penis no bigger—smaller, even—than an eraser on one of her parents' golf-scoring pencils.

Now the intern led them down hallways that Knox didn't recognize. At one point she wondered, Where are the animal cages? They took the stairs instead of the elevator. The intern took the stairs two at a time. Knox was reminded of what it felt like to arrive after tip-off when she went to home basketball games with her father at Rupp: here was a similar concrete stairwell, a frightening exhilaration. Her father knew the back passages of the arena. He was allowed to hustle through them, ahead of Knox; he sat on the board of the university. As on game days, theirs were the only footsteps she heard in the stairwell now, noisy scuffs bouncing off the thick walls.

Behind Knox, someone tripped. She wasn't sure if it was her mother or her father. It was difficult to tell from the thunking sound, the brief "ah" she heard after, like a whispered swoon.

She kept moving.

No one said anything. It may have been that there wasn't enough time or breath to ask questions to the intern's back, or to say, as much to oneself as to anyone else, What is happening?

They reached the OR. The intern turned to them. She said, "I have to go in. Wait here. Your daughter is hemorrhaging. I'm sorry, I tried to find you. Someone will be with you." She swung through the windowless doors.

"All right," Knox's mother said, with absurd calm.

The three of them stared at the place where the intern had just been, stared at the door until it was still.

Knox thought, with some doubt: I'm here. This is where I am.

She didn't look at either of her parents. She realized with a kind of satisfaction that she was capable of obliterating herself to the point at which any further movement was unnecessary. She could just stand, keep her eyes on a fixed place, not think, not say a word. To speak to one another, to acknowledge each other, would be wrong. Better to stand together like those children who close their eyes in order to be nowhere.

They waited. For seconds or minutes.

"Let's sit down," her father said.

Just like that, the fear started. Knox ignored her father, tried to ignore the chill that began to crawl up her arms. He should have known that none of them was supposed to speak, that they kept everything suspended only through that small collusion. Her mother knew it; Knox could see out of the corner of her eye that her mother remained where she was.

"Mina, you've cut yourself," her father said. Knox did glance over then; an inch of her mother's slacks stuck to a place on her shin. It was possible that the place was darkened with blood.

"I fell on the stairs," her mother said.

"Mina." Her father sounded panicked.

"That's enough," her mother said. "I'm fine."

Nothing more was said. Her father sat. Knox tried to calm herself, but the fear was loose now. It occupied that word, *hemorrhaging*, and lit here and there on her body. She tried to shake it loose. It was both outside and inside, growing around her heart and up her esophagus until it felt like she would choke. There was nothing to do but stand there, breathing it in and out.

"Everything is going to be all right," her mother said.

It was. Could hemorrhaging even be normal, a side effect of labor, easily stanched? Anything common must be twice as common with twins. Everything twice, intensified, complications expected but no more complicated, in the end, than the everyday, than a dropped vase that doesn't break and only needs retrieval from the floor. That was the case here. Otherwise Knox would be doing something, someone would be doing something. Otherwise, the feeling she had now of everything having been wrong would be a truth instead of a simple reaction to disorienting circumstances, a way to manufacture hindsight, to reshuffle causes so the effects made sense. With Charlotte, there was always a glitch. She meant it to be so, had to turn back on the sidewalk because she'd forgotten her gloves, left her wallet everywhere, asked waitresses ostentatious questions about their personal lives, locked herself out of her apartment. She had always required a few extra attentions, from everyone. When she was younger it had been much worse. Beyond the wrecked cars, the lost summer jobs—sometimes Knox thought she was the only one who knew how bad it had been.

Her mother cleared her throat. She said, "Don't worry. Someone is going to walk out of that door and give us some good news."

Knox swallowed. She stayed perfectly still. The fear was wild in her now. It was growing out of the crown of her head. She said, "Yes."

Her mother was religious. By her chair, in the corner of the library, there was a black leather-bound Bible and a stack of the *Science and Health* newsletters that came monthly and featured articles, Knox thought now, with titles like "Someone Is Going to Walk Out of That Door and Give Us Some Good News." Hers was a private religion, structured more around quiet study than Sundays in church, though Knox was the occasional recipient of printed tracts that she found on the front seat of her car, or slipped under her cabin's kitchen door, on the days after she confided some hurt or slight to her mother. The last time this had happened she had confessed some guilt related to Ned, referred to the stasis that clamped her whenever he asked her to declare her intentions; the next morning she had discovered, rolled up in her newspaper, an article titled "Wonderful Things Are Happening."

Knox tried to think, the way her mother might: God is here. God is here. Then she let go of thought again.

"I'm going to go in there," her father said. "This is crazy."

They were silent. Her father stood, but he didn't move through the door. He reached his hands up and interlocked them at the top of his head, sighed.

Just then, Bruce came out of the operating room. The cap sat on his head, the mask lay tight over the lower part of his face. Knox didn't look for too long at his eyes, or at the rust-colored streak on the front of his scrubs.

"Bruce, what is it?" her mother said. Knox could tell that she had adjusted her voice; she sounded almost playful, as if she were asking him about a gift he had just handed her.

"I don't— Something is wrong. They're operating." Bruce

spoke through his mask. His voice sounded high pitched. He sounded startled to find them there, startled to be talking.

"For what?" her father said.

"He doesn't know, Ben," her mother said. "Do you, Bruce? You've been in there with her, darling, haven't you?"

Nothing is following, thought Knox. Words are not connecting here.

A nurse pushed out through the door.

"I'm here for you, Mr. Tavert," she said to Bruce. "There's another area we can wait in. Follow me."

"But what about us? Can't we go with you?" Knox's mother asked, her voice rising.

"The doctor will be with you," the nurse said. "Just hold tight where you are, okay?"

She led Bruce through another door next to the OR entrance. Knox and her parents stood, waiting, silent again, for what seemed like a long time. Knox stared at a frayed place in the canvas that covered the door Bruce had moved through, drawing herself more fixed with every breath and contracting her mind until it was temporarily fixed, too, fixed like the frayed place on the door, fixed into a kind of starry point: cold, still, immovable.

Breathe in, breathe out.

When Dr. Boyd emerged, his white coat was clean, and he wasn't wearing a mask or gloves. That's good, Knox thought. He's clean.

"Hi," he said. "Let's sit down." He spoke to her father. Knox felt a burning in her chest that was instant. All the organs in her caught fire at once. She wanted to close her eyes, but instead opened them wider, until she could feel the air of the hallway touching them, drying them out. Freeze, she thought: we are this family, this attentive family, waiting at the mercy of Dr. Boyd. Anybody walking by would be able to see the kind of family we are. If I could only be walking by, instead of here in this family.

"There were complications," Dr. Boyd said, and Knox hated that she'd known he would say that, use that word. "Charlotte's uterus failed to contract, which needs to happen in order for her postpartum bleeding to stop. We gave her medication—" The words were rushing from him. Knox had only met him on this night. She didn't know what his face meant, how to read it.

"You were giving her something when we were in the room," her mother said. Her face was hard; the lines around her mouth seemed to deepen as she spoke.

"Yes. When it became clear that the medication wasn't slowing the bleeding down, that Charlotte was experiencing what's called uterine atony, we brought her to the OR in order to arrest the bleeding."

"How—," her father said.

Dr. Boyd looked at him. "We gave her a blood transfusion. Your daughter continued to bleed."

Knox could see the tiny points of black inside the stretched pores on his nose. She wondered if, at any point, her mother, or her father, or herself for that matter, would smash the nose. That seemed possible. To smash his shiny nose, kick his chest, gnaw at the fleshy parts of his ears, push him, push him away. "Your daughter developed a very rare complication, something I've only seen a couple of times in my practice. It's called DIC, which means that her blood refused to clot. The blood thins, to the point of, almost . . . a watery consistency. It thinned and at that point couldn't respond to medications, or to any of the blood products we could provide, and I'm afraid that your daughter has ultimately lost so much blood that her organs cannot sustain function."

Knox wondered if Dr. Boyd would begin to pant from speaking so quickly, from packing so many words into one breath. He stood fingering the pockets of his lab coat.

"This is what you're telling us," her father said. "How is there time for anyone to have a complication, we were gone for twenty minutes."

"Unfortunately it only takes a matter of minutes for the patient to become incapacitated. We have even—in an emergency, a hysterectomy is performed, and I did perform that as a final resort. I know this is extremely difficult to take in, I understand that. What is important to know is that the clotting factors in your daughter's blood were used up, and she began to convulse. This happened extremely quickly. She was under anesthetic at the time, and wouldn't have suffered."

Dr. Boyd looked down at the floor. Then he looked up, and Knox thought she saw a kind of aggression in his face. "Your daughter has died," he said. "At eleven forty-seven, a few minutes ago. I am so deeply—I'm sorry. This was something so rare and unexpected, it just, every physician dreads this happening, I can tell you. It happens in one out of about ten thousand cases. There are no predictors. It's, I can call someone down to be with you, or to escort you to the chapel, or if you'd like to be alone, I can—"

"What?" her father said. "What?" He stood with his mouth open. Catching flies, that was Marlene's phrase.

They stood together, in the hallway. Knox's mother began to weep.

"I am here to answer any questions," Dr. Boyd said. "To give you whatever you need."

Knox felt aware of her face. She thought: This is the face I have now. She wanted to slap its unreal expression from it, so that her face would be opaque and not show anything to someone who might see. But she couldn't move. The air seemed wetter suddenly; she realized that she had made a tent over her nose and mouth with her fingers and stood breathing through it, like a mask.

"I want to talk to someone else," her father said.

Knox watched the frayed place on the door. She allowed the star of her mind to experience just one glimmer, smaller than a filament, of the reprieve that her father might affect with his words. He was getting to the bottom of things. He was a man of some power; he almost never spoke impolitely to anyone. When he did, something would happen.

Her mother was making a low sound. Knox couldn't go to her. Her deep, fathomless work was not to move. If she had let herself think, she would have wondered whether, when Dr. Boyd spoke of death in his weak and watery voice, he meant a respirator or something, a coma or state from which Charlotte could surface.

Medicine could forestall almost anything. It was ridiculous what medicine could forestall, obscene. But she didn't think.

God is here, God is love—

Suddenly Bruce came out of the door with the frayed place on it, as if Knox had summoned him with her gaze. He was no longer wearing his cap or mask. A nurse was with him. She was touching his arm at the elbow. Knox looked at his face and felt a cry beginning at the base of her throat. It was impossible to look at him and not know.

She thought he might move toward her mother. But he seemed to stop, at the center of the hallway, and sway there. Knox's mother stayed where she was, and continued to weep, her eyes wide, watching him. After a pause Knox's father walked past Bruce to the nurse, and demanded to speak to the doctors. How can this happen, he screamed.

Knox pushed her own cry back down. There was a roaring in her ears. She realized that she was the only person who saw that Bruce might fall; even the nurse was distracted now. A hate was filling her: thick, like oil. Hatred of the fact that she saw Bruce might go down, and that she couldn't stop herself from moving toward him now, and gripping his shoulders in her hands, and holding him upright.

The cloth of Bruce's sleeves moved under her hands, and she could feel the warmth of his skin underneath. She could feel the hairs on his shoulders. He was heavy; she planted her feet until he seemed to still. She could smell antiseptic soap on him, and the odors of the room where Charlotte had been.

"Okay," she said, her hatred of everything making breathing difficult. Bruce began slipping again under her hands; she needed help. But there was no one to help.

"I'm right here," she said, her voice even.

Drowning.

· II ·

KNOX

HERE WERE the three weeks.

Here was her family, now.

She had sat up in the den with Robbie, some nights. Close together on the couch, not touching, until the talk shows were over, and they got up to go swimming, or Knox left for Ned's.

They sat watching programs she couldn't quite understand the purpose of: shows that flew to small towns and picked local teenagers to be made over like their favorite pop stars, behind-the-scenes documentaries about the filming of movies that weren't in theaters yet. Here, on this night, was a tanned crew standing on a coastal hilltop, arguing and pointing to some spot in the middle distance, beyond a few cypresses and a chewed-looking stone house, while an actress in a red dress and forties hairdo stood to one side, laughing. Now the actress was being interviewed close-up; she sat in a director's chair with the ocean behind her. She had changed out of the dress, lost the hairdo—had fast-forwarded a lifetime, Knox thought. She wore yellow-tinted sunglasses; the wind kept whipping tendrils of hair into her lip gloss, where they stuck until she felt them and pulled them gracefully away from her face.

"Who is she," Knox said. "She's pretty."

Robbie cut her a look, then rearranged the blanket around his shoulders. "You know her," he said. "We just saw her on *Letterman*, talking about this movie."

"Oh."

Robbie trained the remote at the screen. "Do you want to watch any more of this," he said. His voice was low and unmeasured; television had sucked the inflection out of it. His hair stood up from his forehead in a cowlick that looked like the result of a sweat-tossed sleep. His skin was ashy in the room's low light.

Knox hesitated. She did want to watch. There was something about the saturated blue of the water behind the woman's chair, the way her eyes remained trained on the interviewer, as if she couldn't wait for the next question to come out of his smarmy mouth. She wondered where the movie was being filmed. On some Greek island? In Italy? Turkey? All places she had never been.

"I guess I don't care," Knox said. "I should go to bed."

"Me too."

But Robbie squinted his eyes, as if the television were backing farther away and he were trying to draw a bead on it. He pushed a few buttons on the remote. The screen went gray, and a question appeared: ARE YOU SURE YOU WANT TO ORDER THIS PAY-PER-VIEW EVENT? Robbie used the remote to scroll down to YES, adding three dollars and ninety-five cents, according to the prompter, to their parents' cable bill.

"I'm ordering a movie," he said.

Knox licked her lips, which were dry. "Okay," she said, though he hadn't asked her permission. Neither of them moved. An image of a boxer receiving a punch to his jaw stretched to the edges of the television screen and remained frozen for a moment before motion began. Then a crowd was all of a sudden booing; a mouthguard flew out of Sylvester Stallone's lips in a swanning trajectory that the camera followed; white drops of sweat erupted from his hairline, the sides of his wet, contorted face; he was going down.

Knox pulled her own blanket up to her chin; the air-conditioning in the house was so cranked they needed help to keep warm. "A-dri-an," she offered softly, going for the South Philly accent, her voice rasping in mock pain as Rocky hit the floor.

Robbie turned up the volume a little, ignoring her. It was one-thirty in the morning. Their parents were asleep upstairs. Two clear plastic containers lay open on the coffee table, still half full of the taco salad Knox had picked up that afternoon from a drive-through place in town.

"Well, I'm going," she said.

The ref rushed to Rocky's side to count: One. The crowd counted with him. Two! He pounded the floor. Adrian looked scared to death in her high-necked cotton dress.

"How many times have you seen this," Knox said. "Ten?"

"I dunno," Robbie said. "Like fourteen."

Knox waited. She herself wouldn't ask. If Robbie wanted to stay where he was and watch *Rocky* for the fifteenth time, then that was what she truly wanted him to do. For some reason, it was completely up to him to ask. If she said anything about it, expressed any desire before he did, she would feel exposed and foolish, she knew.

Robbie glanced at her, then back at Rocky, who was in the process of taking a futile swing, meeting only air with his glove. He clicked the television off. Knox reeled for a second in the dark, the screen's light still firing on her retina.

"I'm going to swim," Robbie said. "You want to? Come on if you want."

Knox breathed out in a rush. She nodded. This was what she looked forward to, though she knew she should make Robbie go to sleep.

She stood, folded both of their blankets quickly, and draped them over the back of the couch. Robbie was waiting for her in the back hall, his shirt blue-white in the gloom. He let himself out first. Knox reached the screen door at the moment before it snapped shut with a whine that might be loud enough to wake her parents—or at least to disturb them; she wasn't sure they were sleeping nights—and slowed it with the palm of her hand. She followed Robbie into the dark.

They walked, and Robbie began to rub his face. When they reached the pool house, he stopped walking and begun rubbing at his face and hair with both hands.

"I feel like I need to get fucked up," Robbie said, trying to laugh. "I feel like I'm going crazy."

"I know," Knox said. She held her breath, hoping Robbie wouldn't start to cry. It was like this, with none of them knowing who would need comfort next, or which way a moment would go. She was thinking of liquor. They had drunk a little wine the night before, but something hard might be better, if that's what Robbie wanted. Tequila wasn't a bad idea, if she could find any. In fact, it was a pretty good idea.

"Sorry to cuss," Robbie said. He swung his foot, brushing the top of the grass with it.

Knox smiled. She felt engulfed by affection—almost nauseous with it—for a moment.

"God. Say what you like. I'm not sixty. No, wait—on second thought, go to your room."

Robbie glanced up. He smiled back at her, though the smile was faint, perfunctory. "Mr. McGaughey came by at lunchtime while you were out. He kept telling me about these old pictures he has of her, from some Fourth of July party I don't even think I was born for. It's like, he wouldn't stop talking about them."

"People are nuts," Knox said lamely. She had meant to say *ineffectual. Lacking in wherewithal.* "They don't know what to say." Now she sounded like their mother. She blinked her eyes a few times. Their mother didn't seem to get it; she didn't seem upset enough that their father seemed so bad off at the moment. Her father fell into the category of things she wasn't capable of thinking about for longer than a moment or two. He had stayed in bed for most of the time since they'd been back, a prone shape in the half dark of her parents' room.

"I almost walked away while the guy was talking to me," Robbie said. "It's like . . . I forgot I was supposed to keep standing there."

"What do you want me to do," Knox said to her brother. She hoped, in that moment, that he would ask her to do something impossible, something humiliating. She remembered the truth-or-dare games she had roped Robbie into during the years right after Charlotte left, when Robbie was too young to protest. She had made him eat raw eggs and dog biscuits. She had made him stand in a locked closet for one hour. She had made him climb into one of the haylofts and stick his finger in a rat trap. She had made him kiss her once, his lips pressed inexpertly against hers for whole minutes, after having watched a salacious evening drama some oblivious babysitter had allowed her to stay up for. Ask me to die for you, Knox thought, and I will. Just ask me to. I want to.

"There's nothing you can do," Robbie said. "What do you think? No one's normal." His voice broke.

Knox went to hug him. He was an inch or two shorter than she; her nose came to rest in his hair, which smelled like cigarette smoke and something sweeter, a leftover shampoo smell. He let her hug him, and then moved out of her arms, wiping his face.

They made their way down to the pool without talking any more. Knox could hear the sprinkler system ratcheting in another part of the yard, its *chicka chicka* and the audible arc and fall of drops as they rained in near unison against the grass. She could hear her own shoes meeting the walk, and not her brother's. He picked his way in front of her in the dark.

They reached the pool deck, stopping together near one of the plastic chaises. The two of them stood in place there for a few moments. Robbie put his hands at the small of his thin back and breathed the night air. Knox squatted, bounced on her heels. The pool water itself was black, blacker even than the darkness around them. It lapped quietly against the tiles that lined the sides of the pool. Trying to maintain her balance, Knox scuffed her shoes off one at a time. The brick had trapped the heat of the day and felt warm underneath the tensed soles of her feet. She kept her eyes on the pool surface as Robbie began to undress with a controlled rapidity. It would embarrass both of them if she spoke or looked at him while he was undressing, so she stayed as she was.

Robbie's jeans and shirt landed on the seat of the chair between them. He moved toward the pool steps in his boxer shorts and descended into the water smoothly, making a minimum of sound, until his body disappeared with a slosh, and his head reemerged. Knox could see that Robbie's eyes remained closed as he rubbed the wet from their sockets, pushed a mess of hair up from his face.

"Feels warmer than last night," he said softly. "Like the heater is on."

He didn't expect a reply. He turned away from Knox and began to stroke away from her toward the deep end, kicking up water with louder splashes now. He would swim a few laps while Knox herself undressed and slid into the shallow end, spending minutes bobbing with the water at her armpits, her head and neck dry, before she talked herself into dropping down, immersing herself in the soundlessness and the uniformity of temperature and the light pressure against all her limbs as they floated up. Knox did this while Robbie crawled up and back. She held in the last of her breath, sprung off the bottom, and corkscrewed though the water once, twice. The material of her bra and underwear grew heavier, threatened to float away from her with their own thrust as she moved. She didn't swim for too long, just let herself flay like that, then hauled herself back up the pool steps and out of the water. She found her clothes, pulled them on over her wet skin, wrapped Robbie's jeans around her shoulders. She walked the length of the pool, passing Robbie as he splashed below her. When she got to the diving board, she stepped out to the edge that hung over the water and lowered herself carefully down until she was sitting, curled, her arms around her shins and her knees close to her face, close enough for her to smell chlorine on her skin. She waited for Robbie to finish. She stuck the tip of her tongue out and touched it to one of the water drops on her knee. It tasted like it smelled: of diluted bleach, of leaves decomposing.

Robbie swam halfway back, then made his way over to the side and pushed himself up and out of the water with his forearms in a deft motion, the pool releasing him with a plunging sound. He got to his feet, cupped his hands inside his armpits, and trotted quickly toward where Knox sat on the diving board, his boxers plastered to his legs and drooping low off his hips in a way that made him look skinny and young, that made Knox think of waterslides and birthday parties.

"I have your jeans," she said to him, once he'd drawn close enough. "Here." She slid them off her shoulders, wadding them together so she could hand them back.

"No, I'm getting back in," Robbie said. Even his voice seemed to shiver. Knox could hear the acquired Virginia in it—the glottal swing and expansion that had rubbed off enough during his freshman year to last him through the summer, that he must have used to shout for beers with in overcrowded basements. She suddenly wondered if there was a girl, somewhere, that he had been calling, a girl who was looking forward to him returning to school. She hoped there was. "It feels better in the water," he said. "God, I should have brought a towel."

One or the other of them said this every night. Knox breathed a kind of acknowledging laugh, a hum: I know, we don't know what's good for us, we don't even think of towels until it's too late. She breathed, too, that familiar guilt: she was the older one; she should be the one remembering what it was they needed.

Robbie hopped onto the metal ladder to Knox's left and lowered himself back into the water, sighing a little. He treaded over to the diving board and reached up, gripped with both hands near Knox's crossed feet, and held on.

A minute passed. Knox could hear a steady dripping under the board.

"I'll tell you something if you tell me something," he said at last, his voice echoing up from the cave of space under the board.

She had been getting ready. This was something they had started doing, after their swims—only she and Robbie talked like this, no one else.

"I have mine," she said.

"Go."

"You may have heard it."

Robbie waited. Knox was gathering herself, trying to remember the details of the story she'd chosen. Any story about Charlotte she knew well was necessarily old, and she couldn't always guide her mind back to the point of it, or separate out what she might have been told from what she'd experienced firsthand. This one was about a moment in which Charlotte had raised her hand to wave to their father in the sales pavilion, briefly confusing the closest auction hand and halting the bidding, causing the auction-eer to joke about the eager little lady with the outsized bank account in the seventh row, causing all heads to swivel, and their mother to close her fingers tightly around Charlotte's arm, forcing it down. They had been warned many times never to do this, to be ever conscious of their movements during an auction, and Knox kept her arms vigilantly pinned to her sides at all times in that frigid arena as the twitchy yearlings were paraded past, lest she forget. Knox had wondered, at the time, if Charlotte had meant to do it—a bewildering possibility given their father's subsequent stern lecture, which she could never have imagined provoking on purpose. Charlotte, though, had let herself be reprimanded, had stood in the aisle after the gavel came down like she hadn't a care in the world.

Finally, Robbie lifted his head to the edge of the board and looked up at her. His eyelashes, shorter, blonder than Ned's, gummed together into wet points.

"*Go.*"

"Sorry," Knox said, and started talking.

BRUCE

THE NICU WAS the only place Bruce knew how to be.

He hated the crowded elevator one had to take to get to it, the pressure mounting in his chest as the box rose. Given another second, he knew, he'd erase the silence around him with the scratch of his voice; but once again the doors slid open too early, and the few people he'd been close enough to touch, had stood closer to than any normal definition of propriety would allow, exited without ceremony into the empty, white air of this place that contained more than any place should ever reasonably contain. He hated the approach, the construction-paper letters on the walls of the corridor, the stupid mural of smiling fish, the waiting room where the day's roster of expectant grandparents and their hangers-on sat waiting for their own news, too confident behind the newspapers they were pretending to read. Every inch of the room, from floor to furniture, was covered in industrial carpeting, and Bruce knew the very thoughts of its occupants, the soup they were anticipating for lunch, the content of the jubilant e-mails they were composing prematurely in their heads. He hated the desk his special badge allowed him to circumvent. He and Charlotte had checked in there, and other couples stood, checking in there, too: the women swaying on their feet, overdressed, too much of the world outside, as if oblivious that their connections to everyday enterprise had already been severed. They were floating in the blackness of space, untethered, in their tasteful jersey maternity dresses with their BlackBerrys on VIBRATE and their overnight satchels packed just so, slung over their tensed shoulders. They made Bruce angry. He knew what was contained in their bags: white cotton nightgown sets and changes of pregnancy underwear and address books and sanitary pads and a few leaves of stationery and a dopp kit and a tiny onesie and hat for the baby to go home in and snacks, probably some kind of gourmet trail mix flecked with chocolate morsels, which no one would ever consume. Trail mix, as if this were a hike, an outing. That's what Charlotte had packed—that and a half-pound bag of peanut M&M's, though on their hospital tour they'd been assured that food was forbidden. Bruce remembered, distantly, his quaint outrage at this: His wife would require some rocket fuel for the epic journey she was about to undertake, wouldn't she? Ice chips? Was that a joke? Had anyone else seen the labor and delivery films? He'd looked around at the other participants on the tour; no one had answered him, though a few shot him sympathetic looks. He'd been muttering. Charlotte had squeezed his hand. He and Charlotte had held out some vague hope that she'd have a go at actual labor, even though the twins she carried all but guaranteed a C-section, and their OB had scheduled one months before, to fall on a date that preceded her due date by one week, though they'd never made it that far. He didn't make eye contact with the couples now as he stepped past the desk, though the men were desperate for him to look at them; he could feel it, feel their eyes on him. They wanted recognition, or pity, acknowledgment—I've been there, dude, it's going to be fine—anyway, they wanted something he couldn't give.

As the men looked at him, angling, the nurses looked away, failing to greet him once he'd pushed the metal panel that admitted him into the private unit through automatic doors. It was clear from their casual laughter and the pauses they indulged in before answering one of his questions, the internal gathering and even impatience they were not afraid to let him glimpse, that they'd made some bargain long ago not to feel. Except for one, Sophia, who seemed to have a different shift each day so that Bruce could never depend on her presence, they failed to smile or exude much palpable warmth. He supposed that, compared with what he needed from them, it was a saner choice to offer him nothing; otherwise they might be consumed, tip into him and be burned up. Yes, that made sense. The room was only slightly larger than the conference room at his office. Tall, metal Isolettes on casters, nubby recliners, and all manner of monitoring machines were its furniture. It was loud; the alarms on the Brady cardiograms rang ceaselessly, printers spat out reading after noisy reading; this was an atmosphere of emergency, as opposed to the hushed haven Bruce had expected. That part, he didn't hate. It felt appropriate, and he dissolved into the hum and activity as if he were falling into water, negotiating the maze on his way to the corner Ethan and Ben's crib occupied, a beautiful, light-filled corner, with a view of the East River that might make Bruce laugh under other circumstances, so wasted was its beauty on him and the other occupants of this floor. A developer would kill for this view. Apartment seekers would ransom their grandmothers for it. Instead, Bruce pictured a face like his own as viewed from outside, the sole face visible from behind an acre of glass, pale, eyes fixed on the barges below as they plowed forward, their progress barely discernible except for the crescent of white churn in their wakes.

What he loved: seeing the boys. Only that. The exhale he was able to produce when the boys came back into his sight after his night away from them—another meaningless night he'd already forgotten, had already voided from the ledger of nights. His miraculous boys.

The chair Bruce sat in was gray. He occupied it for about ten hours a day, if you subtracted lunch, and the inevitable perambulations he had to make when the noise filled his head so that it brimmed. He'd written a report in grade school about the Siberian gulag, where guards swaddled their shoes in cotton and trained themselves to move so silently that their very presence con-tributed to the torturous goal of confusing prisoners as to whether the voices in their heads were actually audible in the pervasive absence of sound. Here it was the opposite, though the effect must be the same; the sound was what pervaded; the thoughts were what you couldn't identify, because you might have spoken them instead of merely thought them; someone was always speaking here, asking you to repeat your story and repeat, repeat, repeat. Bruce had no idea why the doctors and hospital workers from dif-ferent specialties couldn't seem to coordinate information and thus relied on him to stitch the quilt together every time they made their rounds. "Hi, I'm Cassie from social work. So how are the babies doing? Twins, yes?" Cassie would stand there, read-ing the chart, getting up to speed. Somewhere on the chart was typed the phrase *maternal death*, though Bruce suspected it was near enough to the bottom of the page that some people never got to it. When they did, he could read it in their faces, and the satis-faction that coursed in his veins then was as powerful as a drug. He wanted Cassie to know every last detail. He wanted Cassie, well-meaning Cassie, on her knees.

Ethan and Ben were okay—improbably okay, though their stay here would be necessary for another week, until the fluid in their lungs cleared completely and they could handle feedings on their own. Their brains, hearts, and other internal organs were unscathed. Their esophagi were fully attached. They were proba-bly not going to suffer any significant developmental delays; though time would tell on this score, the same was true for any kid. They were beautiful—dizzyingly so—and intact. Bruce had such difficulty grasping this that his pace would quicken each morning as he drew abreast of their Isolette, so that he could assure himself once again that their survival was true. They should look like accident victims, bloodied and deformed by trauma, he thought. But they didn't—aside from the tubes, and the slight translucence of their skin and obvious lack of meat on their bones, they were *babies*, their features tiny but formed, discrete, unblemished. His eyes seared, as if he were looking into the sun.

Ethan was longer. He had a raspberry-colored mark on one of his eyelids, which Bruce had been told would fade as he grew. There was a suggestion of fuzz, which lent a reddish cast to his scalp, though this was covered up most of the time with one of the striped caps the hospital provided for warmth. His nostrils flared as he slept; his fingers were tapered and elegant; he seemed to Bruce to possess a capacity for disdain that made Bruce proud and even more protective of him than he was, if that were possible: You're right, he thought. Everything you're thinking is right. Though Bruce held him anyway, for as much time as he was allowed each day, it was clear Ethan didn't like to be held, not yet; he stiffened slightly within Bruce's careful grasp, and his breath quickened.

Ben seemed dreamier. Phantom smiles animated his mouth while he dozed against Bruce's forearm, his head cradled in his father's left hand. His cries seemed briefer, more to the point, than his brother's, as if he couldn't wait to have them over. He was darker, would have Charlotte's coloring, it appeared—though Bruce was careful as yet not to let his mind extend any further into the future than the next feeding time.

"You're comparing them?" Sophia said to him this afternoon. She sighed, shook her coarse, hennaed curls. She wore a loud smock, printed with Warner Bros. cartoon characters, over her nurse's clothing. Her face was punctuated with moles of different colors and shapes. "I've got two girls at home. Why is it always our instinct to compare them? I can't help it, either. But it'll get you in trouble, for sure."

Bruce watched as Sophia slid Ben's diaper off without waking him, and quickly fastened him into a fresh one.

"How can anyone help comparing," Bruce said. "They're so different."

"The more different they are, the harder you've got to work to pretend you don't notice, otherwise they're going to try to figure out which of them you think is better, or which one is more like you, whatever. It's like a wedge. These things gone off at all this morning?" Sophia pointed at the Brady monitors.

"Ethan's just once, but I turned him a little and it stopped."

"Good. They're too damn sensitive sometimes. A little reflux will set one of these machines off, or the wrong position—I'm glad you know that. Some people around here get hysterical."

"We're all hysterical," Bruce said.

Sophia looked at him, smoothing at her Tweety Bird pockets.

"With good reason," she said, after a long moment. "You been down to the chapel yet?"

"No."

"You're going to need all the help you can stand with these boys. You might as well get some from God."

"I think I'll get a Coke. Would you like one?"

"Go down there," Sophia said. She didn't smile. "It's nice. Nobody will bother you."

"Thanks," Bruce said airily, and he tried to smile as he stood, though he wasn't sure that he was successful, and in a moment Sophia was fiddling with a saline drip, her expression concentrated, inaccessible.

Bruce didn't want to tell Sophia that he didn't believe in God. One might assume that this shortcoming dated from his mother's death, but his mother hadn't believed in God, either, though she wasn't incapable of invoking him as one might a character from one of Bruce's comic books—a bumbling straight man, a Magoo. She railed at God, made jokes at his expense, but she didn't actually believe he existed, nor did his rational, mathematically oriented father. What explanation could Bruce offer to the devout, to someone like Sophia? Sorry, I grew up in Manhattan. Sorry, my family spent weekend mornings debating op-ed columns, while everyone else was in church.

Bruce moved through the doors back into the corridor, past the desk. With each step he took away from the boys, he felt a familiar uptick in his level of unease; to be away from them was to doubt anew their well-being and to subject himself to the clutching sense that he was exposing them to more terrible risk. He tried to ignore the feeling, stretched his stiff arms over his head and pressed his fingers ceilingward as he walked, cracking his knuckles. A woman with a long braid and a baby face sat in a wheelchair, looking pained and abandoned. A man—an overgrown boy, really, in a baseball cap and cargo pants—stood with his back to her, hunched over his cell phone. Cell phones weren't allowed this close to the NICU. Their signals could interfere with the monitors, though everyone seemed to use them. The alternative was the decrepit pay phone in the waiting lounge, or the long, circuitous trek back to the hospital entry. Bruce himself had made calls from here before. He'd called Charlotte's family, updated them on the twins' imminent delivery, called his father, checked his messages, a thousand years before.

"Excuse me," Bruce said to the man's back. He said it softly, the faint smile he'd attempted for Sophia resurrected on his lips.

The man didn't respond, perhaps hadn't heard him. He continued to talk into his mouthpiece, his voice husky, not quite a whisper. When Bruce tapped him and he turned, his eyes were bright. He looked excited. Bruce almost felt bad for the guy.

"Okay, okay," he said to whomever he'd called. "I've gotta go. Yeah, for sure, we'll keep you posted!"

"Hey," he said to Bruce, the word a question, as he snapped his phone shut. He looked at Bruce as if he expected to know him, expected in the next second to receive more good news. His face was open, smiling.

"Hi. I just wanted to let you know that you're not supposed to use that in here." Bruce gestured toward the phone. He felt himself working to keep his own expression blank, to banish the apology from it. His heart raced. What was it that had made him stop for this one, when yesterday he'd ignored another?

"Oh." The man looked around. "Okay. Do you work here?" His eyes narrowed slightly, though his smile remained in place.

"No."

"I was calling my wife's parents to tell her we're about to have a baby," the man said, his voice even.

"I know. Still. There's a rule." Bruce felt an odd thrill—there had been one time at Bancroft when he'd almost fought a boy named Pete Harvey, had experienced those few seconds that existed between a provocation and the moment the response would come, his body taut, alive with a kind of ecstatic, out-of-nowhere indignation.

"Thanks. It doesn't look like anyone's around. But thanks." The man's voice gathered a subtle, progressive edge of sarcasm as he spoke; he turned a few degrees away from Bruce, his eyes bugging at his wife, whose face Bruce decided not to look at again.

"It interferes with the machines. Some people on this floor are hooked up to important machines."

"Ted," the woman said. Her voice was coaxing, even playful. The name emerged from her mouth sounding swooping, pro-longed. *He's clearly a wacko, honey, let's focus on the big picture. This, too, will be part of our birth story, the funny part, the part when Ted almost lost it, brave Ted, keep it together, Ted, I am having contractions right now, this is nothing, a fraction of a moment, it's already gone. I'm over here, look at me, honey, and smile again. Our room is almost ready.*

"My twins are hooked up to heart monitors in the next room. All I know is that they tell me cell phones could interfere, so you see my problem. I know you wouldn't want to be responsible for any interference."

Now the man's features contracted. Bruce watched him. Something was happening. Ted's jaw worked, and he wouldn't look Bruce in the eye. This struck Bruce as curious and caught him momentarily off guard—he'd expected . . . if not an apology, then at least a pass, a connection, a tacit forgiveness. But he felt calm overall—poised, adrenaline having already permeated his body with its false high. He took a breath, measuring the inhale and the exhale deliberately, slowly.

"I'm really sorry to hear that, buddy. Good luck. All I'm trying to do is get my wife through this process in one piece, okay? That's it."

Bruce stood in place.

"Good luck," the man said again to him. He enunciated as if for a child and drew closer to the wheelchair, touching its back with his hand. "God bless." This last phrase he practically spat at Bruce, who recognized it as his dismissal.

I don't believe in God, Bruce wanted to say. He blinked. He felt like a subject of hypnosis who'd been abruptly woken. Of course: his misfortune was a contaminant to these people, worse by far than his meddling had been. He had both courted and been bracing himself against their pity, but he hadn't anticipated such obvious anger. Bruce could feel the couple willing him out of their vicinity, as if the bad voodoo of his own experience here could hurt them. Ted was not going to let this happen.

"Sorry," Bruce said. "Okay."

"Great."

"Okay."

It took no small amount of will to make his body turn and resume walking. And as much as the power of the information he held in him threatened to best him and declare its own, anarchic freedom, he didn't fling a word about Charlotte over his shoulder as he moved down the hall. In the ears of these people her name and fate would ring like a spell, a jinx, the designation of an ancient devil whose name must never, under any circumstances, be spoken. Bruce knew this, and his hands shook with the wish to make them recoil, but an equal part of him knew that as the steward of the most terrible secret on the ward, the Ring to his hobbit, he was charged with making it all the way to the vending machine, step by step, without once revealing to a stranger that his wife had died on an operating table just out of sight, six days ago, and he was now a single father of two infant boys, and no one was going to go out of their way to give him the space and time to understand this, much less to deal with it, and his previously unlimited choices had narrowed to two: either he could force one of the nonoperating windows here open and let himself fall through space toward the barges on the silent, beautiful river, or go through the rest of his life this way. He picked up his right foot and put it down, his throat itching with sudden thirst.

A GUY from the buy side, who Bruce kept up an e-mail correspondence with at work, had sent him a to-do list when he'd heard. Lionel Tregoe was the father of four, and though Bruce had never met his wife (and had only met Lionel himself twice, both at fairly useless conferences held at the Midtown Sheraton), he suspected she'd been the one to type out the directives he'd been following all week, and he was grateful to her in a way he could never be to those responsible for the strange early deliveries of flowers and personalized children's clothing, some of them with attached notes of such brevity and cheer that Bruce felt a kind of vertigo at the possibility that the small detail of Charlotte's death was actually going to be politely ignored in some quarters, at least when it came to the gifts. One friend of Charlotte's grandmother's had gone so far as to phone in an order of blue balloons from her remote Kentucky assisted-living facility, though Bruce wasn't sure how she'd managed it. On the other end of the spectrum, a band from one of Charlotte's acting classes had *already* taken it upon themselves to start a blog in tribute to her life, which he couldn't, and perhaps never could, bear to look at—not least because the people involved, her friend Stephen among them, had always struck him as self-involved twits. But the list was something he could use, and in the eternal space between sunrise and 10:00 a.m, the hour the NICU opened to family visitors, he'd started to go about the tasks it outlined. He had placed an ad for a babysitter in the *Irish Echo*, posted another on Craigslist, and left a message at a placement agency Lionel's wife recommended. He had lugged the car seats to his garage and installed them, after a full hour and a half of wrestling, in the backseat of the car. He had made a trip to a terrifying baby emporium the size of three football fields for cases of formula (Charlotte had planned to nurse), bottles, a steam sterilizer, pacifiers, preemie clothes, and diapers. He let the voice mail fill up, and instead of listening and responding to its contents, went about assembling a blast list of e-mail addresses so he could update the rest of the world, and then promptly forget it existed.

He forced himself up and down the bright aisles of Gourmet Garage and filled the refrigerator with groceries—individual yogurts, sports drinks, pasta sauce, a bag of apples, an arbitrarily chosen pound of orzo salad, marinated steak. He tried to eat. That had been on the list, too. Eat. Lionel's wife must be some kind of clairvoyant, he thought. Or a saint.

KNOX HAD INFORMED HIM that she was coming once the boys were released from the NICU, had written him back in response to his last e-mail. She hadn't mentioned a hotel. When Bruce had finally summoned the energy to call her, trying to gauge the seriousness of her intent (and, he suspected, to put her off the idea, though it was painfully clear he would be in need of the kind of help she was offering until he hired somebody), she'd sounded strange on the phone. Perhaps she felt guilty about Mina and Ben's clear inability to come back to New York at the moment. Though he supposed he hadn't expected his conversations with Mina to go the way they had, and couldn't claim to know exactly why his mother- and father-in-law hadn't yet suggested a date on which they'd come, part of him was admittedly relieved that these recent days hadn't been further complicated by their presence. Was it more painful for Ben and Mina to see him, or to see the boys, or to be in Charlotte's house, where even the smell of her perfume still dominated? Bruce suspected that Ben was the primary reason; Mina had mentioned that he wasn't well, then changed the subject—but it was impossible to be sure. Bruce put his suppositions, and the way he might end up feeling about them, into the category of things to deal with later, and perhaps never. Anyway, he was sure he'd sounded strange, too. How could any of them resemble who they'd been? He'd never known Knox well, at least not well enough to predict her response to . . . this. He'd been surprised, a little, at her offer. It frightened him, actually, though in his dulled state he found he could ignore that and acquiesce to what was practical.

He'd been relieved so far not to have to talk during his hours here, except in response to the questions the doctors and nurses posed. Though he didn't think of Knox as a talker, not as the kind of person who needed to fill a vacuum with noise. Still. The only talking he voluntarily undertook was to the boys—barely above a whisper, and tentatively—while he held them. For some reason he felt embarrassed at the possibility that he would be overheard doing this, marked as clumsy by the people around him who were more experienced with children. He couldn't afford to be learning on the job; he felt instinctively that he needed to know exactly what he was doing, to have been made an expert father through the very appearance of his children in the world, and even to appear vulnerable on this score to a stranger was to have failed. He might have preferred simply to stare at Ethan and Ben, communicating what he needed to in silence, but Sophia had assured him that this was a good thing to do, that they might already recognize his voice, and would feel relief at hearing it often. He didn't know what to tell them, except that they were going to be okay. He described the view, described each of them to the other. During the times when both boys lay in the Isolette facing each other, exhausted from the work of growing well enough to get out of here, Bruce watched them, his arms slack at his sides, and wondered what he was beholden to tell. Charlotte would have known how to direct the parts of their lives that still confounded him toward their places in an orderly line; she was good that way, could take an argument that had left him reeling and soften it the next morning, describe to him the ways in which this happened to everyone, was part of the beautiful bargain they'd made, was *healthy*. She'd be wry and talk about what was natural in life and in death. Now Bruce was left alone to justify and reckon with what they'd had together, without Charlotte to explain any of it, to explain himself, back to him. Theirs had been as fathomless and bewildering and defiant of logic as any couple's shared life, he supposed, before the end. But how could he really know?

They had been married almost five years, tried to have a baby together for three. Finally, insemination—the turkey basting, Charlotte had called it—had worked, a fact that left them incredulous and grateful. They hadn't had to do in vitro, which they'd dreaded equally, after all.

No. Whatever litany of facts he began with, when practicing the telling, turned reductive within seconds. Start again.

In a grassy corner of the park, they would lie on their backs, not unlike Ethan and Ben now, his head flush with her hip, her legs extending beyond his line of vision, and the tips of Charlotte's fingers would gather up folds of her cotton skirt and she would pull it up by increments, inch by inch, so slowly he was mesmerized, he was laughing, waiting to see how far she would go, knowing she wouldn't be wearing anything under her clothes in summer.

Was this their marriage?

Start again.

They had loved each other. He was sure of that. Beyond this, he wasn't sure of much: what her friends thought, what her parents had been privy to, the true measure her siblings took of him. His bond to Charlotte had been a solid thing built on sand, so that he simultaneously trusted in its strength and doubted anew each day whether, when his eyes opened, it would exist. He had no religious faith, but the ecstasy of belief—this had been available to him in the privacy of his bedroom, his kitchen, in conversation held over the noise of their leaky shower. He was a supplicant at his own breakfast table, sipping Charlotte's perpetually shitty coffee. His communions were the toasts they'd made across countless tables in New York, looking each other in the eye with an exaggerated concentration that always made him laugh; Charlotte thought it was bad luck to clink while looking away. Bruce had read somewhere that the tradition of the toast dated from the Middle Ages as a precaution against getting yourself poisoned; the contents of one's cup were meant to spill a little into the cups of one's companions, and a refusal on anyone's part functioned as an instant alarm. "If I go, you go," he and Charlotte had made a habit of announcing to each other, sotto voce, bug eyed, knocking their wineglasses together as hard as they dared without breaking them.

Bruce climbed out of the gray chair. The boys had been asleep in their Isolette (though how they could sleep through all the racket in here was a mystery) for the better part of an hour now. He would take his hall walk, grab another Coke at the vending machine, circle the floor in time to be back before their next bottle-feeding.

Knox was due to arrive the next week. The boys would be home then, according to the doctors. Bruce thought, as he pushed his way out of the NICU doors, aware of the few curious eyes that lit upon him in the waiting area as he emerged, an emissary from the VIP section of the obstetrics wing, closed off to the plebes with a velvet rope fashioned out of everybody's worst nightmare, that his grasp of Charlotte's history within her family had never been total, perhaps couldn't be, because of his mortifying, groveling helplessness in the face of any intact family. It wasn't easy for him to understand why his wife wasn't closer to Mina and Ben and Knox and even Robbie, though he tried, repeating Charlotte's version of events to himself in his head from time to time: Mina and Ben's devotion to each other and their growing business was so complete during Charlotte's early childhood that she'd felt, if not left out, then uncomfortably peripheral. Though she'd been loved and attended to, she was close enough to the edge of the circle the three of them made that she could imagine stepping into the cold territory beyond its circumference. This made her feel both terrified and curious. As she grew, some part of her ceded the insider status to Knox willingly (though Charlotte never seemed to forget the ferocity with which, according to her, Knox had claimed it), and began to look past her family for the kind of affirmation she needed, had always needed, in order to breathe. The money the farm started to bring in thrust her parents further into a world Charlotte viewed as phony and meaningless; though Knox and Robbie were still young enough never to have known anything different, Charlotte recognized the speed with which things were changing. Finally, she'd wanted out, and on some level, it seemed, they'd let her out, which Charlotte felt was right and unforgivable at once. This was the Cliffs Notes account as Bruce understood it, the synopsis Charlotte had arrived at after years spent in therapy and engaged in the burial of her former self under a series of East Village walk-ups, temporary jobs, and pointless left turns. Then came Bruce. He was part of the story, too. He was supposed to be the happy ending.

Of course, this was a story with the blood drained out of it. But Bruce was glad to possess something boiled down that he could invoke at the sight of all that insane beauty on his visits to the farm, and the warm enthusiasm, the trust, really, with which Mina and Ben had taken him in. Otherwise, he would have little idea why Charlotte scheduled so few visits home or could be drawn so quickly into an argument behind the closed doors of her child-hood room during their rare visits—her room with its lone Gau-guin poster still pinned to the corkboard wall, its desk drawers filled with school ephemera and murky, undated Polaroids of Charlotte in Day-Glo makeup, everything preserved so carefully that entering it, for Bruce, was akin to stumbling into a Pharaoh's tomb.

He had no idea what Knox knew, or thought, about his marriage to her sister. He suspected not very much, on both counts. She'd always struck him as someone who remained resolutely single—like certain bachelors did, refusing to wade all the way into the pond of human incident, full of mess and danger and caterwaul as it was. This refusal made sense to him, though he was incapable of it himself. He respected it, even gracefully accepted the judgment inherent in it. Of course, Knox did have that boyfriend. A nice guy; Bruce had met him a couple of times. At the moment, he was having trouble remembering his name.

He reached the vending machine. He stood in front of it, sud-denly baffled as to what he'd thought he wanted. There was a machine for drinks of all colors and caffeination levels and degrees of sugar content—flavored waters, sports drinks, sodas—and another for food: cellophane-wrapped cakes, bags of chips, candy, jerky, small boxes of cereal. He slid his hand into the pocket of his jeans and jangled the change there. He didn't even know if he had enough. The sodas here cost two dollars apiece. He'd left his wallet in the backpack beside the chair, the backpack that he'd balled a receiving blanket into, that held a portable bottle of hand sanitizer, his phone, a work file that he couldn't fathom ever cracking again but nonetheless hadn't removed. (He needed to call Susan, his boss, to find out how many weeks it was acceptable for him to take. Two, three more? However many he needed? Though the firm was small, devoid of the cold, swinging-dick culture that characterized larger shops, it was a business, and he followed a lot of companies. They wouldn't keep paying him forever.) He swallowed against a faint taste of bile at the back of his throat. He wouldn't think about anything now.

THE TURKEY BASTING hadn't happened in the hospital but in the OB's office, all of two blocks away from here. Charlotte had been given a week's cycle of Clomid and had the moment of her ovulation zeroed in on definitively the day before. When they saw each other in the waiting room at the appointed time, they laughed! They were still young! They were fine! They'd fallen into the hands of professionals in the nick of time! Somehow, they both recognized hilarity in the moment, and in each other's relief. The source of their inability to conceive still hadn't been diagnosed; still, Bruce privately suspected himself as the reason for their problem. He wondered if Charlotte suspected him, too, though she'd assured him she didn't, that it was surely her fault if it was anyone's, she was probably defective, marked, the star of their infertility show.

He jacked off into a paper cup. He only had to do it once. The bathroom they sent him into was no bigger than an airplane's, the process blessedly quick—so quick that he lingered for another few minutes after, embarrassed to show himself too early. He hadn't been thinking of Charlotte. Instead, he'd summoned a detailed image of the body of a woman sent into the bathroom to pleasure him. An employee. A fluffer in a tight, white coat. He'd even told Charlotte this, back in the waiting room, as they waited for his issue (*issue*—this was the kind of word that reduced them to more teary, helpless laughter, to obnoxious nine-year-olds at the back of a bus) to be spun, so a nurse could then insert it with a catheter into Charlotte's uterus. He knew Charlotte would ask him what he'd been thinking of. She loved that kind of stuff, loved to weasel it out of him and then tease him with her mock outrage.

That the turkey basting had ultimately become necessary didn't seem as important, in the end, as the fact that it worked (on the first try!), clear evidence that they were charmed. It took weeks for the pregnancy test to confirm it, but Charlotte claimed she knew right away, though it was probably only the effects of the drugs that she was feeling. Between the day of the visit and the day of the bright blue line, Bruce did something he'd never expected to do, that he still couldn't fully explain. He sat at his computer at work one morning and, without premeditation, typed in a string of keywords, chose a site, dialed a phone number, made an appointment for the following afternoon, which he nearly missed when the time came, having sunk into a near-somnambulant denial, perhaps, of what he'd set in motion. At the chosen hour he was listening to the new hire's droning breakdown of the back exercises his chiropractor had assigned him, lingering in the conference room doorway, when he remembered with a start, and, after a moment's reconsideration of the whole thing, made his way calmly down to the street and caught a cab up to the same Sheraton he frequented for work functions. He'd had plenty of chances to back out, then, had chosen and rechosen what came next through the small series of efforts required to show up, but he felt at the time (in the cab, back on the street, adjusting his messenger bag on his shoulder, checking in at the reception desk) like someone who had chosen nothing but was operating from a proscribed set of directives. He'd seen a woman he knew, a broker, crossing the Sheraton lobby on her way to lunch at the moment he entered and felt nothing but mild pleasantness at the sight of her, felt no rush to draw their conversation to a premature close.

They'd found each other easily. In the elevator, he'd introduced himself by name, had smiled in a ridiculous effort to put a twenty-five-year-old prostitute at ease, as if she were the one who was uncomfortable. Two condoms folded together along the perforated seam that joined their wrappers, in the bill compartment of his wallet, purchased hastily at the deli next to his office building. God. He was really in this elevator, he thought, awed. Things like this actually happened. It all seemed normal, ordinary. The magnetized key card in his pocket. The synthetic, cool smoothness of the burgundy-colored spread in the room. The paper wrapper looped around the toilet seat to telegraph hygienic sterility. Come to think of it, that is what the sex had been like, too: hygienic, a performance utterly outside of context, history, or feeling. Sex with Charlotte had always had an intimacy that threatened to cancel him out; he could literally lose track of where he was, feel himself dissolving, while at the same time his mind grew increasingly jumbled and frantic. He loved his wife too much, invested her with too much, feared for her too much; if anything, sex with an indifferent woman, buffed to artificial perfection like a product, was a relief. It was terrible and revelatory at once.

He needed a secret. He needed something outside his life with Charlotte to help him fashion a space, even as thin as a membrane, around himself so he could function apart. Even the guilt that burned in him like a coal provided some ballast to weight his side of the scales—it was his alone; he'd generated it himself. That was something. What he hadn't reckoned on was that as soon as he had the secret he needed, he felt simultaneously compelled to hold on to it and give it away.

Days later, Charlotte lay in bed with a stack of magazines. She'd been there all evening, was "in the weeds," she'd said; the drugs were making her tired, irritable, hungry, restless, and Bruce had made her a cup of tea. The short length of hallway back to their bedroom was dark. Bruce's foot caught on the edge of the runner, and he stumbled slightly; hot liquid sloshed onto his hand.

"Ow!" he said.

"Wha—" When he reached the doorway, he saw that Charlotte had fallen asleep. His cry must have woken her; she sat upright, her hair half covering her face, her eyes unfocused, her pupils black and large. She looked at him as if he were a stranger. The strap of her tank top was falling off her shoulder; one of her cheeks was marked with deep, pink creases. In an instant, her face changed, breaking into a confused smile. The sight of him had oriented her.

"I was having a dream," she said, rubbing at her forearm. The tip of her tongue slid against her lower lip, wetting it. "What time is it?"

"Around nine," Bruce said.

"Nine?" She looked at him pityingly, tenderly, as if she knew. His bowels twisted, and he wondered if he should leave the room. He took a step toward the bed.

"Charlotte," he said. He hadn't planned this; it was something in the moment, in the vision of her there, that was pushing these words from him; now he wasn't sure if he felt sick at the thought of not having told her yet, or of telling her at all, but he couldn't stop himself.

Charlotte looked instantly more alert. She stared at him, not moving.

"What," she said.

"I am so sorry." He was too afraid to reach for her hand. He started to cry.

"Did you sleep with someone?"

"Yes."

Her mouth tightened, but she remained still. Bruce felt every object in the room vibrate. He wiped the tears off his face quickly, not wanting to seem like he was trying to court her pity. What had he done? He wanted only to reach for her.

"When," Charlotte said finally.

"Last week. She was— I paid her," he said. He wanted her to understand, but at the sound of his words, he felt engulfed. He was unworthy of her. She would know this definitively, now.

"Look at me," she said.

He dutifully raised his eyes to hers, his face hot, contorted. She held his gaze, searching his eyes for something.

"You really did that?" she said.

"Yes."

"Bruce. A hooker?"

He said nothing.

"Did you wear a condom?"

"Of course."

She picked at the sheet arranged over her lap. She drew her legs up and hugged them, resting her chin on one of her knees. She hadn't looked away from his face, and he had no choice but to look back, to offer himself whole to her. As she watched him, he saw something evolve within her expression. Her eyes narrowed and then softened. She opened her mouth to speak, then closed it again. Finally, she dropped her gaze and shook her head.

"Charlotte," he said in a strangled voice.

But when she looked back at him, it was like a benediction. She smiled sadly. Again, her eyes seemed to be searching his; in Charlotte's he could read surprise, and something else, something he could barely bring himself to trust . . . a kind of mutual recognition. She hadn't thought him capable of risk, perhaps, or of actual transgression.

"Come here," she said.

He lowered himself onto the edge of the bed, careful not to touch her. He bowed his head and covered his face with his hands.

"I had no idea you were so scared," he heard Charlotte say. Her voice was quiet, stripped of inflection. He nodded into his hands; again, she knew what he hadn't, about himself.

IT WAS shortly afterward that the pregnancy was confirmed. The subject of Bruce's betrayal wasn't closed forever; they returned to it and had different versions of the same conversation on Charlotte's black days, the ones when she couldn't rouse herself from bed in the mornings, when she questioned the veracity of everything that came into her head, but she'd had those days before they were married, before Bruce's confession; they were part of her. Bruce didn't mind these arguments; he welcomed the chance to beg Charlotte for forgiveness all over again, and ultimately receive it. This seemed to reassure them both.

Bruce began to look at couples on the street, in the park, lolling on the steps in Union Square, with renewed interest. He wondered if each of them had undergone a moment—or many—that would remain forever inexplicable to anyone else but was understood within their universe of two, rendering them bound in a new way. After a moment like that, you were helpless, purified, this yet another of the thousand facts his boys would never, could never, be told.

KNOX

AT THE AIRPORT, Ned reached around her waist, hooked his fingers through a couple of her belt loops, and hiked her jeans over her hip bones. She leaned into his chest for a moment.

"These are falling off you," he mumbled into her hair. "You need to fatten yourself up."

"Well, I hear New York has a lot of fancy restaurants."

"You know what I mean," he said. He was keeping his voice light, had been trying to keep it light ever since the last time they were both here, when Ned had picked Knox and her parents up at the nearby private terminal. He had driven them back to the house, seen her parents inside, then brought her back to his dim bedroom, his mouth taut, wrapped her up in the unzipped sleeping bag with the flannel lining he used for a duvet, and rocked her to sleep, talking to her all the while about nothing: the objects in his room, the Earl Scruggs interview he'd listened to on the radio in the barn that day, how the newest stallion was getting along after having kicked at his stall wall the week before, inflaming the hell out of his front left pastern. In the morning, he had scoured his tub with Comet while she slept and then run her a bath, held her hand tight as she descended into the hot, clear water. She had stayed over at his place for several nights, sleeping or trying to sleep, Ned talking to her slowly like he did to his horses. She was sure they had made love more often in the two weeks since Charlotte died than they had in the two months, give or take, before all this happened. Her breasts and stomach were rubbed red; the skin on her upper thighs felt sticky to the touch when she dressed in the mornings. She had her theories. She had lived in his bed and he'd fetched her things from his kitchen: bread and cheese sandwiches, bananas sliced into bowls of milk and peppered with cinnamon; these were the things Ned fixed for her; she was so ravenous all the time.

He'd let Knox push her ice-cold feet under his thigh to warm them while she ate, let her eye the outlines of his handsome, fleshy face as he talked. She had always seen the child in him; that was one of the things she loved about Ned: she could see sweetness and an old petulance at once on his lips and imagine all the things they had begged for and whispered at three, at seven; she could make out, clearly, a willingness to please behind his eyes with their hooded lids, their long, straight lashes that the secretaries in the farm office loved to swoon over, embarrassing him on purpose. Everyone had something indelible in them, lodged deep in their features; Ned's something, she thought, was kindness. It seemed he was doing his best to save her life. She kept meaning to tell him this, but he'd cover her with his warm body, and she'd forget the words to whatever little speech she'd put together. She'd listen to the breath in her ear, to the blood pumping in her own head. She held herself still (how recently she used to pride herself on the energy she could bring to fucking, on twisting herself into positions that would keep them both safe in the knowledge that at least her skill in bed couldn't be questioned, even if her commitment could be), and tried to be thankful that, despite what her head thought it wanted in her worst moments, her limbs seemed to not want to be dead, not yet. This took no small amount of focus. When she came, she didn't make a sound. She closed her eyes. She shuddered.

It would take another month for Ethan and Ben to receive the requisite shots; and after the time they'd had to spend in the NICU, no one was about to rush Bruce or ask him to take any chances, just to get the boys on an airplane. Knox's mother was planning the memorial for just over a month hence, to allow for the twins to travel; and Knox had informed everyone—her parents, Bruce, Ned—that she would be the one to fill in the gap in the meantime, doing feedings, shopping for groceries, lending an extra pair of hands for the pediatrician's visits, and whatever the hell else there was to do, then assisting with the flight home.

"You don't have to do this," Ned said now. "You don't owe her this, you know."

"No?"

"Stay. Stay here with me."

"I can't. What is Bruce going to do? I'm her sister."

Ned said nothing, but watched her patiently, as if waiting for her to recant. She'd sounded melodramatic, and he was too wise to her touchiness on the subject of Charlotte to let her play this role completely straight.

"Yeah," he drawled, finally. "You are. But that doesn't mean you have to overturn your life right now. You're going to mess yourself up, Knox."

"No, I'm not. What about the boys? They're my nephews. They need me."

"If you're going for their sake, then go. That's one thing."

"Why else would I be going?"

Ned took off his glasses, went through the motions of cleaning them, replacing them.

"I don't know." He sighed. "You've got to ask yourself, honey— is this something you would have done while she was alive? Maybe you just don't want to let her go."

"Let her go? She hasn't been dead a month!"

"I didn't mean that, exactly. I think I meant let go of the idea that you're always supposed to fix things. Because you can't, certainly not now. And once you get that idea in your head with her you always end up in a bad place."

"It's not like I'm moving up there. I'll be back in a few weeks, for goodness' sake."

"You're going to be in her house," Ned said. "Among her things."

"I know that."

"You have nothing to feel guilty about, if that's what you're doing."

Knox said nothing.

"You want me to come with you?" Ned looked so worried that Knox was momentarily tempted, and felt her irritation at him lessen.

"You hate New York," she said.

Ned smiled, but his eyes were serious, intent on her face.

"What's not to hate?" he said.

THEIR FAMILY HAD BEEN TOGETHER, all five of them, at Christmas. That was the last time. They sat around the breakfast room table, crowded together on Charlotte's first night home, Charlotte shoehorned between Knox and their father, her place mat overlapping with theirs at the edges. Their mother sat in a low-seated antique chair that had been pulled up to the table's side; Robbie, home too for his winter vacation, had fetched her a pillow to sit on at the beginning of dinner after they had laughed at how comparatively little of her torso showed above the table's surface and torn off little scraps of bread to toss in her direction as if she were an urchin who'd materialized in their midst. "Please, suh," Knox's father said, cupping his hands together and holding them out. Knox's mother compressed her lips, pushed at his shoulder with the heel of her hand, raised her head, and straightened until she sat up taller. She flicked a piece of bread back at Robbie, who ducked. Bruce was to arrive the next day, Christmas Eve; if Bruce had been with them that night, Knox thought, they might have been ranged around the dining room table; it was more generously sized, and anyway Bruce inspired this increased formality in Knox's family—each of them seemed to galvanize in his presence, in the presence of Bruce and Charlotte together, the same way they did for company. Of course, extra efforts were being made tonight, too. Though they sat around the everyday table, they ate by candlelight. Knox's father had opened a second bottle of the red wine his wife had set out on the buffet behind his chair.

"It's not like they *make* you do anything," Robbie was saying.

"Oh no," Knox said. "I'll bet they just show up in your room at four in the morning and put a hood over your head and tell you that if you don't pound twelve beers in a row you're a sorry excuse for a man. But it's not like they *make* you do anything."

Robbie grinned at her. His top teeth were colored pinkish. "I thought you decided not to rush when you were in college."

"So she's right!" Knox's mother covered one side of her face with her hand. "Oh, Rob, not funny. You be careful. No teenager should be forced to drink like that—your little bodies are still growing. Ben, this makes me nervous."

"Thanks, Mama," Robbie said. "It does so much for my confidence when you refer to my little body. Really."

At this Knox, her father, and then Robbie began to laugh.

"What?" Charlotte touched Knox's sleeve. "I didn't hear."

"Not *you*," Knox's mother said to Robbie. "Not yours specifically." Her eyes were bright; she spoke quickly. There was a giddy moment Knox recognized, that, for her, represented one complete definition of pleasure: a minuscule stretch in time wherein they waited for Robbie, having been perfectly set up, to utter a killer line.

"Coming from a dwarf—" was all he had to say. They laughed harder; Knox's father picked up his napkin and swatted at the table; Robbie leaned back in his chair, looking satisfied. "That's it," Knox's mother said, mock indignant, struggling up from her low chair and pushing it away from the table.

"*What*," Charlotte said, the word a high plaint. She held Knox's arm now. "I missed it."

Knox forced herself to look at Charlotte. Her own face, the base of her throat, felt warmed from the wine. Beyond that, she felt good, charged with a kind of invincibility that made her want to turn back toward the other faces around the table, keep herself tangled up in the laughter and talk. She might say anything—there was a momentum to these dinners, to nights like these. Charlotte's lips were turned up at the corners; her eyes planchets, waiting to be stamped with an explanation. They scanned Knox's face. Knox had noticed, when Charlotte first walked through her parents' back door late that afternoon, that she looked paler since the last time they had seen each other, like one of the deeper layers of her skin had been rinsed of its pigment and put back again. Winter in New York, maybe; her cuticles were pink and raw looking where the nail beds met them, her ear ice cold against Knox's cheek when they hugged. Otherwise, Charlotte had looked like herself, her dark, flyaway hair pinned under the strap of a backpack she'd carried onto the plane, the curves of her seeming to extend into the room before her under the layers she wore: fitted army jacket, back-cowl sweater, flannel skirt, tall boots that accentuated an already heavy step. She had changed for dinner, and now wore a corduroy shirt and earrings that stopped just below her jawline and shone like minnows in the light from the candles. She had drawn her legs up so that she sat cross-legged on her chair, her knees resting on its arms, her feet upturned.

Knox sighed. She had no idea how far back to go in order to reconstruct what Charlotte might have missed. The hand on her arm irritated her; her sister demanded a constant inclusion that Knox found rude, that she herself would never have felt entitled to. Charlotte had been watching her for much of dinner; Knox had sensed it, the gaze had made her more than a little ruthless.

"It was nothing," she said. She picked up her wineglass and sipped from it. "Robbie made a joke."

Charlotte waited. Knox took another sip of her wine. She wanted to turn away but couldn't.

"It's too hard to explain," she said, but when Charlotte narrowed her eyes, angled slightly toward their father, and began to open her mouth, she heard herself speaking. "Mom doesn't want Robbie to drink so much at school." She touched Charlotte's hand, and Charlotte's eyes returned to her face. Charlotte smiled and raised her eyebrows; Knox zeroed in on the hieroglyph of freckles that marked the bridge of her nose, so faded with the years that Knox wondered if they had in fact disappeared altogether, if she was seeing them out of habit.

"I heard that part," Charlotte said.

"She said something about growing bodies . . ."

It felt as if she were lifting the words off the bottom of a lake, struggling to push them up, sediment streaming all around her. She didn't want to be talking, but she made herself sound just eager enough.

"And then Robbie said, 'Coming from the midget' or whatever—"

"Oh," Charlotte said. "I got it." She squeezed Knox's arm, then turned to reach behind her for the wine bottle. She topped off Knox's glass with it. She twirled her wrist up at the end of the pour, sending a stray drop into Knox's glass rather than down the bottle's side. "Keep it up," she said, and winked.

Knox kept her lips pressed together. The base of her scalp felt prickly. Had her words come out sounding strange? What was Charlotte talking about? She wanted to protest, but just then Charlotte lowered her feet to the ground, half rose out of her chair, and said, "Mom, why don't you let me do the dishes."

Knox's mother was dragging another chair in from the dining room. She stopped and looked up.

"It's nice just to sit together," she said. "Just leave them. I'll need plenty of help from everybody tomorrow."

"I'm shopping tomorrow," Robbie said. "For all of your presents. So I'll need to help when I get home."

Their mother laughed. She scooted the chair into its place and sat down. "There, is that better," she said, looking around.

"Much," their father said. "Welcome to our world, Min." He reached out to pat her on the shoulder.

"I can do them," Charlotte said. "Believe me, I do the dishes every day in New York, and I never break a one." There was a sudden, insistent edge in her sister's voice.

"It's nice just to sit together," Knox said, enunciating each syllable the way she did with her students.

"Of course you won't break any," her mother said. "I didn't mean—go ahead, if you want to."

Charlotte stood and stacked Knox's plate onto hers. They had been eating off a set of heavy, chipped Provençal dishes her mother had bought during her first trip to Europe and kept stored except at this time of year, red and green, painted with horses, chickens, cows. Charlotte gathered some soiled utensils in one hand and lay them carefully on top of the plates. She carried her load into the kitchen without saying anything else, keeping her eyes trained straight ahead as she walked easily, smoothly, out of the room.

Her parents exchanged a look. Knox, wanting nothing more than to return to the grace she'd been hanging in only minutes before, flicked at the stem of her glass hard enough for her fingernail to hurt. She wanted to follow Charlotte into the kitchen and demand to know what her problem was. Just because she wasn't able to dominate the conversation tonight, was having trouble following—but here was the content of her parents' look, a mixture of forbearance and frustration. Her mother looked away from her father and caught Knox's gaze, smiled sadly. Knox stared back. In doing so, she felt something in her snap into place. She ran her tongue over the back of her teeth, stood too. She picked up her glass and walked around the table, stopping behind her mother's chair, and leaned down and kissed her mother on the top of her head.

"Anyone want dessert?" she said to her parents and Robbie, straightening. "I'm gonna help clear." The peppery, alkaline smell of her mother's hair spray clung inside her nostrils. She was lightening, returning to her proper role, annoyed at herself for letting Charlotte get the better of her. As she spoke she could hear the note of natural superiority in her own voice, the confidence in belonging that she was free to draw on when she remembered to. She reached around to pick up her mother's plate.

"Bring in some of those brownies the McGaugheys dropped off, pal," her father said. "Robbie needs to fatten up his little body."

"I'll be right back," Knox said. She snickered as she said it, hoping Charlotte could hear her. She would laugh as loud, as long, as she wanted to, laugh until her father felt like the funniest man on earth.

In the kitchen, Charlotte was bent over the dishwasher, unloading clean pans. The plates she had brought in from the table sat at the bottom of the sink, hot water from the tap streaming onto them full blast, throwing drops onto the counter. She extracted a colander from the lower rack of the dishwasher and set it on the floor; it wobbled on its metal feet. Knox put her glass down on the counter and bent to pick it up.

"I can put this stuff away for you," she said to Charlotte's back.

Charlotte twisted to face Knox. The color in her face had risen; her hair was tucked behind her ears, flattened at the crown of her head, hanging tangled past her shoulders. Charlotte dragged it roughly away from her face like this when she was in a mood, or trying to concentrate; Knox could see the runnels her damp fingers had left.

"You might as well," Charlotte said. "I don't know where anything goes anymore." One side of her mouth twitched into a half smile. Her bare toes seemed to flex on the kitchen mat, the white polish on them chipped away to nothing. She still doesn't care what she looks like, was what flashed into Knox's mind. Doesn't need to. This familiar thought evoked the old pride and anxiety all at once—her father's proprietary clutches, the exaggerated compliments her mother used to shore Knox up, the need in Knox herself to look, to look, to look, to look, to peer endlessly at photographs, always know where Charlotte was in a room, memorize the way a thin chain fell around her neck, the shape of her head in profile, the way a day's worth of sunburn reddened her eyebrows, the merits of certain colors—pink, black, a bright shade of turquoise—against her skin; like someone who stood too close to a canvas, she had trouble seeing what she was meant to in Charlotte's particular, random alchemy of features, and so kept looking until she had to turn away confused, exhausted; all this mess rose in her now, and she felt sick of it already and glanced down at her shoes. This was part of what it meant to have a beautiful sister (and whether it had to do with proximity or jealousy or both or neither was impossible to say); one could understand it but not ever quite *see* it, however cross-eyed one went trying.

"Ugh," she said, despite herself.

"What?"

"You know," Knox said, taking a breath. She would be too old and wise now to wear herself out. "Just let me do this. Mom and Dad never get to see you. It'll take me one second." She pointed to a tin canister on the kitchen island. "Take those brownies in," and she heard the note of command in her voice, adjusted to protect herself from any accusation of bossiness. "Just don't eat them all before I get back in there, okay?" The water was still splashing uselessly into the sink; Knox moved past Charlotte to shut it off, but Charlotte leaned into her and wouldn't let her pass. She rested her forearm on Knox's shoulder, and Knox had to look into her eyes.

"I want to stay in here with you," Charlotte said. She bowed her forehead until it touched Knox's. The place where their skin met was almost hot, and Knox could smell her sister's oily, bready breath and the apple-scented shampoo she'd borrowed from Knox's bathroom for her shower. Charlotte jerked her head back up and smiled, but Knox had seen real fear and pleading pass over her face. In her surprise, Knox had a clear thought about herself, like a caption: Making her feel punished is never hard like I think, it never feels as good, I never remember this till it's too late. She nodded and turned off the faucet; the subsequent quiet sounded like noise.

"I never get to see *you*, either," Charlotte said, and bugged her eyes out, her mocking composure regained. She arched her back against the counter and folded her hands across her stomach, her fingers woven together. "Plus," she said, her voice sounding happier, more charged than it had all through dinner, "if the brownies are in here, and *we're* in here—"

Charlotte leaned back too far, and one of the heavy dishes slipped off the wet counter and crashed to the floor. She sprang up and away from the broken pieces at her feet, looked down at them, and put her hand to her mouth. She looked at Knox, whose own mouth was open, who could sense her parents and Robbie glancing up at one another in the next room.

"Oh Jesus," Charlotte said.

"You're kidding me," Knox said. They watched each other. Knox felt poised to laugh; sheer not knowing what would happen next wheeled like a bird in her chest, knocking thrillingly against her throat, her ribs, trying to fly out.

"Was that my plate," her mother called. "Charlotte? Tell me that wasn't one of my plates."

Knox and Charlotte kept their eyes on each other. They didn't move. Knox could feel a tiny splinter of glass tacked to the skin of her arm. She could feel her heart beating and feel that Charlotte was tied to her in this moment; she wouldn't do a thing until Knox did, would follow Knox's lead.

Knox swallowed. "I dropped it," she called back to her mother. "It just fell right out of my hands—sorry." Her tongue felt coated; articulation always seemed more difficult when she was lying; this had been true since she was a child. Charlotte made a face and waved her arms as if pressing the air at her sides down and away. No, she whispered.

"I think I can glue it," Knox said loudly. She could hear a lilt in her words that sounded exaggerated; she looked at Charlotte, whose own speech hadn't been accented for years, whose mouth spread into a grin, though her wide eyes searched Knox's face. Oh my God, she was mouthing.

No sound from the next room. Then her father said, "Don't worry about it, honey." It was unclear whether he was speaking to Knox or their mother, but there was a finality in his tone; her father of all people wasn't going to let a small accident mar a family evening. Knox could hear Robbie saying something, though she couldn't make out his words; then her mother's even voice answered him, there was a brief *tink* of silver, a marbling of ice and liquid in a pitcher as it was passed, tipped, and the moment was over.

Charlotte squatted and began picking up the larger shards gingerly. Knox fetched a trash bag from the cupboard under the sink, squatted, too, and held it open for her.

"Always hogging the spotlight," Charlotte said softly. When Knox glanced up at her, she smiled.

"Careful of your feet," Knox said.

When the pieces were all placed at the bottom of the bag, Charlotte walked on the balls of her feet to the pantry closet and returned with a broom and dustpan. Knox took them from her and set to sweeping the floor clean. She scanned for stray chips, bits of glaze along the baseboards, pushing everything into a small pile. It satisfied her, this task. She felt better than she had when she'd first walked into the kitchen. Charlotte bent to angle the dustpan for her, truce ghosting the air between them. It didn't need to be said that Knox could better afford to have broken something; she wasn't leaving in a few days; she didn't fear looking inept or foolish in front of their mother, the way Charlotte seemed to; Charlotte was the one who had let herself become too defensive, had been afraid—wasn't that it?—to go back into the breakfast room alone. And another thing that Knox had difficulty keeping in mind until she found herself in an instant like this: she and Charlotte both understood that they loved each other most purely when Charlotte was slightly in her debt. It inspired this shared quiet in them, a tenderness; it had been like this forever.

Knox swept a final circle around the pile and pushed it into the pan. She felt young, and at the same time much older than Charlotte, which she used to feel so certain was what God had meant her to be; the order of their birth had been an accident he'd committed in some addled moment. Circle, circle, stab in the back, blood runs up, blood runs back . . . She supposed that in no time at all she'd be back to resenting Charlotte for dizzying her with these contradictory pangs. Moments of connection between the two of them never seemed to last long anyway. *Slide down my rainbow, into my cellar door, and we'll be jolly friends, forever more, more, more . . .* They shoved the bag, ballooning with trapped air, into the compactor together.

"Hey, let's go out," Charlotte said. She bumped Knox with her hip.

"If you want," Knox said.

AFTER DESSERT, Knox had driven Charlotte into town. Charlotte had made an effort at charm once they returned to the table, scooped vanilla fro-yo onto everyone's brownie with a soup spoon, despite protests. She told them all a story about one of her temp jobs, a daylong assignment in Yonkers that involved waving convention buses into a hotel parking lot. "It paid ten an hour," Charlotte said, "but for what? I wore one of those reflective parkas for eight hours in the rain, held cones up over my head, the heinous bellboy wouldn't stop asking me out . . ." Knox giggled along with the rest of her family: generously, with relief.

Eventually Charlotte had asked their mother if it would be all right if she and Knox went out for a bit.

Knox's father looked pleased at the question, at the idea of his daughters socializing as a pair. Knox shot Charlotte a telepathic message: *See how easy it is to make them happy when you try? Finally learn this.*

"I never get asked to do anything," Robbie said, but he wasn't serious and excused himself to make a phone call.

"Go ahead," Knox's mother said, dipping a finger into the melted ice cream on her father's plate and tonguing it off with a quick motion, a sheepish look at her father. The broken plate seemed forgotten, at least temporarily. "Have a wonderful time, girls."

Now Knox kept her eyes on the road. It advanced toward her car in sections like fed line, reeling her in. So much wine had been a bad idea; she'd stick to Diet Cokes at the bar and feel better on the drive home. The interior of the car was cold; the vent blast hadn't turned to heat yet. Fields stretched to the left and right of the road in the dark. Yesterday's snow still salted the road in places, snaked in long, perfect tubes down the top rungs of fences that showed themselves in her headlights. A mare standing flush with her paddock gate stuck her neck out over it as they passed, gave them the eye. Knox left her behind, swallowed in the night like she'd never existed, and thought with a kind of awe: She'll stand there all night, just in that spot. That's what mares did when left out in this kind of weather. She wanted to say something about this to Charlotte; though she had to drive carefully now, this road jazzed her even more in the dark, when all that was visible of the properties she knew was contained in the small, jumpy circumference of her high beams. Though she knew it was only farmland whizzing by her windows, she sometimes supposed on this road at night that she understood the deepest wonder of sailors, or African homesteaders, both connected to and unable to plumb the depths that lay, teeming, out of their sight. But Charlotte was burrowed down in the passenger seat, the hood of her jacket pulled over her head so that part of her face was obscured. Knox thought she might be asleep and, afraid to take her eyes off the road to reach for the radio, drove on in silence.

They reached Lexington. As Knox slowed to make a left at the viaduct, Charlotte stirred, sat up a little, and cut her eyes at Knox.

"Where to?" she said in a scratchy voice. She yawned.

"Well, there are so many bars to choose from," Knox said. "Gee, let me think . . ."

"There are more than just the Rosebud," Charlotte said. "Please, Knoxie."

"Ned'll be there later," Knox said. "Besides, you won't see anybody you know if we go someplace else. Come on."

She pulled onto Broadway, then made a left and drove the few blocks to the oldest part of town where the former courthouse stood, where the sidewalks were wide, bricked, and crumbling. The Rosebud, its tiny glass front crowded with neon signs, was one of the few functioning businesses on its block. Cars lined either side of the narrow street it stood on; Knox finally drove around the corner to park. As she walked with Charlotte through the door of the bar she felt a guilty awareness of why she'd wanted to come here; it was one thing not to know how to look at Charlotte at home without feeling stymied by every strange and competitive feeling she thought had evaporated when her sister had left home for good—but quite another to be trailing close behind her as they wove through a crush of people toward the back of the room, under the bolted televisions tuned to the local news, where there was a bit more space to be had and at least the possibility of conversation. Here, among the grooms she knew and the people she recognized as having gone to her grade school, or from the halls of UK, Knox felt not confused or wary but conferred upon by Charlotte's presence. Billy, the assistant manager at Poplar Hill and a friend of Ned's, flicked his eyes upward as Charlotte brushed past his table, following her as she moved; then, seeing Knox, smiled in recognition and half stood from his chair to reach for her hand and clasp it hello. "Buy you a beer later?" he shouted, and Knox jerked her head sideways toward the area they'd be sitting in, nodded, kept moving. She waved to the skinny, underage son of one of her parents' friends who was standing near the brass tap, thought if she found herself next to him in the course of the night she'd tease him about being here in light of the early wake-up he had waiting for him in the morning; he was mucking out at the Horse Park this year in penance for some high school misdeed. She kept close to Charlotte, who must have first begun coming here at sixteen, whose picture was buried among the curling snapshots tacked to the wall by the entrance, who, according to Chuck the owner, warranted careful watching during the period she frequented the place so she didn't "do anything stupid," which Knox took to mean downing a shot or three too many, or perhaps going home with somebody who was sure to brag about it at the bar the very next night. She didn't know, really. She did know that she had tried to use an old license of Charlotte's the first time she herself had attempted to get in here, years ago, and that Chuck had laughed his ass off and turned her away from the door. We already know that face, sweetheart. Come again when you've got your own picture to show and we'll talk. Knox had never really liked coming to the Rosebud; she'd let Ned drag her along occasionally, but preferred her own porch or the next day's lesson plans to this noisy, predictable scene. Yet here she was, preening her way toward the back as if she came here every night of her life. She felt the eyes upon them both as she and her sister—the one whose name people knew, the one who didn't come home all that often—chose an isolated table near the ladies' room door and sat down.

"Well," Knox said breathlessly. "Are we having fun yet?"

It seemed as if Charlotte were still waking up. She blinked, then smiled. She looked Knox straight in the eye, holding her gaze until Knox finally glanced away, at which point Charlotte sloughed off her coat and draped it over the back of her chair.

"Do you want anything?"

"I'm okay," Charlotte said. "Maybe in a minute."

"Me too," Knox said. She would make sure they had a good time tonight, she thought. The jukebox kicked on; a country tune trilled out of a speaker behind Knox's head. I go walkin', after midnight, out in the moonlight . . . A knot of college girls near the bar raised their plastic cups and joined in.

"This place," Charlotte said. "Nothing ever changes." She laughed, rolling her eyes a little.

"Sorry," Knox said, and in that moment she did feel sorry. "In New York you must go to a new place every night."

"No, it's all right." She put her elbows on the table and leaned forward. "I don't mind. Sometimes it's nice when things stay the same. Anyway"—she focused on Knox's face again—"I'm just glad to be out of the house. How is everything, Knoxie?" The emphasis in this last sentence fell on the word "everything," and Knox felt herself flushing at the question, as if she were expected to give an accounting of some complicated life whose reach extended far beyond the boundaries of her own. She pictured the cabin that, just at this moment, stood full of held silence, the eggshell-colored comforter folded down at the end of the bed, the squeeze bottle of dish liquid that was just less than one-third full (she'd buy a spare on her next grocery run) balanced on the edge of the kitchen sink. The car in the parking lot around the corner, its backseat piled with papers, manila files, going cold again in the winter dark; the keys in her jeans pocket; the two rolls of toilet paper in the basket on the floor of her bathroom. What was there to say about any of it?

"Good," Knox said. "Everything is good."

Charlotte didn't rush to fill the pause. She squinted. "Ned's meeting us later?" she said finally.

"He might. He's having supper with his mother."

"How's he?"

"Ned, he's fine," Knox said, glad to have been prompted on a subject other than herself. "Working hard. He's got a new truck. He's so proud of it. It's one of those big, awful ones with a backseat in it that you practically need a ladder to get into."

Charlotte was looking at her with her head cocked. Knox brushed at her mouth, thinking she might have some fleck of dessert clinging to the corners. "He paid too much for it," Knox went on.

Charlotte began to laugh. "I don't care about his truck," she said, and Knox flushed.

"He's—we're still the same," Knox said.

Charlotte nodded, beat a little tattoo on the table's surface with her fingers.

"You know, no one would blame you if you experimented a little, if you feel unsure," she said. "It isn't like you're married."

"But I *am* sure," Knox said. She'd sounded defensive; she checked herself, breathed, glanced around the bar. When she met Charlotte's eyes again, Charlotte was smiling.

"Of course. You always are," Charlotte said. Knox thought her tone sounded vaguely insulting. She chose to ignore this.

Now Charlotte looked around her. "How's work? How are the kids?" she said.

"They're a handful," Knox said. She launched into a story about the difficulty she and Marlene had encountered at the holiday program, the ultimate futility of trying to marshal the ADD-affected students onto bleachers for an hour of singing, when all they'd wanted to do was run. After a minute, it was clear that Charlotte wasn't listening, and Knox changed the subject.

"What about Bruce," she said. Yuppie Bruce, she and Ned called him; her encounters with him had always been awkward. "Will you be happy when he gets here?" Right away she regretted the way the question sounded, the *he* overly stressed, as if Knox had meant to ask whether Bruce had succeeded where the rest of them had failed. But Charlotte's face looked impassive.

"Well, I'm looking forward to picking him up tomorrow," she said evenly. "Having him around seems to make things easier."

Knox closed her eyes for a moment; she felt a sharp, literal wince of pain in her head. "Why," she said, hating what she heard, the word an overanxious bleat. She had meant to say something blithe, like: You know what would make us *both* happy? Two bourbons, allow me. Instead she sounded nine years old.

Charlotte shrugged. "Because he knows how to talk to Mom and Dad, for one thing. And I don't seem to be able to."

Knox inhaled through a small opening in her lips. A dull, familiar anger was overtaking her, and she needed to make it go away. How often did she get to sit like this, talking to her sister, the two of them friends in a bar, and Charlotte was being attentive, doing her best, she'd done nothing wrong by telling the truth. But it was too late.

"You could try," she said. "You never really try."

Charlotte watched her. It was difficult to tell whether or not she looked surprised. She began to say something, then stopped.

"I don't understand you," Knox went on. She was annoyed at herself; she could feel her eyes, her nose, filling as if the very inside of her head, too, were bent on involuntary exposure. "Why don't you like being here? You seem so . . . absent."

She looked down at the table, not wanting to see whatever Charlotte's face might be doing.

"I'm sorry," Charlotte said quietly.

"What is wrong with you, Charlotte?"

"There's nothing wrong with me."

"Then why is it so hard for you to be happy?"

"I am happy."

"Happy with us?"

There was a silence. Charlotte pushed her hair back and shifted in her chair.

"I don't know," Charlotte said. "We really don't have to get into this."

"What is *this*? Tell me." Knox was in motion now; she needed a runway, a half-mile of track in order to slow herself down, not that she was trying.

Charlotte looked at her levelly.

"Not everything is about you. I know you'd like me to be different, but I can't force everything to be perfect just for your sake, Knox. You want your little picture-postcard family scene, but maybe you should just grow up, and stop expecting that from everyone."

"What? I didn't ask you to come. I don't expect anything from you, God knows."

"You're drunk."

"Mom and Dad *love* you. Is it so difficult to be grateful, just for that?"

Charlotte glanced around her, perhaps in search of a bartender, or a closer exit.

"You don't have to speak for Mom and Dad, and you don't have to worry about me," she said. "Worry about yourself."

"I'm fine. I am the one who's fine."

"If you say so."

"Oh, for God's sake." Knox's voice was rising; she made a conscious effort to lower it, to hew closer to an equanimity that had flown from her grasp. Maybe Charlotte was right. How much wine had she actually drunk with dinner? "Don't. You clearly see yourself as some sort of tragic figure. But what did any of us ever do to you? Maybe if you could stoop low enough to actually explain it to me, I'd have a better understanding of it. But as it is, you just seem cold to me. Cold and ungrateful."

"Christ! Where is this coming from?"

Images tumbled violently against one another in Knox's mind like rocks in a stream: of their father's face when Charlotte began excusing herself too early from the dinner table years before, of the rococo margins of the unanswered letters she'd sent to Charlotte at boarding school, thick with spiky ball-point doodles of flowers and vines, of the white undersides of her mother's oval nails that were visible when she overturned her hands in her lap and seemed to forget them, while she wept, her father's arm around her tiny shoulders, her father smiling apologetically at Knox, saying, Come on honey, it's not that bad, the skin at his temples gray. Charlotte couldn't get out of bed. Charlotte needed a higher dosage. Charlotte regretted that none of them understood her. Charlotte couldn't come home, hadn't had time to send the gift yet, was sorry, so sorry, but she couldn't spare the time required to disengage from the consuming fire of her own lot, though she loved them, she loved them all, love ya, Knoxie! Love you!

They drove home in silence that night. Charlotte had given her a glance before climbing back into the passenger seat, but Knox assumed her outburst that night had had a sobering enough effect on both of them to render moot any lingering questions about her ability to stay on the road. The pike they lived on swallowed drunk drivers whole. Knox remembered a boy, a neighbor's child, who'd run off the road at sixteen and killed himself and a friend at the base of their drive. That was years ago. She remembered suicidal games of chicken in high school, friends occupying adjacent lanes, cresting hills that way, the midnight roulette of the bored and high. She was careful, her foot light and jumpy on the accelerator as the miles broke open before them.

Knox had apologized. It was that or subject herself to the sound of the rant in her head, and she didn't want that. As she sat at the table across from her sister, she'd come belatedly to her senses and realized again that the fight with Charlotte might be hers alone. She'd fashioned her existence, in large part, as a staunch against the gaps Charlotte had blown in her parents' confidence, in their image as a family, and done it willingly, but she'd be damned if she'd make herself vulnerable to Charlotte's disapproval on this score by detailing all the ways she might have been different if only Charlotte had. Spoken aloud, that would most likely have sounded ridiculous. It *was* ridiculous. But that didn't make it any less true.

And she'd seen something in Charlotte's eyes, in the bar, that she also didn't want realized in speech—a flash of tired impatience at the fact of her. The very fact of her made things harder for Charlotte when she was here. Maybe always had. Dutiful Knox, watchful Knox, eminently sane, easy Knox . . . she'd quit with the adjectives while she was ahead. There was nothing any of them could do about that, so best to leave it alone.

"Don't mind me," she'd said.

And Charlotte had stared at her, looking pale as a ghost.

THE HOUSE wasn't hard to find. Knox had never had a handle on what streets, if any, might be obscure to a cabdriver coming into Manhattan and had proffered the address tentatively. But she recognized the block when they turned onto it and found herself wishing that her taxi had managed to get briefly lost so that she might have called Bruce for directions and managed to arrive in gentle stages, as opposed to all at once. As it was, she felt like the angel of death. She and Bruce hadn't seen each other since the night in the hospital, though Knox had had a chance to visit the boys in the NICU once more before accompanying her mother and father back to Kentucky. She'd had not one, but two, glasses of watered-down Chardonnay on the flight and felt sleepy and over-anxious at once, as if she'd been up all night. She'd picked at her lunch. She paid the cabdriver and lugged her duffel awkwardly up the steps of the brownstone, scraping its wheels against the concrete as she climbed.

She had to knock for almost a minute before Bruce came to the door. He loomed into view behind the thick glass panes beside it, the beginnings of a beard stippling his face, then disappeared again, and she could hear the sound of several locks being turned. The door opened, and now Knox could see that Bruce held one of the boys—swaddled up in a blanket, asleep—against his chest.

"Hi," he mouthed, and stepped back to let her enter. His blue T-shirt stretched open at the neck, exposing part of his collarbone. His jaw looked sharp enough to cut, under the shadow of beard that, Knox noted, was flecked with gray. It was momentarily difficult to accept that he was real; but then, she saw him rarely enough that she was used to having to reorganize her impressions of him each time they met. Knox thought that the things in his face she'd always recognized might have become more pronounced since she'd seen him last: his dark brown eyes looked larger and his mouth looked more compressed. He was handsome in a way that hinted at a youthful handsomeness that had faded. His hairline may have been high to begin with. He was lanky, his wrists and fingers bony and tapered, and there was a stillness to him that posed a contradiction, given the kinetic energy that seemed to beam off his body. Bruce was the kind of guy who couldn't help bouncing in his chair, or shifting in place where he stood, but who also waited a disconcerting extra beat before responding to something you'd said and tended to stare until you had to look away.

When Bruce leaned down to peck her on the cheek—he didn't have to stoop far; Knox was nearly as tall as he was—she could smell milk, the residue of some powdery baby unction, undiluted sweat. She wondered when he'd last showered. The side of her faced buzzed from the abrasion Bruce's beard made on her skin. The baby's head dipped close to hers, a web of blue veins, narrow as hairs, visible just under the skin of his rosy scalp, which looked chapped. His lips were so pink, drawn in a precise, horizontal line; they twitched, as if even in his sleep he resented Knox's interruption. He seemed to have no eyelashes. Knox stared at him in dumb wonder.

"Ethan," Bruce whispered, nodding at him. "He just ate."

He smiled at her, though Knox could see his face straining to hold the expression until he could see she'd registered it, then relax into a grimmer resting expression. He clutched the back of his neck with his free hand.

"Come on in," he said. "We've been expecting you." He spoke these last words in an exaggerated Vincent Price, Transylvania voice. Knox waited for him to shut the door and flip all the locks back into place, then hoisted her bag up and followed him down the dark hall.

She had tried to prepare herself for the possibility that Bruce would be overcome in some way when he saw her. How this would manifest itself she didn't know, but she had gone so far as to rehearse certain responses in her head. As she peered into the crib he showed her toward now—a wide, white slatted job that had been set up in the living room and into which Bruce lowered Ethan next to Ben, she realized that she had discounted the twins altogether in her assumption that, as perhaps the closest living reminder to Charlotte, her arrival would force a certain level of emotion, for both of them, immediately out into the open. But of course, she wasn't the closest living reminder of Charlotte, not by a country mile, and now could hardly believe the narcissism inherent in the way she'd pictured this scene. She stared at the babies, trying to decipher any features she recognized, now that their faces had cohered into something more than the red, twisting, bright-eyed blanks she remembered from the hospital. They still looked nothing alike to her—and didn't yet look like anyone she knew, either, though Ben looked to have Charlotte's coloring. They were curled facing each other in their swaddle cloths like quotation marks around the empty space between them, so small on the expanse of white sheet that Charlotte must have bought at some neighborhood shop. Ben's fist twisted its way free of his blanket and pressed against his cheek. He twitched, sighed, stilled. Knox's eyes filled with sudden tears, and she was grateful for a reason to keep her eyes trained downward, so Bruce wouldn't see. This was how they were going to play it, she thought. No histrionics on purpose. She was not here to receive comfort from a widower; she knew that much, though it occurred to her that she already missed the version of events she'd pictured, that had them commiserating, comparing losses.

"They're still sleeping all the time," Bruce said. "But I think they're about to come out of that stage. And they're not quite on the same program, which makes things interesting."

"I may mix up their names at first," Knox said. She cleared her throat; the words had come out too coated.

"Ethan's the one with the reddish peach fuzz," Bruce said, quiet, gesturing toward one of the boys. "And the painful gas, unfortunately."

"How have you been doing this?" Knox said.

"I don't know," Bruce said.

SHE ASSUMED he'd taken a leave from work. As far as she knew, there was no other help, aside from the housekeeper he'd mentioned while pouring her some coffee straight out of a glass beaker he'd brought into the living room, where they sat, waiting out the babies' naps. Knox accepted the chipped mug Bruce offered her; it felt good to hold something warm in her hands, though the air in the room was close. Her hands wanted an occupation—otherwise, they might loose themselves from her body and fly away like birds.

"How are your mom and dad doing?" he asked. He took a slurp from his own mug, lowered it, and kept his eyes on the steam that rose from inside its rim.

"They're okay," Knox said.

Surely Bruce could recognize this as a shallow response; she'd left her father staring at the ceiling of her parents' room, her mother starting at every ringing telephone. Knox had even wondered at her mother's lack of fight when Knox had informed her that she wanted to spend this interim, before the funeral, in New York. She hadn't expected her mother, a new grandmother despite everything, to acquiesce as easily as she had. But it was clear that her parents were in no shape to offer assistance to anyone except each other right now. Knox swallowed. The truth would only make Bruce feel worse.

"How are *you* doing?" Knox asked. She'd ventured the question to fill the silence, really; it seemed even more dangerous to let a true silence fall than to say the wrong thing.

Bruce stared at her, running his hands through his hair, ruffling it up on the sides and then smoothing it down again. For a long moment, Knox wondered if he'd forgotten her question, if she should manufacture another. But then he lowered his hands and slapped one against each of his knees, which bounced in place inside his grubby jeans.

"Um. I'm not sure what to say."

"Oh—," Knox began. There was something blank in Bruce's eyes just now, making it hard to fathom his intent. Did he mean to delineate a boundary? Was he angry with her for the question? "That was stupid, of course—"

"No," Bruce said. He opened his hands. "Really, I was being serious. It just feels right now like there's Charlotte, and then there's the boys. And each of those categories sort of requires a different response."

"Okay."

"They even cancel each other out. If the boys' diapers are changed and there's plenty of formula in the house and they're . . . alive, and so am I, then that seems to mean I'm not thinking too much. I can actually block things out for stretches of time."

"I guess that's good," Knox said. She felt some surprise at how relieved she was to assume the role of confessor, how easily the lines were coming. Had she and Bruce ever sustained a conversation of this length before? Not that she could remember, though that seemed hard to believe. She relaxed, just a little, in her chair.

"I always have to be thinking about the next thing I'm supposed to wash, or boil, or get ready. So."

"That makes sense."

"And as far as—I know I don't want to go outside. The idea that I'm going to run into somebody at the deli who knows what happened—or, worse, who doesn't—I don't want that. So I've been staying in. Which is fine, because the boys are still so vulnerable to . . . well-intentioned strangers who'll paw them, I guess. I saw an old lady on the subway stick her finger in some baby's mouth, once."

"I can take care of errands for you."

Bruce was silent. He breathed in deeply, as if he'd extended himself too far and needed to rest.

"Thanks," he said.

Knox sipped her coffee, glancing about her. Her sister had always lived like a magpie, among random, gathered clutter whose meaning Knox had to question: Once Charlotte had tacked up another postcard, did she forget its origin? Did it retain its significance, or just become part of the wallpaper? Everything looked *temporary*. On the mantel, which was carved from a black, veined marble and would look handsome in an apartment where it was afforded the dignity of a clock, maybe a pair of urns, sat a few candle stubs ensnared in a mess of petrified wax drippings. Snapshots fluttered from the edges of the mirror frame, a garland of paper flowers was hung asymmetrically over the door that led into the kitchen. Knox knew that the cabin was barer than it needed to be because she agonized over the right of any object to its own display, but the profusion of stuff that filled any room Charlotte had ever called a home made her dizzy.

"I still can't believe it," Bruce said. Knox looked at him. His face was contorting; he covered it with his hands. Knox sat there wondering: Should she go to him? Put her arms around him? What were they meant to expect from each other, now? She held her breath, thinking of the platitudes she'd rehearsed, unable to speak them. The moments during which she sat, deciding, felt charged, and endless. Her teeth were clenched together in her mouth, and she held her body so still, ready to spring up at the slightest suggestion that comfort was what Bruce required. But he could just as well be needing her to freeze, like a statue, blind, deaf, dumb, as good as gone while he dispensed with this latest shudder of mourning. There was an etiquette, surely; they would have to fashion it together.

After a minute, the question answered itself; Bruce sighed and rose to his feet.

"We should go over some things, I guess," he said. "While we still have a chance to talk."

Knox's nod was emphatic.

Bruce reached for a pad of paper from Charlotte's desk. He shuffled around for a pen and finally found one after rattling open the desk drawer.

"Okay," he said. "I'll just start at the beginning of the day."

He sat down again, paper in hand. Knox got up and peered over his shoulder as he wrote, a good soldier, relieved to have somewhere to look. Bruce's handwriting was cramped, and his letters leaned markedly to the left, as if shying away from the right margin of the paper. Knox was used to looking at a child's grip when she tutored children; dyslexic kids often grasped their pencils like three-years-olds did, with every finger wrapped around. Bruce's grip was an adult one, but it was awkward, not fully resolved, and he bore down too hard as a result.

> 5:00 a.m.—wake and bottle. Four ounces boiled, cooled water,
> two level scoops formula.
> Back down.
> 7:00 a.m.—wake up, dress
> 8:00 a.m.—another bottle
> 9:00 a.m.—nap
> 11:00 a.m.—bottles
> 1:00 p.m.—nap
> 3:00 p.m.—bottles
> 5:00 p.m.—nap
> 7:00 p.m.—bath, feed, rock, try to get to sleep until 10:00 p.m.
> 1:00 a.m.—night feeding
> 3:00 a.m.—night feeding

Bruce glanced up at her. "This is partly wishful thinking," he said. "It usually turns into a big blur at some point instead of a schedule. But I'm trying to get them on the same routine."

"Wow," Knox said.

Bruce's smile was strained. "Is this overwhelming you? I could keep the monitor in my room at night."

"No, no! I really want to help. I'm just—I'm still amazed you've been doing this alone."

"It's only been a week since I got them home," Bruce said. His jaw worked. "A couple of nights, I've stayed here on the couch. Or had at least one of them in with me."

"Do you—" Knox stared at the list. She felt that no matter how hard she looked at it, she wouldn't be able to hold its information in her head. The babies ate and slept; that was all she understood. She would have to follow Bruce's lead and rely on him to tell her hour by hour what she was supposed to be doing, it seemed. "Do you want to take turns at night?"

"I think we should do those feedings together, if you don't mind. It's just easier. Trust me; you'd want the extra pair of hands if you were doing those by yourself."

"Well . . . when will you sleep? Don't you want at least one night off, after a week of this?"

"I don't want to sleep," Bruce said.

THEY WOKE THE BOYS for their evening bottles, and Knox held each twin in turn while Bruce gave them their baths in a baby tub he'd placed in the kitchen sink. Knox watched as Bruce lapped water against the sides of Ethan's belly; the stump of his umbilical cord was still attached, protruding from his white abdomen like a spot of old dung. Bruce was careful not to get it wet. He rested Ethan's head against his forearm, and Ethan blinked at the overhead light. He was the longer of the twins; seeing him so naked and helpless, droplets of water beading on his wrinkled forehead, Knox couldn't help but think of him inside Charlotte's womb. *He was just there.* Knox believed it, but she couldn't feel it. Her mind made little forays, little attempts to feel it: these were Charlotte's sons. They were made of her. Any movement Ethan made in the bath now, Charlotte had felt from within her body, his shifts and hiccups, the jerk of his elbows. Knox thought of her mother's faith, her ability to be impassioned by what she couldn't see. It was like grabbing hold of something warm in the dark, and Knox both wanted and didn't want to find the truth in these circumstances, in her brother-in-law's barely scrutable presence. It was terrifying—but somewhat thrilling, too—to inch forward, feeling her way.

Ben burrowed against her, snuffling at her cotton shirt with his nose. Knox didn't know if she was holding him the right way, if he was comfortable. She cupped the back of his warm head with her palm; Bruce had reminded her to do this before she'd picked him up. He'd also asked her to wash her hands. She wondered if Bruce—and who could blame him—was the kind of father who would turn out to be protective in the extreme, ready to do battle with every sharp corner and potential contagion that entered the boys' sphere. Either way, it wouldn't do to impose her own views on the boys' care, since she had none. She'd washed her hands and held on to Ben as tight as she dared.

"What I do is have the towel ready, like this," Bruce said. He'd tucked a corner of a hooded towel under his chin. He grasped Ethan under the armpits and lifted him into it, wrapping its sides around him quickly. "So he doesn't catch cold." Ethan peered out of the opening the top of the towel made, his eyes and nose visible. "Now I take him into his room, and I'll show you what to do next."

They walked single file, babies in tow, into the room at the far side of the stairs that Charlotte and Bruce had designated as the nursery. There was another crib set up against the left wall, and a changing table and bureau opposite. The room had the same haphazard quality that Knox recognized from the rest of the house; only one of its walls was painted; perhaps Charlotte had still been deciding on the right green, thought she had more time. Some do-it-yourself shelving leaned against the chair in the corner, hardware scattered on the rug below it. Knox felt the thrill of fear again, of reaching toward a flame, getting close enough to touch it, but withdrawing just before contact. She found herself rubbing Ben's back as Bruce talked.

Bruce let Ethan's towel fall open in sections, rubbed lotion into his skin, then wrapped him up again. He smeared some A&D ointment on the pink slope of Ethan's butt and diapered him, showing Knox the importance of tucking his minuscule penis under so his piss got absorbed into the diaper instead of leaking onto his pajamas. He snapped him into a footed outfit that looked too warm for the evening to Knox, though she said nothing. Ethan lay still, letting his father work on him, his eyes darting around. The snapping seemed to go on forever. Bruce put another cream on the chapped places on Ethan's face and head. He threw the towel and the outfit Ethan had been wearing before the bath into a pile next to the changing table, which Knox resolved to scoop up and wash later. Did Charlotte and Bruce drop off their laundry at a service? Did they own a machine? She felt a sudden pierce of longing for home. She was terribly hungry, with no meal in sight, and no end to the evening that she could perceive—or chance for a pause during her time here that she could imagine. Any delineation between the basic concepts of night and day were artificial at best, according to the list Bruce had made.

Ethan began to cry, a repetitive, coughing cry that Bruce told her meant he was hungry, that she should go prepare a bottle for him and, if she had any questions, just yell from the kitchen. They traded babies. Knox would feed Ethan, and Bruce would empty the bath of its soapy load of water and refill it, and they would start again.

In the kitchen, Knox cradled Ethan with one hand while she ransacked a drawer for bottle parts. She found a bottle, a nipple, a plastic sleeve to twist onto the bottle's mouth, and some apparatus that looked like a sieve. She had no idea how to fashion them into a whole. An empty grocery bag stood open and upright next to the garbage can. Ethan was crying in earnest now, stringing the coughs into a continuous wail, the heat of him rising against her body. She kicked the bag over to the counter and began to drop the various parts in, along with one of the cans of formula, so she could carry it all into the babies' room and have Bruce show her. She'd look like an idiot, but she didn't want to get it wrong. She had to work quickly. As she aimed for the bag, she felt her hand shaking.

AT LAST, the boys were down. Bruce ordered a pizza for them.

"We should pray they don't wake up before it gets here," he said. "That keeps happening to me, and by the time I get to eat, I'm not hungry anymore. I've gotten to where I can't tell if one of them is crying or I'm just hearing an echo in my head."

He smiled at her. "Do you want some wine? You look a little rough."

"Yes. Wine."

"Coming up," Bruce said. He disappeared into the kitchen.

"Red or white?" he called.

"I don't care."

"Charlotte never wanted a TV," Bruce said, reentering the room with two wineglasses and an open bottle of Cabernet. "But I told her we would want one once the babies were born. I even got cable for us."

Something about the casualness of this, of the way Charlotte was introduced into the conversation as if she'd just stepped outside for milk, quickened Knox's blood.

"What have you been watching," Knox said.

"Anything," Bruce said. "Mostly *Forensics* reruns. My low point came last night, when I realized I had already exposed the boys twice to the same *Forensics: Philly* episode in the span of their short lives."

"Robbie and I watched that," Knox said.

Bruce flipped around, then settled on a show in which young men who looked too old for their clothing took turns hurting themselves and each other for laughs. One of them waded his way into the middle of a swamp in an animal refuge, picked up a baby alligator the size of a house cat, and offered it his bare chest, at which point the alligator bit one of the man's nipples and held on. The others bent double with mirth.

"Is this stupid enough," Bruce said.

"Perfect," Knox said

They sat together. Knox felt the wine and the abdication of talk wash over her. It was easy to imagine that she was sitting here with Robbie instead of Bruce if she let herself, and as she digested that thought, she felt something click into place. Her sense of what her relation to Bruce in the coming weeks was supposed to be had been vague: Was she here to keep up his spirits with forced cheer? Fade into the background like a servant? Ignore him altogether in favor of the boys, so that he could grieve in relative peace? But Bruce was her brother-in-law; perhaps it was time to begin thinking of him as a brother, insofar as she could. That would help to dilute the strangeness of being near him.

It was easy to have Robbie as a brother. Maybe she loved him as she did because he proved that she could get along with a sibling, that not everything had to be fraught where her role as a sister was concerned. She'd be a sister here, then, too—the kind she was with Robbie, and leapfrog somehow over the history required to make this natural.

KNOX WAS CONSCIOUS that night, as she dressed for bed, that she needed to be appropriately covered up when she appeared in the boys' room for their 1:00 a.m. feeding. She dug in her duffel bag for the leggings she'd packed to run in, a long-sleeved T-shirt she'd brought in case the temperature dipped. It was stifling here in the room Bruce had assigned her, a second-floor space that Charlotte had used as an office during the times when she fancied herself consumed by some project. She'd been part of a neighborhood fund-raiser for a Democratic senatorial candidate, once; the man had lost spectacularly; he was a sculptor and poet who seemed committed to pursuing just causes in the little time he had to spare outside his studio. She'd tried her hand at a play; Knox knew that.

And there was the research she'd put into the fertility treatments she'd eventually come to need. Lists of doctors to contact, insurance forms, success rates, appointments to be made. Knox pulled on the leggings and shirt, as hot as it was. A bare nightgown would be inappropriate, a prim one embarrassing. She felt a flash of surprise that she cared either way what Bruce thought about such a trivial thing, but she was a guest here; attention to these kinds of courtesies would help things go smoothly.

She stretched out on the futon Bruce—or someone—had made up for her. She felt too tired to arrange the sheet over her, or get back up and pry open a window, let some air in. Tomorrow, she'd see about a fan, unpack properly. At least she and Bruce hadn't seemed too uncomfortable around each other tonight. It had been okay, sitting up together with their pizza and wine. Bruce didn't seem to dislike her close up, the way she realized she'd feared he might. Though surely the subject of her had come up between husband and wife. He might have had some preconceived notions about her, too. But being here was as good as being anywhere. She thought she might have been right to come.

KNOX

KNOX WOKE, the sun on her face. She felt plastered to the bed; the effort to raise herself left her nearly breathless, and she sat up, panting. She was so hot; she began peeling off her shirt before she was fully cogent of where she was; in this makeshift guest room, in Charlotte's house, Bruce downstairs, the twins to look after. What time was it? She added alarm clock to the mental list of things she needed, then crawled over to her duffel and fished out her mobile phone. Ten o'clock. Fuck! Bruce must have been the only man on duty for the last several hours; Knox had fallen back into bed after the last feeding she'd helped him with, at 5:00 a.m.

The phone buzzed right there in her hand, startling her so that she nearly dropped it.

"Hello?"

"Hi, honey."

"Mom, I can't talk long. I've overslept."

"All right, I won't keep you."

Knox heard the hurt in her mother's voice and cursed herself for sounding rushed. And yet, crouched on the bare floor, in her bra and jogging pants, her day barely begun, she also felt a twinge of resentment for this intrusion, and a childish desire to make clear to her mother, who wasn't here, who surely had no idea what her night had been like, the demands that had been placed upon her in the last twelve hours. Knox's mother had never been the type to harass her children about milestones like marriage and children; if anything, Knox suspected, keeping the roles the way they'd always been, with Knox the child and Mina the mother, brought her a kind of pleasure. But Knox had seen the elation in her mother's face when she'd gotten the news that Charlotte was finally pregnant, the drugs had worked, and it occurred to her that she wasn't above punishing Mina for this in some way, if she wasn't careful. See? This is how it would be, Mom. Your daughter harried, inaccessible, unmoored from any destiny she could control or call her own. Got your wish? As soon as she had the thought, Knox hated herself for it. She resolved to grow up. She'd been in New York less than a full day, and wanted martyr status?

"Sorry, Mom. I'm coherent now. I have a little time to talk."

"If you're sure. How are the boys?"

How were the boys? Knox had held them until her arms were sore last night. At Bruce's direction, she'd rubbed Ben's back for a full ten minutes until he burped, after he'd drunk a bottle around 2:00 a.m. Ethan had been restless at the 5:00 a.m. feeding and uncomfortable going back down; Knox had finally soothed him back to sleep by placing her pinkie in his wet mouth until his eyes closed. She thought of Bruce's old lady from the subway. Another item to add to her running tally of needs: pacifiers.

"They're good," she said. Was there anything she could say that wasn't laughably inadequate? "Healthy. Bruce has been doing a good job."

"Do they look different already?"

"They do to me. Ethan is longer. He looks like the older one. And Ben is so—he seems like the less fussy of the two."

"I wish I could be there."

"Well, we'll be home in a few weeks."

There was a silence on the line.

"How is Dad?"

"The same." Her mother sighed. "Well, I'd better let you go."

"No—" Despite feeling so inconvenienced at the outset of the call, Knox couldn't help herself; she was a prisoner of the old song and dance, the routine she'd long ago perfected, in which she kept one or both of her parents engaged until their mood lightened. She'd talk as long as she had to, use any number of stall tactics and funny anecdotes until she was assured that nothing was wrong, no one was really mad, she wouldn't have to go through the rest of her day shouldering the burden of another's negative emotion.

"Mom," she said now. "I'll keep checking in with you. I know how important it is for you to feel part of things, up here. Don't worry about anything."

"Thank you, honey. You know, I wish I was there. I wish I could help."

Her mother sounded so far away.

In the kitchen downstairs, the coffee was still hot. Knox gulped some down before joining Bruce in the living room, where she could hear one of the boys fussing. Ethan lay prone on his back in front of Bruce, who knelt on the floor, wiggling some cotton pants onto Ethan's legs. Ethan lay red-faced, his cries thin and sporadic, as opposed to sustained; maybe this was his complaint, Knox thought; maybe she'd become capable of discerning meaning in the babies' noises, instead of freezing up at the sound of them, wanting only for them to stop of their own accord. Ben was strapped into a complicated seat nearby, looking concerned and a bit engulfed by all the fabric and padding around him. There were toys fastened to a bar in front of him—ridiculously so, Knox thought, as he wasn't mature enough to reach for them, or perhaps even see them; they hung more than a foot away from his face. A colorful, plastic key set. A striped fabric doll with googly eyes that Knox instantly hated without justification. She sat on the floor beside Ben. It seemed only polite to speak to him.

"Your brother doesn't like that," she said.

Ben's mouth worked. His fingers fluttered against the blanket that had been draped over his lower body.

"He wishes he could stay in his pajamas all day. But that would be uncivilized."

At this, Ethan unleashed a howl that sounded born more of pain than protest.

"Ugh!" Bruce said. "I hate these things."

"What happened?"

"I just pinched his leg with the snap."

"Do you want me to try?"

Bruce looked at her.

"I think I've got it under control, thanks. Why don't you run out for some bagels for us?"

"Okay," Knox said, though she could only remember having eaten a bagel once before in her life, and once had been enough. "Listen, I'm sorry I slept in. I'm going to get a clock today."

Bruce was back at the snaps, his mouth twisted in concentration. "It's okay, buddy, almost done," he murmured.

"What time did the boys get up?"

"I got them up at seven-thirty. Don't worry about it. There's a bakery on the corner. Do you need some cash?"

She resolved not to oversleep again.

KNOX HADN'T PREVIOUSLY experienced days that were lived at two such completely different speeds at once, so that the feelings of extreme tedium and of the hours disappearing so quickly that there was no accounting for them were inextricable from each other. The week passed. Messages piled up on her phone: from Ned, from Marlene, her mother. Each evening, Knox planned to call them back, and instead was lost in a fug of TV, takeout, and last-minute tasks. She learned to boil a kettle of water at the end of each day to have at the ready for the night bottles. To wash the bottles themselves out by hand throughout the day, so they didn't pile up—the hot water required for this was cracking the skin at her knuckles already; Knox added dish gloves to her growing mental list, even as she realized that these phantom objects she had planned to shop for at some phantom hour of leisure might have to be procured by a phantom servant, whose characteristics she took pleasure in imagining. She learned to keep a burp cloth on her shoulder for feedings; Ben had a habit of spitting up. She learned that Ethan burped most easily when his back was rubbed in circles while facing forward on her lap, and Ben needed little finessing beyond being lifted onto her shoulder and patted once. She learned how to close off pockets of time, as if she were tying off tourniquets; during the feedings, during the times afterward when she burped one or another of the boys, during the times they needed rocking to sleep, or to be walked the length of the living room, up and down, because they needed calming or something to look at or some sense of motion to distract them from their help-lessness; she'd already become adept at needing nothing in the present, and at forgetting the past and the future—even a future so immediate that it would afford her the gratification of a trip to the bathroom to pee, the sustenance a slice of cheese hurriedly stuffed into her mouth in the kitchen might provide. She could check out, become invisible to herself; she was a pair of arms, a shoulder, and a brain during these times, and her brain was not hers but a uni-versal brain, a database she'd accessed the password to that held specific information on housework and child care: clean pajamas, yes; crib sheets, change; pacifiers, sterilize; within the coming hour: wake, change, and bathe. Knox motored through the apart-ment like she had been programmed. This afforded her more sat-isfaction than she would have anticipated. Her accomplishments were small and almost immediately rendered necessary again as soon as she'd achieved them, but, like the steps that made up one of her long runs around the perimeter of the farm, they added up to something. She was tired—stupidly so—but was able to rouse herself, stand, and perform at the points she needed to. She kept going. The balls of her feet were sore from crossing the wood floors, the muscles in her left shoulder tender. She didn't think.

On Friday, she and Bruce bundled the boys into their double stroller for a checkup at their pediatrician's office. Throughout the week, Knox felt, she'd been able to stay out of Bruce's way fairly well, offering him wordless company at night, in front of one of his police dramas or A&E biographies, but otherwise orbiting as opposed to colliding with him during their days. Their exchanges had been about the babies, about chicken tikka masala versus chicken vindaloo, about whether or not it was time to do another load of whites. Her thought was that Bruce wanted it this way, that they were existing together in a kind of purgatory which, due to its brevity, made small talk superfluous. They were waiting together to board a train, having just witnessed a shooting in the station. They could exchange glances of horror and bewilderment, defer to each other during the police questioning. But they wouldn't try to *know* each other; what was the point of that? Knox had even thought to feel relieved that Bruce's old jumpy eagerness seemed to have leaked out of him—his eyes left her face now before she'd even finished answering one of his questions. And this was fine; had he needed anything from her beyond what she was giving, she would have failed him.

This morning, though, she'd felt almost constantly in Bruce's way. She'd been standing in the wrong place when he'd opened the refrigerator door, and he'd bumped her with it; they'd both raced to be the first to apologize. In the boys' room, they'd been reaching at the same time for diapers, for clothes, and had to finally agree to take turns dressing the twin they'd assigned themselves to, leaving each other alone to work in the small space. And at the front door, she'd had to stand aside while Bruce fitted the stroller through the opening; the carriage was too wide for her to stand abreast of it as they left the apartment.

"Just let us get through first," he'd said, and Knox felt startled at the sharpness in his voice. She watched him struggle, shifting the thing from right to left in an effort to wiggle it over the threshold, the boys impassive in the car seat pods that were secured to the frame. Knox could just make them out under the sun canopy Bruce had already pulled over them, made of some navy-blue nylon that cast them into a safe gloom. No possibility of skin damage under *there*.

"Are you sure I can't help you?" Knox said. She had the feeling of lighting a long fuse for the purpose of finding out how powerful the explosive was that lay at the end of it; getting Bruce to engage was surely better than remaining passive if she was going to be snapped at.

"It's sort of like changing a tire, I think," Bruce huffed. "Only one person can do it."

"Okay."

When they reached the bottom of the brownstone steps at last, having carried the stroller down together, urging each other not to let it tip, Knox said, "Do you want me to take them to the appointment by myself? I think I can handle it." She wasn't at all sure she could handle it and felt a bloom of anxiety, as well as surprise, when Bruce drew himself up to his full height, looked past her toward the end of the block, and seemed to consider her offer. A street cleaner approached while she waited; she wondered how the boys were reacting to the noise, heat, and sensation that had assaulted them as soon as they'd been hauled outside. Had she remembered their bottles? Yes.

"No. They're getting shots today. An MMR, I think, and the DTaP. I'd feel bad not being there."

Knox had to shield her eyes from glare in order to look into his face. His beard had gotten fuller over the course of these few days, and his eyes looked red rimmed, whether from fatigue, or some darker emotion, she couldn't be sure. He pursed his lips, exhaled. He'd put on a denim-blue T-shirt and a pair of battered corduroys, some shoes that looked more appropriate for the office than a hot stroll through the Village. Perhaps they'd been the only pair he could find. Knox felt struck by her ability to see him in that moment as a kind of archetype: man in crisis. She wondered how she looked; she'd purposefully avoided mirrors for the last few days, not that she spent a lot of time gazing in them at home. How many times *had* Bruce left the house in the preceding week? She knew he'd run the trash to the curb. He'd popped out for some paper towels the other night.

The words came before she had a chance to check herself

against overstepping. "I can do all the talking. If you're afraid. If we see . . . anyone you know."

Bruce seemed about to speak, but didn't. He nodded, then raised his shirttail and wiped it quickly against his forehead, where Knox could make out a glitter of sweat. His stomach was exposed only for a moment, long, with a light stripe of hair bisecting it at the middle, almost concave at its center, muscled at the sides. The glimpse of it evoked a gentleness in Knox that she put immediately to one side; it would embarrass Bruce, and there on the sidewalk, they stood close enough to each other that Knox was prey to the ridiculous notion that he could read her thoughts. Though she had nothing to hide; she'd merely realized that she had the power to help him, right now, and, just as she'd been in the habit of with Charlotte, this power helped her to see whomever she wielded it over in a better light, behave like a better person, she thought, than she naturally was.

"Hi," the boys' doctor said when she entered the exam room. She was attractive in a bohemian, born-in-the-neighborhood sort of way, Knox thought, dressed in a snug halter top and vivid flowered skirt, sandals that looked as if they'd been tooled in some Greek marketplace in the seventies. She paused in front of the standing scale and held her arms out to Bruce. He entered them and stood in her embrace for a few seconds while Knox extricated Ben from his onesie. Bruce's face was pale.

"And you are," she said, after rubbing Bruce's bare arms as if they were cold, giving him a last long, fraught glance. The bangles on her wrist chimed against one another as she extended her hand to Knox.

"I'm the sister," Knox said, shaking. The doctor's hand was cold and dry. "The sister-in-law. The aunt."

"Well, it's good you're here. These guys need lots of calm, happy adults around them, after what they've been through. I'm Dorothy."

The doctor's ability to refer right away, with such openness, to the fact that the boys' mother was dead came as both shock and relief to Knox. She suddenly wanted to be hugged by her, too—or to lie down on the paper-covered table, turn toward the Sesame Street wallpaper, and let the woman stroke her hair, maybe sing. "Kumbaya." "Michael, Row the Boat Ashore." "Big Yellow Taxi."

"You want to keep him in your lap while I examine him? Hold his arms," she said, referring to Ben. She scoped his eyes, ears, throat, checked his reflexes, rotated his thighs to check hip flexibility, measured his head circumference. After he was weighed and measured, a nurse came in and administered the shots, which sent Ben into such a rage that Knox found herself urging him to breathe while his lips turned indigo. She walked with him into the waiting area and jogged him up and down while he screamed. The receptionist kept her eyes trained on her computer screen, unfazed. There was only one other mother in the toy-cluttered room—an older woman—with a girl of about ten resting against her side. The woman smiled sympathetically at Knox, who kept bouncing. Amazing, how quickly one got the hang of bouncing. She felt as if she'd always been doing it, though she could count on one hand the times she'd even held a baby before, much less one this little. Ned's old, bad joke: you could even count on *his* hand, and still come out accurate.

Dorothy's cool fingers touched her shoulder, and Knox felt momentarily confused; was she getting that hug after all?

"Why don't you come into my office," Dorothy said instead, all business. Knox followed her into an adjacent room, decorated with an O'Keeffe image on a poster from the Santa Fe Music Festival.

Dorothy rocked back in her ergonomic chair.

"The boys look great," she said. "Considering. I'm happy with their growth. When did the umbilical stumps come off?"

"Um—Ben's, I think, on Tuesday. Ethan's hung on a little longer."

"Mm. Well, talk to them a lot. Just narrate what you're doing around the house, read the newspaper aloud—it's good for them. Make sure to use the A&D at every change; they both look a little red in that area to me. They sleep together?"

"Yes."

"That's okay for a little longer, but start phasing it out. Maybe for the naps. They'll be turning and covering ground in that crib before you know it."

"All right."

"No stomach sleeping, I'm assuming."

"No."

"Now." She fixed Knox with a look. Her hair fell in perfect corkscrews around her pert face. "About Bruce. You need to watch him for any signs of posttraumatic stress. You're in the best position to do this. If he seems at all confused by events, forgetful, strangely agitated or withdrawn, if he shows weird signs of temper, changes in behavior, abuse of alcohol or drugs—these are all things you can come to me about, and I'll get a referral for you. Is he seeing anybody now, anybody professional?"

"No—not that I know of," Knox said. He doesn't leave the house, she thought. Who could he see?

"Well, try to get him to. He certainly needs that."

Ethan wailed from somewhere outside the room.

"Sometimes grief over maternal death can manifest itself in aggression—even toward the infant. I don't mean to scare you. It's just that it's important for Ethan and Ben that you watch him, too. Do they have a baby nurse?"

"No. We're the baby nurse, so far."

"More outside help would be beneficial, too. Try to talk him into that. Is he going to sue the hospital?"

"I haven't heard any talk about that."

"Well, that's admirable. A lot of people would sue the shit out of them, even though from what I understand there wasn't any malpractice involved. Just a terrible, terrible thing. A freak thing. I learned about DIC in med school, but I've never seen it. Never had a maternal death in childbirth like that in our practice before. And she was so nice. I met her, of course, before the birth."

"Yes."

Knox thought she could begin to see, now, what Bruce had feared: that out in the world, it might become clear that their situation was even more devastating than they'd feared, that there were repercussions they hadn't even considered. As opposed to offering the benefit of their perspective, people with cooler heads, objective people, might simply have the time and space to grasp how fucked they really were. It scared Knox, the idea that her sister was a point of discussion among obstetric and pediatric professionals throughout the city. Charlotte as cautionary watercooler tale. As downtown Manhattan myth, chat room ghost story. This story belonged to her family, surely, and didn't have the breadth to shelter any stranger who might want to huddle under it. In her arms, Ben began to whimper, perhaps echoing his brother's agitation. Did they worry about each other, Ben and Ethan? Did one's distress become the other's distress, this early in their lives? She could probably ask Dorothy, but she wanted to get out of this office. She rose from her seat, dropping a burp cloth and Ben's pacifier in the process, then dipping at the knees to try and retrieve them without jostling Ben. And why did Dorothy assume that Knox had any ability to persuade Bruce to do things like enlist psychiatrists and baby nurses to his aid, when she couldn't even seem to convince him to let her help eke the stroller through the door?

"I am so sorry about your loss," Dorothy intoned from her desk as Knox contorted further to reach and gather Ben's little set of accessories. Knox could picture her jamming at a Dead show, her taut little body writhing in ecstasy, her corkscrew curls bouncing in time with the relentless drumbeat. So sorry for your loss so sorry so sorry for your loss sosorrysosorry.

"Yes," Knox said, for the second time. "Thanks."

SHE FOUND BRUCE at the receptionist's desk, paying the bill. Ethan was already strapped into his seat; Bruce had left his cotton pants off, so the round camouflage-printed Band-Aids that covered the places the needles had poked Ethan's soft thighs were visible. His eyes were closed, and each breath he drew contained a leftover shudder from his earlier crying fit. Ben's eyes were bright as Knox strapped him in, too; suddenly, he looked owllike to Knox. Rapt and full of understanding. His cheeks were blotchy.

"Try some infant Tylenol," the nurse called to them as she crossed into another exam room. "Point eight—the lowest amount in the syringe. That'll make them more comfortable after the vaccinations. And make sure those Band-Aids come off in the bath tonight. They end up in the funniest places if you leave them on—you'd be surprised."

"Okay," Knox called back when it seemed clear Bruce wasn't going to answer.

Bruce scanned the credit card receipt the receptionist handed him and signed. Soon, after another brief struggle with a set of stairs and a heavy door, they were out on the sidewalk together.

"Should we go home?" Knox said. She was reeling. The crying, Dorothy's efficient delineation of directions from which further calamity might strike, the coffee she'd drunk that morning, refilling her cup from the coffeepot the several times it had cooled while she'd been distracted from her breakfast. They stood together, in the sun, the gargantuan carriage between them. Knox seized the handle and began pushing it back and forth, just a little, while they waited for Bruce to say something. She did it as much to steady herself as to soothe the boys with the movement.

At the end of the avenue, a block south, was a park. Knox thought she recognized the stone arch at its entrance from film scenes set in Washington Square—had Charlotte lived so near to Washington Square? It was funny, in New York, how Knox always questioned her recognition of the iconic places; when she'd first seen it out the window of her taxi at Charlotte's wedding, Knox didn't believe her father's assertion that they were passing the Empire State Building, simply because it was right *there*. And she hadn't exactly made a banner effort to get to know the city on her few visits here—she could even admit that there had been something almost defiant in her cluelessness that she couldn't seem to help at the time. A black woman, pushing another double stroller, made her way past the arch, a tote bag with a plastic shovel protruding from the top slung over her shoulder. Another woman, cell phone in hand, followed her, holding the wrist of a little boy—was he two, three? Knox didn't have the experience to tell, and the kids she taught at home were older. The boy held his crotch with one hand, and tripped after his mother, his legs pressed together.

"They don't have to go down again for an hour or so, yet," Knox said. "Maybe we should take a walk."

"That was hard," Bruce said. He traced an arc against the dust on the sidewalk with the tip of one of his heavy, polished shoes. It occurred to Knox that he might be lonelier in her presence. Was he making a greater effort than he would to keep things together, all for her benefit? If she hadn't been there in the room, would he have collapsed, sobbing, in Dorothy's arms?

"A walk would be good," he said, attempting a smile.

They entered the park, a concrete bowl flanked by a few grassy areas and a low wall on which clumps of self-consciously counter-cultural high school kids sat in the shade, their teeth showing white through a haze of pot smoke, their tattooed and pierced bodies and beaded hair lending them a ceremonial aspect, as if they'd gathered for a ritual offering to the Sun God instead of the highly amateur rendition of "Little Wing" that Knox could hear one of them picking on his guitar as they passed. The sound of clapping reached her ears, like rainfall; a crowd was gathered on the far end of the fountain, watching someone perform. She smelled grease, sunscreen, the reek of urine. The leaves on the few trees were dusty. Pigeons waddled out of their way; ahead of them was a small, enclosed playground where a few parents stood listlessly pushing their toddlers in swings. The black woman Knox had seen before stood next to a shin-high painted donkey on a spring, while a girl with perfect French braids rocked back and forth on it, singing to herself.

Knox, who was pushing the stroller, paused in front of the playground gate, which looked like it might have been originally meant for a medieval jail. It looked eight feet tall and was finished at the top with a row of fussy iron spikes. A padlock hung open on a limp cord that someone had draped through the bars. Was there a fear that the clatter bridge would be stolen? she thought. The children? Or maybe that some of the showy troubadours from the wall, a few of whom she'd bet used to play here not so many years ago, would leave baggies of unsavory things on the ground at night if they got in, open for little explorers to stick their noses in.

If she'd been asked, why the playground? at the moment she pushed the gate open and began to back the stroller in, she might have produced an answer about the comfort that a picture of the future, of life going on for the boys, might provide. This would become a familiar spot for Ethan and Ben; soon they would be climbing onto the donkey, wrestling each other for the next turn on the slide. As it was, she was operating on instinct, fueled by a nascent fear. Bruce wasn't talking, and this suddenly worried her. The idea of returning to the house and diving back into their ocean of tasks with an unbroken silence to contend with—silence that Dorothy had alerted her to the possible dangers of—seemed like something to avoid, if she could find a way to do it. There were benches here, and something to look at, and bottles for the boys if they kicked up a real fuss again.

Knox rolled the boys to a stop in a bench by the swings and sat, without asking Bruce whether or not he cared to.

"It seemed a little cooler over here," she said. "We don't have to stay long, if you want to get home."

"I'm fine," Bruce said, though that wasn't exactly what she'd asked. He sat beside her and stretched his long legs out in front of him.

"It's strange," he said, after they'd spent a full minute watching the French-braid girl laboring to stay upright while she pushed a dirty plastic lawn mower up a ramp. "I used to pass by here all the time, and now here I am, inside."

Knox nodded. The fact that Bruce was initiating conversation made her wonder at herself; maybe the silences between them had been comfortable, and she was worrying over nothing. They did, after all, need to maintain some space within the confines of the house.

"We don't know each other very well," Knox blurted, the confusion over where she stood suddenly overwhelming her.

Bruce looked at her.

"No, we don't," he said simply. Knox couldn't say whether she'd expected him to make a joke or protest by asking her what she was talking about, they were family—but that he seemed so unmoved by her remark was unsettling. Bruce sat up straighter, peered under the boys' sun canopy.

"I'm not imposing, being here, am I?" Knox said.

"What?"

"I'm here to—I guess it's important for me to know I'm helping you. If not, then I hope you'd tell me."

Bruce scratched at his chest, raking the thin material of his shirt back and forth over his skin. He pressed his lips together, squinted, then looked at Knox again. She had trouble meeting his eyes, but made herself; she didn't want to seem chicken.

"You're helping," he said.

A couple entered the gate then, pushing a stroller of tangerine canvas, its chassis poised ridiculously high off the ground. The woman came toward them first, sat down on the opposite side of their bench; the man struggled to catch up with her, bumping the stroller over the rubber matting that covered the blacktop where they sat.

"If you'd listen to what I'm saying," the man said. He was so average looking in his baseball cap and baggy shorts that, even staring at him, Knox wondered if she'd be able to pick him out of a lineup five minutes hence. His wife, however, was memorable, if not beautiful; her red hair was tied up in a messy bun; her tortoise-shell statement eyeglasses were oversize for her tiny face.

"I have been listening, and it sucks," she said. "If you want to go, then go, but I'm not going to fight about it anymore because it's upsetting to Susannah."

Susannah, if that's who she was, sat like a dissolute queen in her palanquin, tongueing the spout of a SpongeBob sippy cup.

"I'm not going to go," the man said. "I'll just stay home if you're going to act this way."

"Susannah, do you want to go get some pizza? Daddy has to go do Daddy things with his Daddy friends." The woman took hold of the stroller handle and began walking with it out of the playground as quickly as she'd come in. Her husband stayed behind for a moment, his hands working visibly in his shorts pockets, the coins in them clinking together, then followed, leaving the gate ajar behind him. The black woman quickly moved to shut it before her blonde charge pushed her lawn mower through the gap.

Knox and Bruce watched them go.

"God," Knox said. "Makes me glad I'm not married."

As soon as she said the words, she regretted them.

"Well, you don't know what marriage is like," Bruce said. "That's just a few seconds in their day."

"I'm sorry."

"You fight, but you keep coming back to the same resting place. And when you get back to it, it's where you want to be."

Knox drew her knees up to her chest and wrapped her arms around them. She dug her short nails into the skin of her thighs, but couldn't manage to press them in deep enough to hurt. She'd wanted Bruce to confide in her, she supposed, though now that words were actually coming she was afraid where they would lead.

"I used to follow her, you know. Around the neighborhood. If she'd leave the house, I'd find myself doubting, after a while, that she'd come back when she'd said she would, and then I'd just shadow her like a loser until she came home."

"Bruce—"

"My mother said to me once that she'd been taught when she was a girl to look for a man who loved her just a little bit more than she loved him. Of course, she thought it was bullshit, and was the kind of woman who wanted to be head over heels in love, all the time. But the strange thing is, I *did* become that guy. I might have loved your sister just a little bit more than she loved me. And I didn't mind—or I wouldn't have traded it. Of course I *minded*."

"I'm sorry."

"So, I wouldn't judge. You might get a glimpse of something, but you may as well be reading one line of a play. You won't really understand."

Bruce was right. Knox had never understood Charlotte's marriage, or really—aside from her parents' union—marriage in general. Had she tried? Ned wanted to figure out what their future together was meant to be, but she preferred her pocket-sized life. The kind of existence in which you could experience the gamut of human feeling in the course of a day sounded like hell on earth. Why had Bruce let himself in for that?

"Why," she heard herself asking, "did you love her so much?"

Bruce watched the couples at the swings.

"I couldn't make a list for you. I just loved her," he said. "That's it."

Knox sat still. She pretended to check on the babies, who she'd thought were asleep but were still blinking in the navy-blue light that filtered onto their naked heads. "It's okay, it's okay," she whispered to them. Ben twisted a balled fist against one of his eyelids. Ethan's pacifier had dropped from his mouth.

"What about you and Ned," Bruce asked. "You've been together a long time, right?"

"You sound like Charlotte," Knox said.

"You don't have to talk about it."

"No—it's just that he's just such a . . . fact. It would be like describing my relationship to gravity."

Bruce nodded.

Why did she feel guilty, saying this? She'd simply been caught off guard by the question. She missed Ned, actually. Surely it was because she was unused to being away from him that she felt incapable of a fuller response than this one. How did you take the measure of what a person meant to you? What you meant to them? It was impossible, she thought. Better not to try.

"I don't believe in God," Bruce said.

"You don't?"

"I mean, I have no idea where Charlotte would be, aside from the crematorium. Nothing else seems plausible to me."

"Well," Knox said. She braced herself against the wave of trite language that threatened to engulf her, let it break and flatten over her until she could say something true. She waited for one beat, two.

"You believe in that," Bruce said. "Can you tell me what you think?"

"I've always thought what my mother thought," Knox said, surprising herself. "Thinking about God was all tied up in my love for her early on, because every time she talked about him, it was to comfort me. God is like a bedtime story, for me. I think of God, and I hear my mother's voice."

"There are worse things than that."

"I suppose."

"I hear my mother's voice when I see a picket line," Bruce said. "Never cross a picket line, never cross a picket line," he whined. "What opportunity did she think a kid was going to have to cross a picket line?"

Knox laughed.

"Just not getting to say goodbye," Bruce said. "Not getting to say anything."

"I know."

"How can that be?"

He started to cry, more motion than sound, his body shaking slightly.

After a time, Knox handed him a baby wipe she'd dug out from the diaper bag; Bruce accepted it wordlessly and blew his nose into it. He was still watching the swing area, where a father who looked all of nineteen was struggling to extract his son from one of the rubber bucket seats. The boy's shoe had caught in one of the leg holes, trapping him, as his father tried to lift him out by the armpits. "You're hurting meee!" the boy called.

"That'll be Ethan and Ben soon," Knox said, though she had trouble conjuring the image, or believing that they'd ever have real words at their disposal, or grow big enough for shoes.

"Maybe we should try it," Bruce said. He'd recovered his voice. Still, Knox didn't know if he was serious.

"I don't think—they can't even hold their necks up," she said. Ugh, she sounded like a killjoy, even to her own ears. But it was clearly a bad idea. Surely Bruce hadn't meant it.

"The seats are so deep they'll be supported, see? Maybe they would like it."

"Aren't those things crawling with kid germs?"

"We'll wipe their hands down. We can just hold on to them and let them feel the motion of it—not even let go. Come on, let's do it. For one second."

He was fumbling with the clasp of Ethan's seat harness. Knox looked at Ben; he appeared ready to close his eyes at any moment. But the realization that Bruce was in motion, spontaneous motion, whatever her thoughts on the matter were, was enough to generate a lift within her that was physical. Whether from relief, or curiosity, or something less readily defined, she felt her heartbeat accelerate, and began to unstrap Ben in turn. So, they would do something that wasn't on the schedule. Bruce had his own reasons; she didn't need to know what they were.

Bruce had stashed two sun hats in the mesh bag that hung from the stroller's handle, and handed one to Knox. She tugged it onto Ben's head; under its wide brim he looked to her like a ninety-year-old man, dozing in his back garden. She smiled at him. He was light in her arms as she walked behind Bruce, the soles of his shoes slapping audibly against the rubber matting. They found two bucket seats, side by side, and lowered the boys in—slowly, carefully, as if into water.

When their bare feet stuck out, and they sat slumped against the fronts of the seats, their arms limp, their faces just visible above the chin straps of their comical hats, Knox and Bruce began to push the boys forward and back, only a touch, never letting go, watching each other with smiles playing on their lips. Knox took her cues from Bruce, and never lifted the seat higher than he did. The boys were silent. Their eyes darted; they looked shocked by this new experience. Knox breathed a deep draft of the fetid, smelly air and held it, taut with anticipation of any expression either of the boys might relax into, any clue as to what they were thinking. This anticipation was as close to happiness as she'd come, she thought, in the last three weeks. She was glad that she noticed.

Ethan's eyes widened; then his face twisted into a mask of anguish, and he began to wail. Knox could see the white rims of his gums, the ridges at the roof of his mouth. He was terrified; his arms stiffened until he seemed to be holding them apart from his body, opening them to the park like a tiny infante from a seventeenth-century painting. Ben took up the cry, and until she and Bruce were able to react and raise the boys into their arms to quiet them, Knox was aware of the image they presented, of a man and woman pushing two frantic newborns back and forth in the park. The image was so desperate, so obviously a misguided, willed attempt at Family Fun, that Knox found herself giggling once she'd pressed Ben against her, and stood rocking him in the sun, separated from the traffic at the northern edge of the square by only a scrim of dead trees and a fence. This was a public humiliation; surely the boys' screams had registered by now with the hippies on the wall, the crowd by the fountain, the homeless man trying to catch a nap on the floor of the dim men's room. As Ethan's sudden panic had been contagious, so was Knox's laughter, and soon Bruce joined her, his laugh higher in pitch than she would have expected it to be, a silly cartoon twitter that only added another layer of ridiculousness to their circumstances.

"We have no idea what the hell we're doing, do we?" Bruce said, rubbing Ethan's back.

"Doesn't look like it," Knox said.

Knox

Knox had been gathering up laundry, balling it into her duffel bag, where a pile of the babies' soiled, weightless clothes already waited. She paused, rocking on her haunches on the floor of her attic room, her hair hanging irritatingly in her face, reminded of all those madwomen in books, the hidden, dangerous ones, stashed in sloping cubbies like these. Rochester's wife. Cinderella. She was clammy with sweat, pitying herself. The only time she wasn't in motion in this house was when she slept, and God knew sleep had been impossible to come by. The attic smelled like sour milk and cardboard.

She squatted in place. What would she say now to Charlotte, if she could?

They were who they were. Ned had told her she didn't owe Charlotte anything, though surely the truer thing was that they owed each other everything. Would she assure Charlotte she was here, that the boys were okay, that Bruce—though she wasn't at all sure of this—was okay?

Bruce. He wouldn't leave the house. Though his pretext for the time he spent on the living room computer was work, Knox had glanced in passing at the screen the other day and seen him scrolling through some text on the hospital's Web site. What was the working definition of *survival*, for Bruce? Was this it? She was used to Ned, to her father: men who expressed pain only under duress, as a kind of shameful last resort. But that day at the playground, he'd struck her as a vessel rigged to spring open at the slightest touch. This both unnerved and intrigued her, though they hadn't had another conversation like the one they'd had that day. Still, the possibility of disclosure seemed to hang like a scrim in the rooms they passed through, floating overhead but low enough to brush against, should they wish to raise their hands toward it.

Would Charlotte even be comforted by her presence here? The thought of her sister tending to those she loved after her own death made her jealous, actually, though she wasn't proud of it. "Mom and Daddy are fine," she heard Charlotte saying. "Ned is getting along." Her voice sounded smug as it ricocheted through the halls of Knox's imagination.

She should have tried harder. She should have answered all of Charlotte's calls, instead of picking and choosing the moments that best suited her. She should have gotten more involved during the pregnancy, when it was suddenly clear that Charlotte wanted her to. But whenever this kind of guilt threatened to push her under, she'd proven capable of grasping on to a justification to hold her afloat. When Charlotte had first left home, she hadn't answered any of the letters Knox had sent her at Walton, though Knox had primed herself to wait the four days it would take for a letter to arrive, then checked the mail daily for a response. Wasn't that true?

She felt infinitesimally small, even as she thought it. Well, she was trying harder now.

Last night, Ben flashed a smile at her while she struggled to pull a sock onto his twisting foot, and Knox had stopped what she was doing to peck at his cool cheek with kiss after kiss. It was too early for smiles, but she'd seen one. When she looked up, Bruce was watching her, and it occurred to her to feel guilty. This wasn't hers. But as soon as the thought came, it was gone. Thank God she was here, thank God the boys had someone else to love them, right now. Bruce seemed to thank her, too, with his look—she hadn't imagined it, she thought—and the moment passed.

She and Bruce had developed a routine of their own, which shaped itself around the babies' emergent schedule. They'd put the boys to bed a half hour earlier on successive nights this week, letting them cry for short bursts until they'd established a fairly consistent bedtime of eight-thirty. When the door to the boys' room was closed and the baby monitor switched on, Bruce dialed a neighborhood place for hummus, warm pita, lamb sausages. Knox would open a bottle of red wine; she'd taken to stopping at a nearby liquor store on her short, daily walks with the boys (she'd appointed herself for this job after the last pediatrician's visit; Bruce hadn't volunteered to come along, and they didn't discuss it). They would unfold a frayed tablecloth and drape it over the ottoman, sink onto the couch with their glasses and food containers to watch another installment of Bruce's crime show, which seemed to run simultaneously on nine different channels as far as Knox could tell. She found herself missing Robbie as she ate—too quickly, without truly tasting—and watched more bullets entering skulls in slow motion, more bodies being dissected by teams of nubile forensic pathologists in tight slacks. She would refill her glass and vow to call her brother, her parents, Ned, as soon as the show was over—at which time she could only summon enough energy to climb up to her futon and arrange her body upon it, often without having brushed her teeth.

In the mornings, Bruce fetched the boys first; they were diapered and bouncing in their little seats on the kitchen floor when Knox appeared, dressed for breakfast. She finished making the bottles before sitting down to coffee with Bruce, who leafed through the *Times* without speaking to her while she fed one of the boys, then handed her the paper to read while he fed the other.

They moved through their days in this kind of silent, increasingly efficient compromise, taking turns, trading off. For some reason, Knox found herself holding Ethan more often, and Bruce holding Ben, but otherwise it was like they'd been twinned, too, completing each other's actions, sharing the whole of their days. Two weeks from the last one, there would be another pediatrician's appointment, after which, if the boys were healthy, they could fly. Knox organized the changing table's drawers. Bruce bought some faster-flow bottles, and the feeding times shortened.

The laundry needed doing now, though, or neither of the boys would have clean pajamas for their next nap. Knox pushed her legs up to a standing position and hoisted the duffel onto her shoulder. She remembered the towels she'd thrown into a corner of the room's closet at different points in her hurried mornings over the past week and nudged the door, already slightly ajar, farther open with the toe of her boot.

The box she'd tossed them behind was too large to nudge aside without setting down the duffel; she dropped it to the floor and decided to drag the box out of the way altogether. She winced at the scrape the cardboard made against the wooden boards and stayed in a crouch as she impulsively opened it, lest she need to spring quickly to her feet and explain herself. She was trying to get at her towels. Was that all right? Did anyone mind?

On the top: Unopened bank statements, dog-eared magazines, birthday cards. A cocktail napkin with a phone number on it, a brochure from a small French hotel, a blank W-2 tax form. There were several Walton alumni magazines with covers that featured savage-looking girls wielding hockey sticks, or pale figures in theatrical costumes and stage makeup ill suited to their youth, captured during some soulful soliloquy. Knox rifled downward, discovering nothing of note but the all-too-familiar version of herself, still poking at objects as if *they* were alive, instead of the family members she'd investigated through the little spy missions she'd gone on as a kid. Why had she thought she could better find her family on her own, by sifting through the things that belonged to them, instead of trusting what she saw and heard in their presence? It was the secrets she trusted more, she thought. Here she was, looking for them again. What secrets? To what end?

She stopped herself and stuffed the damp towels into her bag. When she stood again, she found herself noticing the clothes, obviously exiled up here for various reasons: there was a sequined shift that looked like it might have been a one-off for a party, a thick, uncomfortable-looking fisherman's turtleneck, several coats. A pale yellow silk slip hung by one strap from a metal hanger. Lopsided like that, it made Knox think of a pretty drunk, hanging on to the arm of someone who'd insisted he take her home. She fingered the soft material, picturing it against Charlotte's skin, set off by her dark mass of hair. There was a yellow ribbon that tied at the neckline, and a half inch of yellow lace at the hem. This was the only thing that Knox drew to her face. On impulse, she reached for it, pulled her T-shirt off over her head, and shimmied the slip over her breasts, tugged it down, and stood in place, her heart beating fast. The stale perfumes of cedar chips and dry-cleaning fluid were a comfort to her, somehow—chastening, humble, familiar. She grazed her hand against the silk. Had Charlotte slept in this, worn it under her dresses, packed it for the delayed honeymoon she and Bruce had taken to Ankara? Had she bought it, then regretted the color? Charlotte's laugh had been deep and knowing; she'd kept her mouth closed. The slip was loose on Knox at the top and hit her farther above the knees than it would have on her sister, whose height had been the only average thing about her appearance. Goddamnit, Knox thought, frightened by the images in her head, the power of them. What was wrong with her? She was wearing her dead sister's clothes. Knox fished an old, dirty shirt of Ned's out of the duffel and buttoned it onto herself quickly, tucked the hem of the slip into her jeans, thrusting her hands in a circle at her waistband until the material was smoothed out of sight. She began to cry.

.   .   .

"KNOX! There's coffee."

"I'll be right down," she called. She rubbed her palm against her face, and turned. As she moved down the stairs, the house phone rang.

In the kitchen, Bruce stood at the sink with his back to the door, the cordless in his hand. His free hand tapped against the leg of his jeans, and he looked over his shoulder as Knox came in, then turned back.

"I'll think about it, Mina," he said. He rocked on the balls of his feet. "I can tell you've put a lot of thought into it. Okay." He paused. "Yeah, she's been a lifesaver," he said. "She just walked in. All right. Nice talking to you."

Bruce's face looked pinched when he turned fully around to hand her the phone. Knox took it, and he walked out the door.

"Mom?"

"Hi, honey. How are you doing?"

"We're okay."

"It's not easy to get ahold of you. But I'm sure you're very busy."

"I'm sorry, Mama."

"No, don't apologize. I know how it is. How are the boys?"

Knox thought an apology was exactly what her mother had needed to extract before the conversation could move forward; as soon as Knox offered it, her voice had warmed, her speech had sped up a fraction.

"Hanging in there." Did her mother really know what her days were like here, or want to, in much detail? Knox wasn't sure how much to offer; she felt she could either provide her mother with some variation of *fine*, or give a thorough reporting of the diaper rash they were trying to prevent from spreading on Ben's bum, the possibility that they might have to switch Ethan to a soy formula, the fact that she and Bruce had finally located the button on the bouncy seats that caused them to vibrate under the boys' backs, which Ben liked and Ethan seemed to fear. There was no in-between.

"I was talking to Bruce just now about the memorial service." Knox couldn't prevent her stomach from dropping; speaking to her mother about this felt like admitting that there was nothing Knox could do to prevent or protect her mother from knowing that this had happened and would continue to be true. Knox's old habit of reassuring and jollying when her sister's name came up had been rendered impotent in a fell stroke, and now that she couldn't do her job, Knox would rather avoid talking to her mother at all than failing her so utterly.

"How's Dad," she ventured.

"He's—wait, let me finish."

"Okay. Go on."

"I need to know whether or not you, or Bruce, or just one of you, want to speak at the service, and if you do, roughly how long it will take and, I suppose, something about what you plan to say, or read, if you'd like to do a reading. I need this for the printer. We're doing it at First Presbyterian because it's just big enough, and you may remember we went to Dr. Houlihan's funeral there since the new minister took over, and it was so lovely."

"I remember."

"It will be a full house, but if you want any of your friends there who might not be aware of the day, you're responsible for letting them know. Anyone here will know from the paper, I suppose— Lindsay Acheson and Beth Foreman have called to see what they can do, and I think I'll set aside several rows up front just for special friends of Charlotte's, so if you think of people I might be leaving out, let me know. I can give you the full list once I've finalized it. Lindsay Acheson is so sweet."

"Mama," Knox said.

"Yes?"

"Those are Charlotte's friends from grade school."

"I know."

"Well—has she even kept in touch with them?"

"They're some of the oldest and dearest people in her life."

"I just—are you inviting anyone from up here? Is Bruce doing that?"

"Your father and I don't really *know* her New York friends. I'm sure Bruce will mention the date to anyone he thinks is important.

Otherwise, maybe he's planning to organize something up there, at some point."

"I don't think so, Mom. He hasn't talked about it. He doesn't even have time to sleep, right now."

"Maybe not, but if you both could find time to help me with the program, I'd like to know what your contributions will be by the end of the week. Then I can send the printer the final version."

"What about the wedding list? I could call information for a lot of those phone numbers—"

"Don't do this, honey. I've been very busy with the arrangements. If people want to find out when and where a memorial service for one of their friends is going to be held, they certainly have the resources at hand to do so. I can't worry about everybody."

"Okay."

"Thank you."

Knox stood looking around: there were unwashed dishes tilting against one another in the sink, the sandy, yellow residue of dry formula on the counter. A cotton undershirt no bigger than her hand hung limp over the back of a chair rung. She was suddenly so, so tired. Fatigue raked through her like a swoon, but she steadied herself.

"Have you talked to Ned?"

"No."

"I saw him at the barn; he mentioned he's been having trouble getting hold of you."

For years, Knox thought wryly, and her shame instantly compounded.

"Don't worry about that. He knows I'm all right."

Knox's mother breathed into the receiver. Knox could picture her at the desk in her beautiful library, the tarnished light there, the daintiness of her crossed ankles, her leather flats on the carpet. She could smell her flowery perfume. Had she finally allowed herself to get far enough away to be homesick?

"I think it's wonderful what you're doing, Knox," Mina said. "We all do."

They hung up. Knox looked around, rolled up the sleeves of Ned's shirt, and started in on the mess.

SHE FOUND BRUCE stretched out beside Ben, on a blanket that had been laid on the living room floor. Bruce's feet were bare, his long body arranged in a straight line. He held a gaudy, rhinestoned compact open in front of Ben's face, and passed the mirror back and forth in front of his eyes.

"This was in the bathroom cabinet," Bruce said, looking up. "Don't worry, I'm not putting makeup on him."

"I didn't think so," Knox said, wiping her hands, still damp from cleaning, against the front of her jeans. She smiled.

"I thought it would be interesting for him to see himself," Bruce said. "He seems to like it."

Knox watched Ben's face. His mouth hung open in what looked like astonishment. His tongue worked against his bottom lip, and he didn't look away from the mirror once. Who did he think that was? In the world he existed in, did he think his reflection was just another baby, hovering and staring?

"Is Ethan still napping?"

"Yep. The phone didn't seem to wake him up."

Knox sat in the chair opposite Bruce and Ben and closed her eyes. Even as she did so, she told herself not to get too comfortable inside this reprieve; Ethan would be up soon enough.

"So, your mother."

Knox opened her eyes. Bruce wasn't looking at her.

"She seems to have a lot of plans," Bruce said, his voice even.

"She's worked up a head of steam, that's for sure," Knox said. "She wasn't like this when I left."

"The service. Where I'm going to stay. How long. She mentioned some place across the road where we could have our own space. A guesthouse or something."

Her parents had recently acquired a pocket of land that lay catty-corner to the yearling division. There was a house on it that her mother had yet to redo, a hollow relic from the thirties; the architect had referenced a much older Georgian style with some skill, but neglect had left it a mess; the last time Knox had walked through its rooms, she'd wondered how they could ever recover.

"She didn't mention that."

Bruce smiled at her from the floor, but there was something hard in his features, too. "She's been working to get it ready for me. She wanted a list of everything I thought the boys would need for the 'nursery.' "

"She must think it's important not to have us in your hair while you're down there."

"That's the thing. I have this weird feeling that she plans to keep me there. It's a lot of trouble to go to for a few days."

"No. I'm sure it's just something for her to put her energy into right now," Knox said.

"I just wish—"

Knox waited.

"I wish we didn't have to put the boys through this, so early. Make them travel. Everything feels like it's happening too soon."

"Yeah."

"I wonder why we all have to go through it. Wouldn't it be easier not to put ourselves through it? All those people."

We, he'd said. Knox's mind caught. Of course, she wasn't necessarily included in the *we*.

"I think the boys will be okay," Knox said, not wanting to think, right now, of Lindsay Acheson's plump, smiling face, of Beth Foreman—who'd called Knox "stork" in school—attempting to wrap any of them up in her arms, of Mrs. Howard's lisped condolences.

"They're portable," she continued. "They'll roll with things."

"That's not what I mean."

"I know." Knox sighed. "But my family needs this. My mother needs this, it seems." Knox felt herself returning to her usual role of loyalist, of translator. She felt like contradicting herself and her automatic explanations.

"Part of me is afraid that I don't. That gathering a million rubberneckers together won't make me feel better. It's supposed to, right? I'll do it, but I'm not going to say anything. There's nothing I feel ready to say. Jesus."

"It's what has to happen next, Bruce. It might as well be now, as opposed to a year from now." A year from now, where would they be? The boys walking, or trying to. Laughing, speaking. Would they have lost the grave suggestions of understanding that Knox felt she recognized in their faces now—especially Ethan's? Would they move further away from the knowledge of how they'd come to be here, instead of closer to it, as they grew? Knox couldn't picture herself a year from now, back in her cabin, driving to work, writing evaluations. Bruce, she supposed, would be writing out instructions for the nanny before he left for work. She could only glimpse this if she concentrated very hard: there he was gnawing on a piece of dry toast as he chased two squealing toddlers down a hallway, his tie looped around his neck. It seemed more like an image from a movie, or an advertisement for deodorant, than something real and foregone.

Bruce sat up, rubbed his face all over with one hand. He shook his head, like he was trying to dislodge something inside of it, then picked Ben up and held him to his chest, kneaded his diaper briefly to check for heaviness, see if he needed to be changed.

"Do you want me to make the list for you? Not that I could promise you it would be totally thorough. Mom's probably already got three of everything anyway."

Bruce smiled sadly at her. Knox suddenly wanted to brush at the hollows under his eyes with her fingertips and erase them. He looked awful, really.

"You've been great," he said, his voice quiet. "Thank you."

Her mother had called her wonderful, and now this.

"I'm not great," Knox said. "I'm here for the wrong reasons."

Bruce settled Ben on his lap so that he faced forward. He looked improbably alert, as if waiting for the proper moment to contribute to the general conversation.

"Well, whatever you're here for, I'm grateful," Bruce said. He rubbed at Ben's soft scalp. "I wasn't sure I would be, to be honest. I didn't want anybody around. This is going to sound strange, but I didn't want to leave the hospital."

"I don't think it's strange."

"In school, I had a friend whose mother went missing. I remember hearing later that he hadn't wanted to move out of the apartment where she'd lived with them, in case she came back. It's something like that, I think."

"What happened?"

"She died."

They watched each other. Knox was conscious of the possibility that her face might be blotchy from before, from crying. She was holding her breath.

"You didn't give me much choice, when you told me you were coming," Bruce said. "But you're good with the boys. I can see that you love them."

"I'm not a baby person," Knox said.

"Well, you're good at pretending, then."

"Actually, I lack imagination."

"Okay," Bruce said. He cocked his head. "Clearly you refuse to take a compliment."

"I don't know what Charlotte ever said to you. But I shut her out. I was not a good sister to her for a long time."

Bruce closed his eyes. Something about the oddly intimate sight of him this way provided Knox with a brief moment of comfort, even though this was only a facsimile of him in sleep. She'd been worried about him; she felt the full weight of this now.

"What's a good sister? Is there a definition in the dictionary for that?"

"A friend. I was angry with her all the time."

"Well, she wasn't easy."

"No."

She wanted to ask: Not easy how, from your perspective? But she was aware that she was talking to Bruce about his wife and needed to quell the bounce of excitement in her chest at the unexpected possibility—the most far-fetched possibility on earth, it had seemed—that Bruce understood her.

"I think she just wanted to know you were on her side," Bruce continued, and Knox's small hope turned despairing in an instant: here was confirmation of complaint, of bad opinion pooled between husband and wife that she would never be fully privy to.

"I know." She pressed against her eyes with the palms of her hands. Peekaboo. I see you. "And I wasn't. I should have been, but I wasn't after a certain point. Honestly, it was easier once she'd left. She made our mom cry."

"Well, that was a long time ago. She was a teenager."

"She made my father feel bad. She forgot about me when she went away. She never even really knew Ned." She took up all the oxygen, Knox thought, she left no room for anybody else's problems, she was always the beautiful one— What was she doing? She sounded pathetic.

"I love your family, Knox. I'm not going to act like I understand everything about it. It's yours. But I don't want you speaking like this in front of Ben, okay?"

Bruce broke off. At the same moment, Ethan began to cry softly, without having fully committed himself, in the next room. He was waking up.

"I've been careful not to let them see me breaking down. I don't think it's good for them, and neither is this." He wasn't looking her in the eye.

"Of course, I'm sorry."

She had scooted herself to the edge of the chair she sat in. As Bruce shifted to go to Ethan, Ben appeared to bobble in his arms, and Knox reached forward to steady him, though immediately Bruce corrected Ben's angle as he rose. As she moved to sit down again, she noticed another change in Bruce's face; the muscles around his brow contracted and his thin lips parted slightly in surprise.

"Is that . . . Charlotte's?" he said.

Knox followed his eyes downward, where the hem of Charlotte's yellow slip had come loose from her waistband and dropped into sight below her shirt. She felt her chest prickle with sweat.

"I know. I was wearing it. It's so weird," she blurted. "I forgot I had it on."

Bruce said nothing. Knox wished she could make them both disappear, absenting them completely from the moment so that only Ben was left, lying peacefully on his blanket, opening and closing his tiny hands. She was a freak. She had no business. She guarded against the defensiveness she knew could ride right in on shame's back, against saying to herself: But she's mine, too, my sister. No—there was no excuse for this violation.

"Bruce, I'm sorry," she said. "It was in the closet upstairs. I should have asked. I just threw it on."

"Don't apologize to me," Bruce said. "It wasn't mine."

She nodded. Bruce watched her for a moment, then turned and carried Ben out of the room. Knox remained where she was, her hands clasped in her lap, numbly wondering how much time she should allow before following Bruce. Despite everything, he would need help with Ben while he changed Ethan and got him dressed. But she remained where she was, turned to stone.

THEY GAVE each other a wide berth during the week left before they flew to Kentucky. Knox wouldn't have called them wary of each other, exactly. Once again, it was easy for them to avoid one another if they chose, with the necessities of the boys' care hanging between them. They were polite, and on the surface of their shared, work-filled hours, it appeared that little had changed.

"Ugly, it's me. When do you need me to pick you up?"

She and Ned had hardly spoken at all since the first week she'd been in New York. At first, she'd attributed this to an abstract understanding he must have of the wormhole she'd fallen into; he'd been with her every moment in Kentucky, hadn't he, before she'd come. Then she remembered the awkwardness between them before this all happened, the way he'd behaved the day after the bluegrass festival, and wondered if he was giving her room or, justifiably, taking some room for himself, now that she didn't need him to bathe, feed, and rock her to sleep. Of course, she wasn't exactly available now. If he had the energy to chase her down, he'd find her; otherwise, he wouldn't. Today, he'd found her: hustling by the hall table, Ethan sprawled against her chest in his carrier, his long, bare, skinny chicken legs bouncing against her stomach.

"Well, speak of the devil," she said, the lightness in her tone belying the way she felt, even upon hearing his voice, which was lonely.

"Your father told me you were coming on Thursday, so I wanted to be of service."

"How nice. But we'll have car seats and a lot of gear, it looks like. I think Mama should fetch us in her car."

"Oh. Okay. I hadn't thought of that. How are the boys? I can't wait to see them."

"And me, right?"

"Naturally."

False, easy cheer. Why did she feel so guilty about it? Knox rubbed her fingers up and down one of Ethan's calves, tickling him. He stared up at her from his place under her chin, serious as a heart attack, his lips slick with drool.

The memorial was scheduled for Saturday. Ned read her the announcement in the paper.

The next pediatrician's appointment came and went. Ethan contracted a fever after the shots this time, but it broke within a day. They spent the night before the trip back home packing the boys' clothes, bottles, bottle brushes, blankets, pacifiers, diapers, wipes, formula, special laundry detergent, hooded towels, bath liquid, lotion, thermometer, gas and fever medicines in case, infant nail clippers to keep their faces from getting scratched during the course of their time away, burp cloths, the music player they relied on at night. The double stroller stood by the door, unfolded and ready. There was hardly enough time between the moment Knox zipped the suitcase Bruce had allotted for the twins' things shut and the midnight feeding to fit in a trip to the bathroom, much less a coherent conversation.

On the airplane, though she and Bruce sat side by side, they spent their time trying to joggle the boys into sleep and keep their hands and faces from touching the armrests. Knox must have knelt down twenty times to pick something up that had fallen onto the floor or into the aisle, bracing Ethan in her lap all the while. She didn't see the land changing, thousands of feet beneath them, settling into the green, undulating country she knew best. She could feel herself descending at the end of the flight, feel that they were about to touch down, but until the plane bumped onto the tarmac she couldn't have said exactly how close they were to the ground. She wished there was some way to know whether or not Bruce absolved her. She was carried forward and placed her hands over Ethan's ears as the brakes screamed and they hurtled to the end of the runway, then slowed, rolled, turned, and reached the gate, where she and Bruce would gather their things and carry the babies into the airport; somewhere inside, her parents stood, she thought. Though perhaps just her mother had driven to get them. When she finally was able to glance at the field beyond Bruce's window, she was startled by the layer of frost that lay over the grass as they moved past, graying it slightly. She could see the racecourse in the distance, on the far side of the highway; the rows of stately old trees there were beginning to turn. Overnight, it seemed, autumn had come.

· III ·

BRUCE

THIS IS HOW CRAZY manifests itself, Bruce thought. Like this.

He was standing in his suit and tie in the beautifully appointed library of his mother- and father-in-law's house, holding a glass of white wine, surrounded by people. An employee of his father-in-law's, a short, muscular man in an unfashionable tie, stood at his elbow, the tops of his ears pink, clearly alarmed to find himself in such close proximity to the bereaved husband. He rattled the ice cubes in his own glass and gazed along with Bruce into the heart of the gathering, where Mina stood beside her husband's chair, her small hand draped protectively over the back of it, smiling in thanks as someone gripped her shoulders and leaned closer to speak to her, the picture of a gracious hostess, except for the slight dapple of mascara that sooted her cheek, and the downward pull that seemed to weight her features, even as they forced themselves into expressions of gratitude, understanding, and welcome. In another society, it would be acceptable, Bruce thought, for her to burn herself in effigy, to swaddle herself in white and take to the streets, to keen. In this one, she was throwing a cocktail party. The dining room table was cheek to jowl with sterling chafing dishes, manned by handsome-looking women in dark bouclé. This was the time for special friends and family to gather before climbing into their assigned cars. They would leave for the church in half an hour.

"Southern funerals," the man said. If he'd introduced himself, it had taken Bruce only an instant to forget his name. "You really need a football stadium. And a doggie bag."

Bruce nodded, tried to smile. "All the food," he said.

"My wife brought the cheese straws," the man said. "Try those, if you get a chance."

Neither of the boys had slept much the night before in the guesthouse, which Mina had decorated every inch of for them, even ordered furniture for. The room she'd designated for the babies was much more luxurious and finished than their room at home. Everything matched, was swathed in cream and pale blue. Ethan and Ben looked dwarfed in their gargantuan cribs and clearly were going to need a few days to get used to them.

"How're your boys doing," the man asked, and Bruce momentarily wondered if he'd spoken aloud.

Bruce glanced at the man, whose flush had expanded to include the whole of his broad, frightened face. Bruce wished that the two of them inhabited an alternate universe, wherein he could acknowledge and thank this person for his obvious valor. I wouldn't want to talk to me, either, he thought. Thank you, this is good of you, and I know it.

"We're all hanging in there," he said instead, his voice duller than he'd wanted it to sound. He cleared his throat.

"Yep," the man agreed quickly, as if this was the response he'd expected to receive and he was pleased now to have it. "You know, it's a funny thing. In mares, twins aren't ever allowed to come to term. They just don't thrive, aren't robust to race. Could be dangerous for the mare to have them, too, I imagine."

"Oh. Well. That's not why Charlotte died. She hemorrhaged, but that could have happened with one baby, too. It didn't really have to do with twins." Even as he spoke, Bruce questioned himself. This was true, wasn't it? He'd been over and over what the doctors had said. Disseminated intravascular coagulation; he'd revisited the same pages multiple times on the Internet on various medical sites. He'd wondered if he was remiss, a fool, not to be filing a lawsuit, though he had found no fault so far in the records of Charlotte's care he'd been provided with. But declaring this, out loud, forced Bruce into a new disorientation; how could he be sure of even the most basic facts? It was just so much jargon, in his mouth. Jargon had killed his wife.

"I see. You know, I shouldn't have said that," the man said, touching his arm. "I hope you don't think I was being rude."

"No. Don't worry."

"She was beautiful," the man said into his highball. He rocked forward onto the balls of his polished wing-tip shoes. "Just a beautiful girl."

On the far side of the room he saw Knox. She was leaning against a section of wall in an ill-fitting gray dress. She'd been careless with her hair, pulled it back into a ponytail; strands escaped from its sides, glinting redder than usual in the sunlight that poured in through the casement windows. She, too, held a wineglass and raised it now to her lips. Bruce had been on his own, essentially, with the boys since they'd arrived the day before yesterday, and he had to admit it was strange, to be suddenly without Knox's presence in his orbit, during the feedings. She'd been staying away, he thought, and that might be good.

There had been that day, in New York, when he'd seen she was wearing a nightgown under her clothes, a nightgown he himself had bought for Charlotte and that she'd worn only once, before pregnancy forced it into the back of some drawer. She'd worn it to appease him; he had seen, as soon as she pulled it from its little box, that it was a color she never wore. He'd been annoyed with himself then, and frightened that Charlotte felt, uncharacteristically, that she couldn't say what she obviously felt, which was that he'd missed his mark. Things between them were still fragile in those days immediately following his confession. Their marriage had shed its skin and was still in the process of growing a new one over the tender flesh it was made of. They'd clung to each other, unprotected and careful.

When he'd recognized it on Knox, he'd been shocked. Not that she had it on, necessarily, but by the plainness of what he'd never seen before: that Knox and Charlotte were sisters, physically. In a kind of flash, he could see them superimposed upon each other, their parts corresponding as he'd never thought they could. Not three feet away from him, there was Charlotte's look, there was the same sloping nose, there was her *family*. He could see it. He wondered then if the wives' tale that applied to couples about growing to look more and more alike the longer they were together could apply to siblings, too. Though Knox and Charlotte looked at first glance to be made up of different strands of their parents' DNA, surely the experiences they'd shared here in this house, on this breeding farm, had shaped within them a certain set of identical traits that could show themselves to the keenest observers. Ethan and Ben looked nothing alike, and yet it was impossible for Bruce to imagine that anyone could fail to see them for what they were: brothers. That Knox and Charlotte were sisters was instantly, uncannily clear.

He'd been unnerved. Knox had assumed he was angry, and he supposed it was easier that way. But what he'd really felt was too close to something: a chimera. A dangerous thing.

She was lovely, Bruce thought, watching her now. She should really take more trouble with herself, carry herself like she gave a damn. He knew this was unkind, and wondered why he cared to hold such a thing against her, at this of all moments.

She looked up and caught his eye. She raised her glass into the air in a barely perceptible motion and frowned.

THE VESTIBULE of the church was crowded and dim. Ned threaded his arm around Knox's waist, and something about this proprietary gesture angered her. She took a breath, moved out of his grasp under the auspices of reaching toward the center table for a program. She was shaking. She didn't want to do this. Ned moved a step toward her, shadowing her like a point guard, aware of her position at all times. He was taking her jumpiness to mean that she needed his support. What was it about that that was so hard for her to accept?

Something pulsed at the edge of her consciousness, some bloom that had yet to open; as soon as she tried to fix upon it, it eluded her, inaccessible. What? It had to do with Ned, but she couldn't retrieve it now.

She smiled at Ned, who was speaking to one of the ushers about something. She took another breath. He was good. He'd tucked his maimed hand into the pocket of his suit pants. He looked handsome; something about the sight of him scrubbed up like this was poignant to her. His hair was still wet, the grooves the tines of his comb had made glisteningly visible. She took another breath. Bruce, her father, her mother, Robbie, the solemn officiant—all of them seemed to be moving about the chill space to little purpose, addressing one another with brief and meaningless phrases that they immediately forgot. Her father was medicated with something; this seemed clear, though to confirm it would signal to Knox that the world was, in fact, ending.

Her mother was hurrying toward the door to greet someone; Knox saw the woman she'd hired for the day to bring the boys to the service, then bring them home again once they'd made their appearance. Her mother had—gently, it's true—insisted to Bruce that Ethan and Ben would want to know, later in their lives, that they had participated in this day, even for a few minutes, and solved the problem of who would look after them by providing the name of the lady who stepped into view now, the soft wave of her hair frosted gray around her face, holding one twin in each plump arm. The boys were dressed identically in navy blue jumpers over white shirts—also provided by her mother.

Knox was momentarily overtaken by the sense that this was a

play, and they the actors, hushed in the wings. She felt sick. Perhaps if she'd thought to drink another glass or two before leaving home, she'd feel calmer.

Ned was at her side. He whispered in her ear, "You okay?"

She nodded. Her mother drew the woman holding the twins closer, and when Ben saw Knox, he began to whimper and wriggle against the woman's chest. Knox reached for him without thinking.

"This is my younger daughter," her mother explained to the woman, who smiled pityingly, and handed Ben over. Knox gathered him up and kissed the top of his head, her eyes briefly closing. Ben stilled, and quieted.

"You have quite a way with that little man," her father whispered, standing close to her now. He seemed smaller, diminished in some way, his jacket too loose on his frame.

Knox's eyes filled with tears.

"I love you," she whispered back.

It was time to move into the church. The place was full of people and murmur and dusty light. There wasn't any music yet; Knox shuffled down the aisle in her appointed place behind her parents and Bruce, abreast of Robbie, who kept glancing at her as if for affirmation that he was going through the correct motions. As she walked, she was aware of the looks she and Ben were receiving, the sighs emitted when people saw the baby in her arms. She hadn't meant to draw further attention to herself in this way, to have this special status conferred upon her, and felt some mild shame that Bruce's arms were empty; Ethan would be brought to their pew through a side door; the woman holding him was behind them somewhere.

They slid into the pew. Ned and Robbie had switched places at some point; now Ned's hand was at her back, guiding her. She braced her legs and sat down with care; Ben was drowsing in her arms, and she didn't want to jostle him. Her stockings chafed her at the waist; she was hot. A current seemed to be moving through her, threading through her arteries like a wire, humming with an extraneous energy that was too much for her body to contain. Was she going to have some sort of episode? She tightened her arms around Ben and felt grateful for the curve and solidity of the wood under her, for its smoothness. It was cherry, she thought, suddenly. Hardwood with lethal flower, horse killer.

The minister led them in prayer. Lindsay Acheson was slated to speak. After the hymn, she made her way to the gilded lectern, her round face streaked with tears.

"Charlotte was my best friend as a little girl," she began in a reedy voice. "And though the years thrust us apart in some ways, I will never forget her high spirits, her sense of mischief and fun. Once—"

Knox glanced to her right, at Bruce. He looked frozen in place. She grazed Ben's back with her fingers; he stirred, then rearranged himself on Knox's breast, completely asleep now.

Lindsay continued. This is a memorial for Charlotte's youth, Knox thought, not for Charlotte herself. The flowers at the altar were pink and fluted. The picture of Charlotte that had been chosen for the program looked too young, too innocent, to really be her. Knox had no idea where it had been taken. Had her mother asked Bruce to provide it?

The minister touched Lindsay's arm as she descended from the lectern. He looked hollowed out to Knox, devoid of color, his robe furling around him as he moved as if there were nothing substantively corporeal under it. He smiled before speaking.

"I did not know this young woman in life," he began. "Though it has been my pleasure to get to know the Bollings recently, and to get to know Charlotte through the recollections of those who loved her. This is one of the most difficult tasks a minister can be faced with: the memorializing of a person whose hand one never shook, whose face one never saw animated in conversation."

Knox stole a glance at her mother, who sat rigidly upright, her fine hair teased into a gossamer cloud around her face. Her eyes were rapt; Knox could see this man could break her with a word.

"The artist Piranesi was trained as an architect. He was famous for his etchings, which took existing Roman ruins and restored them to their original glory. He re-created what was missing, through his art. I suppose you could call this some version of my job, to fill in both my gaps in knowledge so that I may do full honor to Charlotte's life, and to fill in the gaps in each of you today created by her loss, so that we may feel more whole, and our celebration of her more whole."

The minister paused to sip from a glass of water that had been placed somewhere at his elbow; it took him twice as long as it should have to accomplish this small thing.

"A series of Piranesi's etchings, though, called *Imaginary Prisons*, were different from his other works," he continued. "These were also of architectural structures, but instead of visions of perfection, they were mazes without exits. Staircases led upward into stone walls, doors were placed without purpose. In these works, the edifice became a trap, a trick, a nightmare."

What is he talking about, Knox thought. That he'd referred so openly to the fact he'd never even met Charlotte made her feel anxious. Couldn't he have lied about that?

"Such is life with and without God. With God, we have the power to realize the vision of the great architect of our lives, and to realize the fullness of our relationships with others. Without God, the most magnificent of structures—mainly, us—becomes devoid of meaning and purpose. Perhaps Piranesi understood these distinct possibilities. But what it's important to know is that without God, the process of assigning the life and death of this cherished young woman her proper place and meaning in each of your lives may become a maze from which it is impossible to discover any exit."

Knox felt her thoughts crowding through her; she was unable to slow them down. Her knee grazed the pew in front of her as she shifted, and she found herself focusing on the place of contact, where there was a nick in the varnished surface of the wood, which glowed like something vital.

Too quickly, it was her turn. She looked down at Ben, his transparent eyelashes fanning against the skin of his cheek. His lips, the color of the altar flowers, were parted. God, he was dazzling. A perfect thing. It was clear to her that she couldn't wake him, that she needed to bring him with her up to the lectern now. She formed a basket with her forearms and, pressing him to her, negotiated her way over Ned's knees, and past Robbie, who was trying to stand to make way for her, his young limbs a tangle, a puzzle he had to solve.

There was a microphone at the lectern, a dark bulb at the end of a small arc of brass, beckoning her. If she spoke directly into that, she would wake Ben, would frighten him, she thought, so she positioned her mouth slightly to the left of it, bending down, her body mirroring the shape of the brass rod, a long, slim, curved thing, live, electric. Knox rested one of her elbows on the wooden edge of the stand, to steady herself.

"I wanted to say something about love," she said, looking up at last as the final word proceeded from her lips. There were hundreds of faces staring up at her, expectant. There were Marlene and Jimmy, their shoulders touching. She could hear she'd been too loud, despite the precaution she'd tried to take; the mike was picking her up, and Ben shifted in her hands.

"I wanted to say something about family, also, today," she went on, though she knew it would happen, and it did: Ben's dark eyes blinked open; they were Charlotte's eyes; and he opened his mouth in a wail that gathered volume and urgency as it came; he had no idea where he was, or what was happening. Knox raised the top of his head to her lips, began whispering into his ear, bouncing in place. In a moment, Bruce was moving toward her, his hands splayed, his face full of understanding. She met his eyes. They'd been part of a sacred dance, the two of them, and she hadn't understood until she was back home that it might be over for good.

"Hey," Bruce mouthed. His face twisted into a half smile. "Let me take him."

Knox stepped toward him, and the delicate handoff was under way; Bruce's tapered hands closed around Ben, who started to calm in his father's presence. Bruce moved aside, toward the side aisle; he'd stand out of the way in lieu of returning to his seat. Knox bit her lip, resolved to gather herself. What was it she'd wanted to say? That she needed to recover? Her eyes scanned the front pew, the faces of her people, and lit on Ned's, with his strong clean-shaven jaw and pretty eyes behind his glasses, telegraphing such encouragement in his expression. Go on, he seemed to be saying with that face, as well known to her as her own, and suddenly it came to her, what had eluded her, before. I don't love you, she thought. Not the way I'm supposed to. When she was too overcome to continue speaking, she thought she registered forgiveness in his look, and she wanted to tell him that he didn't understand, and that she was so sorry, so, so sorry, but then she felt the minister's hand resting gently on her back, and she was waving her hands in front of her face, and stepping aside.

KNOX STOOD on the porch of the guesthouse where Bruce and the boys were staying, a baking dish in her hands. She'd spent the last two and a half hours making lasagna, though what she'd wanted was to lie down in her dress and sleep and perhaps never wake up. Instead, after the reception at her parents', she'd driven out of the field where the car guys—the same group, with the pimples and lazy smiles and self-deprecating manners and blinding white dress shirts she remembered from all her parents' summer parties, now gone silent, their gazes sorrowful and kind—had parked her, and made her way straight to the Kroger's in Versailles, where she'd powered up and down each wide aisle, surprised at what she seemed to be doing. The place was a psychedelic whirl of color, vast as a midway; at this time of the evening it seemed peopled by the aimless and elderly, each customer more tragic, sunken, and shambling than the next. Her cart was overly large and difficult to keep on course. Her uncomfortable heels smacked against the linoleum to the time of the piped-in music all around her. Canned plum tomatoes, no-boil noodles, bags of shredded cheese, ground beef, oregano, cumin. She needed everything.

She could smell dust here on the porch, the sour odor of

decomposing leaves. A breeze touched her face, and she knew from the weight of the air that it would rain soon. She'd finally changed into jeans while the lasagna baked, filling her cabin with an extravagance of scent that made her ashamed of the lacks it had suffered on her watch. She'd never cooked. There was so much she'd never done. The dish she held was too hot, too heavy for her to bear gracefully; she raised one foot off the ground and tried to balance it on her knee, where it teetered, the foil she'd laid over the top and forgotten to crimp under the handles sliding partly off. She'd made enough for eight people, but she hadn't known how to reduce the one recipe she'd found in the cabin in a *Joy of Cooking* that her mother had relegated to a shelf there, probably for the sake of decoration rather than out of any real faith that Knox would put it to proper use.

Bruce opened the door. He wore a loose T-shirt with the suit pants he'd had on earlier. A burp cloth was slung over his shoulder. He held on to the edge of the door, as if he wanted to be prepared to close it after her, once she'd gone.

"Are the boys down," Knox asked. She whispered out of habit, though the room her mother had prepared for the babies was well out of earshot.

"Hopefully," Bruce said. He didn't smile. "They're in their cribs, anyway."

Knox stood still, waiting to be invited in. Bruce watched her.

"I made lasagna," she said stupidly.

"Thank you," Bruce said.

"It was a long day," Knox said. She took a breath. "It wasn't what I wanted, either. I just wanted you to know that." As she said this, she became so dizzy with sorrow for herself that she felt she might have to hang on to the door, too. Her throat pained her, and she knew she was going to cry.

"It doesn't matter."

"It does." She squeezed her eyes shut for a moment and tried to compose herself. At least she could show Bruce she didn't mean to be crying, and was fighting to stop. "I'm—could you take this fucking dish?"

Bruce laughed, then, a laugh that degenerated into coughing and then renewed itself while he moved to relieve her.

"Sorry," he said. He opened the door wider, still laughing. It was a laugh she hadn't heard in New York—there was something reckless in it, as if he might have given himself permission to go mad. He looked straight at her, one of his hands balancing the lasagna. Knox ducked past him, though she hadn't formally been asked inside. Where else did she have to go? Robbie was headed back to school the next day; Ned was lost to her; it was too cold to swim. What she really wanted, she knew the instant she entered the desolate hallway, was to hold one of the babies. She wanted her arms filled with them, to smell their heads and their lotioned, still-skinny bodies inside their pajamas. She wanted to rub her index finger along the ridges their spines made, over the brief jut of their shoulder blades, rest one of their soft, diapered butts on her forearm, press them against the length of her torso, and stay. She resolved not to stop moving and crossed toward the stairs. She could hear Bruce set the dish down somewhere behind her, and his footsteps on the bare treads climbing after hers, but he made no effort to stop her.

The door to their room was open; a humidifier hummed somewhere inside. In the glow from the nightlight stood two round cribs, trussed up with gingham and eyelet, along the walls of what Knox remembered now was a former study, paneled in some cheap veneer. The trappings of the nursery were incongruous with the soul of the room, but the preparation her mother had put in was everywhere: there were two matching hampers, a storage system with coordinating baskets, an elaborate mobile hung from a hook in the ceiling. The plush rug underfoot muted her entrance, and she didn't even know which twin she was lifting until he was in her arms: Ethan, just a touch lighter, the slight knob at the top of his skull discernible under her palm, which was gliding over him, reading his form like Braille. She held him against her and swayed in place, nuzzling his scalp.

Bruce stepped into the room. He seemed to consider each piece of furniture in it. Knox felt strangely embarrassed for him, for a moment, there among all the baby comforts; the fact that he—and, indeed, Charlotte—would never have been responsible for the existence of a room like this, yet was forced to make it his temporary dominion, emasculated him somehow. It was as if her mother had turned Bruce himself into an infant by creating this frilly environment for his sons. God, she was tired, thought Knox. She had better put Ethan down again, before she fell asleep right here and dropped him.

There was a knocking sound; Knox looked and saw the diaper pail rolling on the floor; Bruce must have stumbled against it. Immediately, Ben started to wail. She began jogging Ethan up and down in her arms by instinct, but after a few seconds it was clear he wouldn't wake. Bruce reached down into the other crib for Ben; when he raised the boy to his shoulder, Ben gave a loud burp and lowered his head against Bruce's T-shirt, asleep again as quickly as he'd roused himself. Bruce began to rock him, just as he might if Ben were still awake, dipping low at the knees and moving from side to side about the room, drawing U's in the air with his long body. He traced a slow, rhythmic circle around the place where Knox stood with Ethan, his eyes trained straight ahead, his face expressionless. Knox put Ethan down and waited until Bruce had lowered Ben into the opposite crib, then preceded him out of the room.

Bruce left the door open a crack. They stood on the landing that overlooked the front hall. The only light here was from a lamp Knox's mother had plugged into a corner below them.

"I'm sorry," Knox said.

"For what," Bruce said.

"For needing that. I almost woke them both up."

"You know," Bruce said. His face looked severe. "I think you apologize too much."

"I'm also sorry for today. There was just—there wasn't enough that honored you, and how much you loved her."

"What are you talking about?"

Bruce's brown eyes flashed; he looked suddenly capable of hitting her.

"Your wife was just . . . frozen in time. Didn't that bother you? It bothered me, and I contributed to it."

"So you're fixing it with a casserole?"

"It's lasagna."

They stared at each other.

"Knox," Bruce began slowly, as if he were speaking to a child. "Charlotte is dead. Ethan and Ben's mother is dead, and they'll never know her. I will never talk to my wife again. I am fucking terrified. Do you honestly think that what got said or not said at a church service makes any difference to me? I'm trying to get through the day. Your guilt over . . . whatever. It doesn't help me."

Knox lowered her head. She was nodding, though her eyes were welling with tears.

"I don't know what I'm supposed to do, or what is going to happen to my life. So if you can help me with that, you're welcome to. If you can't, then I honestly don't need anything extra to worry about. A memorial is an hour and a half of my existence, all right? Not life and death. Neither is one of the boys waking up, or—much of anything else, come to think of it. Not after . . . I can't even fucking say it again. Maybe once I can even say it, I'll be better off."

Knox was starting to sob now, her hand over her mouth, trying to be as quiet as she could. Her chest felt as if it were exploding; it felt good, actually. Good and terrible at once.

"Hey," Bruce said, grazing her hair with his long, tapered fingers. "Come on."

She tried to stop, or to indicate that she was going to stop soon, but she couldn't get her breath.

"Your lasagna helps me. Your lasagna helps me enormously."

Knox attempted to smile, and failed.

"Knox."

Something about the sound of her name in his mouth made her cold, and she stood shivering in front of him.

"I wish she could see you with them." The words seemed to jerk out of her. "It's not fair."

When he wrapped his arms around her, the warmth came as a

relief. This was her first thought. Then his chin was resting on the top of her head while he held her, and by the time he lowered his face to kiss hers, she had an understanding of what was happening and had chosen it. She couldn't claim not to have chosen it, or to have been swept up into something she wasn't conscious of, or couldn't control. No, she had chosen it, and in the moment, she was glad.

KNOX

THOUGH IT WAS STILL EARLY, Knox was surprised at the deep quiet in her parents' house when she entered. She crept up the stairs like an intruder, trying not to think of her mother and father, openmouthed in sleep at an hour she would have normally found them at the breakfast table, if life were in any way proceeding as usual. She should turn around and let herself out so as not to risk the embarrassment of waking them. But the idea of returning to the cabin now, to the forced companionship with herself she'd have to endure there, sat like dead weight in her. She wanted ballast, and company—or, at least, the familiarity of her old bed. She made her way slowly, carefully, to her room.

She opened the heavy door off the landing, and paused. Something about the sight of the space, arranged like a shrine to her girlhood, shamed her. She was so tired; she'd planned to lie down on the eyelet coverlet that hung down to the floor, grazing the carpet with its scalloped edge like a veil, but to disturb it now struck her as a violation; the pillows were arranged in such a smooth symmetrical pile; Knox thought of a bier, floating away on the lake of soft carpet. She turned away from the bed and took inventory in a squint; the light streaming through the windows was already too bright. There was her desk, an expanse of bleached pine on which sat the framed pictures of her family; while Charlotte had displayed an array of snapshots on the corkboard wall in her own room, always of herself with various friends and always changing, Knox remembered curating this select group of photographs at an early age and framing them herself: a wedding photo of her parents, a shot of herself and Charlotte bursting through a corona of hose water in the side yard, their bathing suits puckering across their flat chests, and a posed shot of the five of them standing together in front of a fence, Robbie in a bassinet at their feet, pried loose from a Christmas card she'd begged off her mother one year.

On the sideboard that functioned as a bookshelf: a tilting hodge-podge composed of the stuff of school reading lists, forgotten library books, academic texts for the anthropology major Knox had switched halfway through her years at UK. She blinked, then brought her hands together and rubbed. Surely there was a box somewhere up here. She hunted one down in the adjacent guest room and carried it back across the landing, floating it, full as it was of air, onto the rug in front of the shelves. She'd set to work gathering books the center could use; there was an anemic library there, and the classrooms were always hard up for books the students could practice with. Yes, this struck her as a legitimate way to spend the morning. She'd even alphabetize as she sorted. She took a breath and began.

She'd fed the boys this morning and let Bruce sleep. To even touch on the image of herself in the half-light in the babies' room, shushing Ethan as she waggled the bottle gently against Ben's gums to entice him to suck faster, made her feel like her blood could catch fire; her face was hot with the memory even as she worked to push it aside. What had she been doing there? Once the boys were both topped up and burped and drowsing again in their cribs, she debated waking Bruce, but left the partially empty bottles at the threshold of the room as evidence of the feeding, snatched her clothes up from the pile they'd formed at the foot of

Bruce's bed, and left. She hadn't worked overly hard at being quiet; she was conscious of a certain, albeit weak, defiance in the way she'd clattered down the stairs and let the screen door spring shut behind her. She supposed the idea of skulking around like a fugitive from her life, trying not to make a sound, was all too familiar to her. But as soon as she'd reached this house she'd been at it again, trying to minimize her presence, the affront of it, to the point of rendering herself invisible. Wasn't that how she behaved?

Knox slid a handful of paperbacks toward her and balanced their spines against her palm, then fanned them out. The dust reached her nostrils and pricked them; she sneezed. She had no idea how she would feel when she saw Bruce again. She supposed, if she were honest with herself, it would depend on how he felt when he saw her, and this shamed her all over again, but it seemed immovable. Perhaps he would decide, then, how things would be. There was little in between that Knox could discern: she had done something terrible, or she hadn't. Her mouth was dry. Her heart was doing that thing it sometimes did when she ran: beating too hard and too irregularly in her chest, frightening her.

Knox put the paperbacks down on the sideboard shelf, wrapped her arms around herself. It was freezing in here. Maybe she needed to eat something. Instead of making the necessary motions toward the door, Knox knelt beside the box, then lay fully down beside it, twining her fingers over her eyes. Just for a minute she thought. I won't move.

She heard someone pushing their way through the open closet that linked her parents' dressing room to hers; her mother had had the closet's back removed when Knox was born, so that night visits could be accomplished more quickly. There was the scrape of clothing being pushed to one side, a rattle as the neat rows of slacks and blouses her mother kept there swung back into place. Knox knew she should sit up, that the sight of her on the floor might be alarming, but she couldn't seem to initiate the set of small, bodily tasks that would accomplish this.

"Honey?"

Her father's voice. Knox did sit up, realizing how sure she'd been that it would be her mother who would appear; she felt guilty at the sight of her father's ashen face. He loomed over her in the oversize navy bathrobe he'd worn on Sunday mornings ever since she could remember, his features clean shaven—he must have showered already—this evidence of routine reestablished relieved Knox somewhat even as she organized herself and scrambled to her feet.

"Daddy, I'm fine! I was just—lying on the floor." She laughed nervously. When she reached to touch his arm, he batted her fingers away lightly and gathered her into a hug. Knox had long been as tall as her father, but she reflexively bent her knees a bit and lowered her head so that it was flush with her father's shoulder and stood like that, buried in the fragrant, dark blue plush of the robe, so that after a few moments she forgot if her eyes were open or closed. She felt her throat constricting and forced herself to pull back and smile at him, her hands clasped around his upper arms. Her father smiled at her as if from a great distance, as if he were smiling into a camera with the sun before him, unable to make out exactly where the lens was.

"What are you doing here?" he asked her.

"I don't know. I just didn't want to be at home, I guess."

"That's right," he said, patting her cheek and then settling himself into her desk chair. Knox noticed he was moving stiffly, that he grasped the sides of the chair with both hands. Please don't get old, she thought. Not yet. "You should have slept here last night," he said. "I don't know why I didn't think to make sure of it."

Knox flushed, despite herself.

"You stay right here," he said. "You just move right back in here if that's what you want to do. Goodness knows Mom and I would love it." His eyes were the color of the cornflowers that grew wild at the back of the property, such a clear, delicate color, a surprise in an otherwise rugged face. He seemed to stare right into her. Knox remembered again how elemental, steady, and unquestioned her love for her father was—as much a part of her as those photographs on the desk were part of the room.

"Do you want some breakfast," she asked him, though of course he was perfectly capable of getting breakfast for himself, if he wanted to.

"Couldn't eat," he said. He patted at his stomach, hidden somewhere under the folds of the robe. "Maybe I'll lose some weight." The skin around his eyes crinkled; he seemed to wince at his own poor joke.

"All I want to do is eat," Knox offered.

"Lord knows there's plenty of food. I have no idea what we're going to do with it all."

"Well. You can take it to the office."

Knox's statement hung in the air; she wondered suddenly when, even whether, her father would go back to working full days again, he who'd built everything here. She was still standing; she lowered herself back onto the floor. Her father looked about him, taking in the details of the room.

"I come in here to sleep sometimes, did you know that? When your mother is snoring." He grinned. "I like this room. What's going on there?" He pointed to the box.

"Just packing up some books for the center. I don't read them anymore."

Her father looked stricken for a moment, then recovered. "Don't take too many. I like things in here the way they are."

He smoothed his hand across the wooden surface of the desk, then picked up one of the picture frames, the one that held the photo of their whole family together. He studied it. Knox kept expecting him to put it down, but he seemed to peer closer at it as the seconds ticked by.

His eyes swung back up to her face, appraising.

"You've turned out," he said, surprising her. If anything, it seemed inevitable that the comment he'd make would be about Charlotte, her presence in the picture versus her absence now.

He handed the frame to her, and she forced herself to look at the image it contained. She might have been eleven or twelve; pale and freckled, her strawberry hair cut unflatteringly and caught up by the wind, she stood next to her sister, the slim stalk of her arm protruding out of the cap sleeve of her Easter dress to touch Charlotte, as if to guide her sister back into the group. Charlotte had drifted into the foreground and her mouth was open, partially smiling; she appeared to be giving direction to the photographer, or attempting to complete a story she'd begun before they'd all assumed their poses. Her sister wore a gauzy peasant skirt. Whereas Knox looked embattled by the weather, which was obviously a bit too chilly for the clothes they all wore—her cheeks and knees reddened, the skin on her bare legs mottled and vaguely blue—Charlotte looked like some gypsy on a heath. She looked . . . resplendent. The energy in her body and swirling hair seemed to strain away from Knox's touch, away from all of them. There was no weather that wouldn't suit her and no contest here, never had been. Her sister's beauty and vitality jumped out of the picture, eclipsing all of them: the pink suggestion of Robbie in the bassinet, her mother, hip cocked, in high-waisted jeans, her father with a nearly comical abundance of hair.

"What do you mean," Knox said, looking up.

"When you were born, there was something fragile about you. I can't explain it. It wasn't like the boys—you were skinny, but you weren't premature, you were *healthy*. It was more like you had a tenuous hold on things. It felt like we could see through your skin, sometimes. You didn't grow as fast or as early as your sister had, I guess, and she was all we'd known. You clung to us like a little weed. We worried about you."

Knox nodded, unsure how to respond.

"And look at you now," he went on. He smiled at her with such love that Knox had to will herself not to glance away.

In her mind, she implored: Tell me. What do you see? She had no idea how people saw her; it often surprised her that they saw her at all.

"I got tall," she said instead, calm as she could. "You're biased, anyway."

"You turned out," her father said. He rocked forward in the chair, effectively closing the subject. "You've always been hard on yourself."

The thought entered her consciousness: She could confide in

him. He would understand, better than she did, certainly, why she'd gone over to see Bruce last night and stayed, whether or not that constituted a betrayal or one night out of many spent trying to caulk a wound.

"Honey, you all right?" her father asked her.

"I don't know."

He cocked his graying head, considering. Knox sat alert, ready to incriminate herself. She set the photograph down beside her on the rug, faceup.

"You think the boys are going to be all right?" he said.

Knox cleared her throat. But before she could muster any words, her mouth flooded with saliva; she wondered, suddenly, if she was going to be sick.

"Knoxie? You need a glass of water?" Her father raised himself halfway out of the chair.

She shook her head, first slowly, then faster before she stopped. She rubbed at her face with her hands, ordering herself to recover. She'd come this close to burdening, bewildering, her father with a needless . . . God. The smile on her face when she raised her head again was as dazzling as she could make it.

"You know what? I think I do need some breakfast," Knox said. "I just got a little shaky."

"Okay," her father said, watching her.

She didn't need his benediction—or if she did, it wasn't fair to ask him for it. This was a moment in a lifetime of moments. She'd move through it. It occurred to her that this was how Charlotte might have felt within her days, ruthless within a self-generated propulsion that kept her from getting caught up in every small exchange. Was this the greatest difference between them? It felt revelatory that she might simply move through. Though it was possible that lack of sleep and the sense of incredulity that had been dogging her for days was responsible for the punchy relief that was filling her now, filling her very lungs with air.

"Dad," she said, after a pause. "Are you going to go to work?"

"Not today," he said.

"Soon?"

He scanned the ceiling, and sighed.

"I suppose. Setting yearling reserves doesn't really seem to matter right now."

"Sorry."

He drew the lapels of his robe closer to each other with his fingers, and tucked his hands into his armpits.

"Cold in here."

"Yeah."

"Let's go downstairs."

They made their way to the kitchen. They sat across from each other at the table, the cereal in their bowls untouched, and outside the crows, who wintered together in the bare locust tree near the house, numerous as leaves, strutted in the yard. It would be another hour before her mother appeared, noon before Robbie, dressed for his flight back to Virginia, slipped into his chair and joined them.

KNOX'S MOTHER reached into a suede purse she'd drawn out of the coat closet, extracted a brush no bigger than her hand, and started dragging it through her hair. She dropped it back into the purse, fished out a lipstick, and applied it blind with an expert touch to her puckered mouth. Her face looked grim. Earlier, she'd said to Knox, "I think I should go check on the boys." The way she'd looked at Knox as she spoke, then nodded after, as if something had been decided, seemed to Knox to signal an unspoken invitation or a plea for an escort. Had Knox become the caretaker, as opposed to the overgrown cared-for, so quickly? She nodded back, trying to convey her understanding. Like that, they were readying themselves, letting themselves out into the cold, headed for the garage, though the walk to the guesthouse would take no more than a quarter of an hour. Perhaps her mother needed to seize the moment, lest her resolve fail her; Knox could tell that the proximity of Ethan and Ben was somehow frightening to Mina; from her place in the passenger seat, she watched her mother jam the keys into the ignition.

"Dad seemed good this morning," Knox said. "Better."

"Really," her mother said loudly, her body turned to peer out the back window as she waited for the garage door to grind toward its apex. "That surprises me."

Knox swallowed. She was used to reflexive comfort from her mother, not cold truth. She resisted the urge to press her mother further, to wheedle some reassurance out of her. She stilled her foot, which was tapping in the well; she felt as if she'd drunk a pot of coffee when she'd had none at all this morning. There was the question of how she should act when she saw Bruce, separate from, but related to, the question of how she should feel. As her mother navigated the sloping drive, signaling at the bottom despite the fact that they occupied what might be the sole moving car for miles around on this quiet morning, she sensed a growing giddiness in herself that felt tied up in her childhood memories of being driven everywhere by her mother, in her desire to distance herself from whatever her mother had meant just now, from the weight of . . . everything. It might be crazy, but why couldn't she imagine a trajectory in which the night before played toward its best and furthest conclusion? The momentum she'd sensed during her conversation with her father seemed to be taking hold of her. What if she just capitulated to it, completely? What would happen? What if she tried not to care? She failed to recognize herself in these questions, which was good. Even exhilarating.

They wound through a stand of bare walnut trees, straight as flagpoles on either side of the access road.

"Mom," Knox said suddenly. "Do I smell smoke?"

"No," her mother said, her face expressionless.

"I'm not going to ground you."

"I quit years ago. Anyway, it doesn't matter."

"Okay," Knox said. She kept her voice gentle. It wouldn't do to let any more of this in than she could help. She saw that now. It wouldn't help any of them.

"Just, if you have anything you need to get off your chest, anything at all, I am here to listen. I can't promise I'll like what you say, but I won't leave you alone with it."

It was, deliberately, the same speech Mina used to give Charlotte, so many years ago. The barest hint of a smile flickered across her mother's face, then was gone.

When they pulled up to the guesthouse, Bruce stood out front with the double carriage, one of the boys bundled in his arms. He drew his unsmiling face close to the twin's, and pointed at their car, then pumped the baby's mittened hand into a wave. Mina took one of her hands off the wheel and waved back.

"Look," Knox heard herself say, pointlessly. But she wanted to claim the tableau with a word somehow, to direct attention toward it as if it were hers. She and her mother climbed out of the car.

"I was going to take them for a walk," Bruce called. He seemed isolated against the landscape; it was lonely here; they should have come earlier. "Of course it's only taken us an hour to get ready."

"Let me see," Mina said. She strode toward the carriage where Ben lay, then straightened and stood on tiptoe, her flats falling groundward to expose her pink heels, to see Ethan. She reached to touch his face, and Knox thought of the way she'd always been taught to approach a horse that might bite: slowly as opposed to tentatively, palm flat and open. As Mina stroked Ethan's cheek, her face seemed to relax a little, though the set determination Knox recognized in her features hadn't completely dissolved.

"He doesn't know me," Mina said.

"Of course he does," Bruce said, looking straight at her. "Don't you, Eth?"

"Maybe you should take them, Mama," Knox said.

"I don't know where there is to go," her mother said. "Down to the yearling barn? Isn't it too cold?"

"They just like the motion," Bruce said. He settled Ethan in beside Ben; Knox noted how much more efficient he'd gotten at the strapping since she'd first arrived in New York. He drew a blanket from the basket under the chassis and tucked it over both boys so that only their heads, swaddled in the hoods of their fleece buntings, were visible. "It would be a real help, Mina. They're bored of the sight of me."

"Is there a bottle for them? What if they start to cry?"

"There's a warmed one right here," Bruce said, gesturing to a little bag strapped over one of the carriage handles. "But if they really fuss, just head back, and Knox can deal with it."

Knox laughed. Her mother looked lost. She glanced from Bruce's face to Knox's, and back again.

"Okay," she said, wrapping her fingers around the push-bar. "Wish me luck, then." She picked her way down the walk and headed right, back onto the access road they'd driven in on. The only sound they heard was the squeak one of the wheels made against the blacktop.

"Do you want some tea?" Bruce said, startling her. Now that they were alone together, she had no idea what to say or where to look.

"That sounds great."

She followed him into the kitchen. It was odd; she couldn't think of a moment they'd ever been alone together. Her family, the boys—there was always another presence, somewhere in the house.

"That was nice of you, to nudge Mom like that."

"Not at all, it's good for me. I can use the break." Bruce opened a cabinet. A layer of checkered shelf paper winged its way to the floor and rasped against the linoleum; there was nothing else in the cabinet.

"You know," Bruce said, sounding surprised. "I have no idea if there's really tea."

"Bourbon?" It was Knox's attempt at a joke, an allusion to the awkwardness she sensed in them both, but when Bruce turned to her, she couldn't be sure how he'd taken it. He looked pale. He was wearing the same clothes he'd worn last night—as was she. He crossed his arms over his chest and rubbed at his upper arms; a shiver seemed to run through him.

"I could look," he said.

"Oh, I don't really want any." Knox watched him. The energy in her limbs had no place to rest; she wished she could stretch her arms around him, or dance, or take charge of the tea making if in fact there was anything in the cupboard to fix, which she knew there wouldn't be. There was only her lasagna, and some milk and juice in the fridge, the fruit in the bowl, and formula. Nothing else. She made herself sit. Her palms were clammy; she rubbed them against her jeans. Her brain and body seemed to be apprehending things separately and by degrees: Bruce was panicked. This was the way it was going to be. It was her job, now, to make him feel otherwise. Because there would be no convincing him that what had occurred between them was the beginning of something new, something else.

As that thought penetrated her, she felt herself calming.

"Bruce," she said, once she felt assured that she could keep her voice from shaking, "you don't have to worry."

"I love your sister," he said simply and with relief, finally meeting her gaze.

"I *know*."

"I'm sorry," he said.

"There's no good and no bad," she said. Her voice sounded resonant in this airless space, convincing.

"It has nothing to do with you," Bruce said, taking a step toward her, then stopping himself. "I just can't—I shouldn't have—"

"Bruce. You didn't do anything wrong. We're the same people as before. There's no good and no bad and you don't have to worry."

She was repeating herself, as much to apprehend her own words as to make him understand. This was a change, this calm stealing over her in the midst of complication. She'd never denied herself the right to sort things into categories of right and wrong. Yet here she was, as much a moral relativist as she'd ever accused Charlotte of being.

She patted the seat of the chair beside her, and pushed it away from the table with her foot. Bruce sat down. She reached for his hand and held it chastely, briefly, before releasing it. She was balancing Bruce's doubt with her own certainty, and this felt right. She could sense his gratitude. Her setting aside the alternate universe she'd allowed to take rough shape in her mind earlier, if only to test her own audacity, felt like a physical undertaking; her blood itself seemed to bow for a moment under the weight of it, and then every cell in her body felt abruptly free. She knew it couldn't last, even that the very lightness in her might be a measure of the distance she had to cover when she crashed back to earth, but she felt she could lift the gloomy house they sat in from its foundations if she wanted to. Bruce was beautiful, his face a study in hollows and sadness and concentration. He'd been Charlotte's, but, in an irrevocable way, part of him belonged to her now, too; this had been true, hadn't it, even before they'd come back to Kentucky. He took her in with his eyes.

Knox's mother burst into the kitchen.

"Come and help me get them out," she said. Her face was exultant. "I don't know how to work the strap thingies. Oh, we've had the nicest walk!"

There were moments in everyone's life, Knox supposed, that showed you that you weren't the person you thought. Maybe these moments taught you something good about yourself, or shamed you. Whether you kept them to yourself or spent your time talking to anybody who'd listen in an effort to decode their meaning, or to reshape the truth until it became something you could live with, depended on the person. Marlene loved to talk about the moment her mean-as-dirt mother-in-law died, and she (Marlene) found herself supporting her even meaner-than-dirt father-in-law by the elbow at the internment as he cried, shocking herself most of all when she reached one arm around his stooped shoulders and stood there rubbing at his back, half expecting him to shake her off right there in front of the minister, when instead he folded himself into her embrace. She didn't tell the story to brag on herself— more to illustrate, Knox thought, the possibilities in people, the unseen forces that could nudge us further open, or further toward kindness, than we might expect.

Bruce smiled at her. They followed Mina outside. Later, they would bring the boys back to Knox's parents' house, arrange them on the sofa, watch them, begin to think about dinner, discuss, tentatively, the rhythm of the days ahead. Ben would appear; Knox would allow herself the briefest moment of curiosity: had it been her grace that made these small steps forward possible?

I'll tell Marlene, Knox thought, feeling dizzy as she rose, the depth of her exhaustion making itself fully felt for the first time since early morning. She'll be the only one.

·IV·

KNOX

KNOX COULD REMEMBER a day in New York, before they'd flown home for Charlotte's memorial, when she'd tried to imagine life a year hence. Now here she was, the leaves stirring overhead, pausing between each step she took along the serpentine path that led through this section of Washington Square Park, holding the boys' hands in her own. At fourteen months, they were walking, though Ethan, his ankles flexible as a dancer's, had only just begun to, his face cohering into a proud, secretive smile each time he pulled himself up and propelled forward without stumbling.

"Woof!" Ben squealed. He pulled at her hand, trying to speed her along. "There!" A woman who was passing them, pushing an elaborate pram, smiled at Knox, a smile of beneficent inclusion. They were drawing closer to the dog run. Knox tousled Ethan's hair—curly and coarse, now, grown past the tops of his ears, and stood close behind him so she could brace him against her shins if he toppled backward in his excitement. The boys pressed themselves against the link fence, exclaiming over each animal that ventured close enough to nose at them through the wire. This was their safari, she thought, while she sipped her coffee out of a paper cup, her arms drawn close to her sides against the early morning chill. They'd been up since six. When the boys began to stamp and chatter, Knox would set her cup down and rub her hands up and down against their sleeves, then against their cheeks until they laughed. She'd lead them all to the nearby diner Bruce had pointed out for her on Sixth Avenue, where they'd jostle together in a booth and she'd treat them to hot chocolates and the chewy, golden pancakes it seemed possible to procure on every corner in New York.

In the past year, Bruce had left his company and taken a salary cut to work at a firm that agreed to let him follow his accounts from home one day a week. The nanny he'd eventually hired was named Maya; she came from Tbilisi, where she'd known war on the streets and the disappearance of two uncles; and yet she was so full of the purest love for the boys, and joyful in their presence, that Knox wondered that she hadn't been more obviously damaged by her short history. It seemed sometimes to be luck, to Knox, whether or not one was scathed. And at other times, she felt it was a matter of deciding. Bruce told her that Maya came every day to the house on Bank Street, at eight o'clock, and left after the boys were in bed.

Bruce and Charlotte's house was different on this visit than it had been before; the clutches of toys on the floor of the living room, the smells of Maya's cooking for the boys, had infused it with a different kind of life. Knox's attic was still hers, though, as she'd hoped it would be. After she returned this morning with the boys, she would sit in the window seat and wait while Bruce fussed with the coffee in the kitchen. She would watch the street: the strange people, coming and going, different people every day, the odds stacked against their appearing before Knox at any point in the future. This had been Charlotte's view, so different from the one Knox had had, at home, of her swan, her withered catalpa, her still pond, the tractors crawling in the distance.

It was a mystery, having a sister.

Her father's career had been focused on a kind of translation of genetic possibilities into reality; he knew as well as anyone that the same set of parents could result in a bafflingly disparate set of siblings, one fast, one knock-kneed, one easy, one rambunctious under the bit, difficult to break. She had worked as a translator in her own small way, though it was pretentious to call herself one, organizing symbols and sounds that made no sense to her students into symbols and sounds that did. Now Knox felt herself struggling to apprehend the meaning of her life thus far: her life with Charlotte, and her life without. For so long, she had assumed that the fact that Charlotte was one way necessarily meant that she was another. To admit that this had been a falsehood was to admit that she was charged with starting over, and didn't know word one of the language.

She pictured Charlotte, down there on the sidewalk, hurrying by, dressed as she had been in the picture on Knox's desk all these years, her skirt and hair whirling after her as she zigged around a low grate, the kind New Yorkers put in to establish parameters around trees. Knox almost wanted to knock on the window, so compelling was the vision. Instead, she whispered Charlotte's name, over and over.

BRUCE WAS finishing a story he'd begun from the kitchen, though why he'd chosen to yell at her from another room instead of waiting to settle beside her before commencing any kind of conversation she didn't know. Nerves, probably. Finally, he reappeared in the room where she sat with one eye on the boys, who were thrusting the contents of one of their toy baskets onto the floor and exclaiming at each other in nonsensical syllables. For the umpteenth time this weekend, Knox felt a rush of gladness that they had each other.

"So Iris, the neighbor, has another name for me, it turns out. She slipped an e-mail address under my door yesterday."

"Women will flock to you," Knox said, accepting her coffee. "Tragedy is sexy." Terrible jokes were the province of the bereaved.

"Well, I'm not looking," Bruce said. "Obviously."

"Not so obviously," Knox said.

Bruce took a sip from his mug. He may have been pretending he hadn't heard her.

"Sorry," she said.

Bruce had a friend coming for dinner, a guy named Toby he'd recently gotten back in touch with.

"Do you want Maya to stay?" Bruce asked her. "You could read to the boys and put them to bed instead, if you want to."

"I don't know," Knox said. "I don't want to confuse anyone's routine."

"It would be great," Bruce said. "The boys would love it." Knox searched his face and judged him sincere. She nodded.

"Okay," she said.

"What about you," Bruce asked. "Tell me."

Knox cast her mind back to the times Charlotte used to use that phrase with her, snuggled up next to her in bed, appeasing. There were few times when Charlotte had paused long enough in the narrative of her own becoming, one she seemed bent on sharing with Knox in childhood, even when her young ears felt too small to contain it, to ask such a question; but those times had obviously meant something, because Knox remembered them with such clarity.

Ethan was suddenly at her feet. He tugged at the hem of her jeans, wanting to be picked up and gathered into her arms. Knox swung him into her lap, looked at Bruce, and shrugged, smiling. She would get back on a plane tomorrow for the return leg of a trip that would become terribly familiar to her over the coming years. She supposed that, somewhere in the spaces between Charlotte's home and hers, she might begin to find out the answer to Bruce's question, if she were lucky. She knew she was grateful for the ease between herself and her brother-in-law—for he would always be that—that allowed him to ask it, an ease made possible by their tacit agreement, made that distant afternoon in the kitchen of the farm's drafty guesthouse, never to touch each other again.

· · ·

IT WAS ONLY LATER that Knox questioned whether or not she had been present at all in the hospital the night Charlotte died. Just a halfway question really, not true delusion. She would think about absence. About how, in a certain kind of story, a photo is examined and the people who have let a ghost walk among them, and thought it human, exclaim over the blank space where the ghost's image should be. She'd seen movies where this happened, or maybe heard the trick described in the scare stories that so often got retold for cheap thrills whenever girls got together in the dark. A picture, a smiling group, and in the middle, where the affable stranger (the one whom nobody had been able to get enough of) should be standing, would be just some blurry thing, some corona, with cars or houses or oblivious pedestrians exposed behind it. From within her own blank and disappeared space Knox would wonder where she had been at the moment that intern first rushed up to them and began speaking. Sometimes she thought of the intern as time itself, approaching too quickly, taking her arm and speeding her away.

The foaling season began in the spring and lasted through the early summer. Regardless of their particular birthdays, per a long-standing mandate of the Jockey Club, each foal on her parents' farm—on any Thoroughbred farm, anywhere in the world— turned one on the first of January. This was the first day of their lives as yearlings, all; though the foals born in March looked nearly ready to race, and the June foals looked so runty it was a judgment call whether or not they'd be entered in the sale or kept back six months and sold privately. Back in Kentucky, Knox could probably count on four fingers the times during the last decade that there had been snow on the ground on New Year's Day, and today was no exception; there was a gray-yellow light suffusing the sky, the sun showed thin, and the grass was the color of weathered cardboard, rough under her boots. On their communal birthday, the new yearlings had no notion that they'd become artificially older overnight. Their breath steamed from their mouths; they stamped as Knox came into sight. What was time to them, or change?

They had moved toward Bruce's bed in the guesthouse that night after the memorial and lay down together, Bruce's mouth rough on hers. Knox hadn't been surprised by her own urgency; she had just given way to it, as if it had been expected, as if she'd felt it before. Nothing could surprise her now. Her mother had made up the bed in the cold room with her own hands, and Knox thought of Charlotte at every moment; when her fingers pressed against Bruce's ribs, she thought of Charlotte's fingers there; when Bruce's knee thrust itself between her legs and parted them, she thought of Charlotte's legs, parting. Yet despite these thoughts, her desire was her own. She couldn't slake it fast enough. She gripped Bruce's lean back with her hands and rocked under him. She slid her hand over the inseam of his pants, and then under the fabric to feel him there, her hand gripping him, so different entirely from Ned, or from anyone, longer, smoother under her fingers. He was so hard. And in that strange house, he was suddenly beautiful. Knox never closed her eyes. She strained, in the dark, to see everything: his long thighs, the singular concentration in his face.

They made love twice, and after the second time, when Bruce had covered the length of her with his body to shield it from the cold and they lay there like that, silent, perhaps shocked at last, one of the babies started crying.

"Oh my God," Knox said.

"It's time for the next feeding," Bruce said.

They got up together. Knox snatched up Bruce's dress shirt from that day on her way out of the room simply to button up against the chill; Bruce stayed as he was. In the kitchen, they poured water from an old kettle into two clean bottles, working side by side. By the time they had mounted the stairs, the boys were in full cry.

They had to sit on the floor to feed them; there were no chairs. The boys opened their mouths like birds, then closed their lips around the bottles Bruce and Knox offered them, silent at once, except for the odd swallowing sound, and the intermittent little hum that Ethan tended to make when he was drinking.

After a few minutes, Knox said, "In a Victorian novel, we would get married." Her voice rasped as if she'd been awake for days.

"Read a lot of Victorian novels?"

"Some."

Bruce smiled at her.

"Don't worry. I don't want to marry you," she said.

"Thanks."

"Why am I happy," Knox said.

"I don't know. Me too."

It was strange, but there it was.

She would be kidding herself if she denied having pictured other things in those moments. She pictured herself back in her attic room, having claimed it for herself, then in Bruce's room, having been claimed by him through an act of magical transference that circumvented all questions, all obstacles. She knew this was fantasy. But for Knox, even the most impossible of projections felt like the result of a process she'd hitherto felt incapable of, maybe *been* incapable of. She had an imagination after all.

She'd found a family, and it wasn't hers. Call it tragic irony or a positive sign; whatever name it went by wasn't going to make the next part any easier.

Bruce had stayed out the week, then packed up the boys and taken them back to New York. He'd had no intention of staying on any longer, and though he'd exacted promises from each of them for extended visits later in the fall, Knox could see that the life he'd known with Charlotte and would return to now—inasmuch as he could—held far more pull than this place did. Than she did. And that was only right. Still, he'd left the boys with her parents and some soft toys on their living room rug and walked down to her cabin on his last afternoon to talk to her.

"I've been thinking, I want you to come every other month for at least a day or two," he'd said. "If you're willing. I think Ethan and Ben would benefit from that. I'd like them to know you and for you to be part of their life."

He'd spoken so formally, she'd wanted to laugh. At least sit down, she'd been thinking. At least ransack my refrigerator. Don't stand there like a stranger.

She stopped herself from referring to the center. Fall term was fully under way now, and she knew Marlene had been snowed from taking up her slack, but she didn't feel like pretending, even to herself, that her work there constituted a career she couldn't turn away from when she wanted to. She was good at the kind of teaching she did, but she was replaceable; this summer had proven that. And hadn't that been part of the appeal of her position, if she was being honest?

"I'll see," she told him, simply.

"Would Ned—"

"No. Don't."

Bruce blinked. It was strange, having him here; as if reading her thoughts, he looked around.

"I've never been in here before," he said. "It's nice."

"Thank you."

He looked at her.

"Charlotte knew you loved her," he said. "It was hard for her to absorb things like that and trust them when she was at her worst, but I wouldn't worry about the kind of sister you were or weren't. Just worrying about that at all is more than some siblings do."

Though this felt like cold comfort, Knox nodded.

"Thank you," she said.

Bruce rubbed at his chin. Like her, he made the rooms and furniture in her cabin look diminutive with his height. He sighed.

"I am so tired," he said, and smiled. "So, so fucking tired."

"I know."

"Knox. I'm really grateful to you."

"I know," she said. And though it wasn't all she wanted now, if she told herself the truth, it was best. She needed to sort out her reasons for wanting anything before she proceeded into the next day, and the next, it seemed. On the wind-blasted tundra that was suddenly her life, it was important to stand still and gather her bearings before she took her next step.

Every year, her father repainted these fences, set the budget for mowing, plowed the muck pile under, and sowed it with lime. The horses that were gathering at the fence line to get a good look at her now were birthed, raised, sold. Some were bred or buried here, too. The whole life of Four Corners was conducted in cycles, from the menses and gestation periods of the mares to the seasons sold for each stallion, and of course the farm, under her family's stewardship, had had a life, too, a life that was only a fragment of a greater, longer existence. If her parents decided to sell— and they'd been talking about it, she knew, though they were trying not to let her hear—another family would live here, raise Thoroughbreds here, or not. If the easements held, the acreage would survive undeveloped, though who could say whether or when larger parcels would be sold off, their boundaries changed, refenced, replanted, built out in various ways.

The defining misapprehension of her life, Knox now saw, was that one could work to protect a private world, to encase it, arrest it. How, when she'd grown up here, surrounded by sex, birth, and death, by live, fallible organisms everywhere, had she allowed herself to fall for this idea? But she had, while all the time, the animals around her moved through their infancies, childhoods, middle years, declines, deaths; the grass faded and browned and was reborn. Knox had worshipped the ascension, the foaling season, the spring, without recognizing the point on the arc at which things naturally gave way.

Charlotte would have died on another day, if not on the day Ethan and Ben were born. Before Charlotte died, Knox hadn't known, really known, that any of them would die; she supposed this was one definition of childhood. The way Charlotte changed everything, in life *and* in death, felt accelerated, shocking, but of course change was the very stuff they were made of. Last night she had rung in the New Year alone, having begged off the party she and Ned had agreed to go to months before, a predictable balloon-drop thing at a local country club, the kind of event made more palatable by the ease with which they could make fun of it, back when there was ease between them to speak of. Ned was a gentleman; though she'd steeled herself and explained to him as best she could about how she'd known nothing, not even herself, and thus couldn't be expected to know that the unspoken promises she'd been making him were hollow at their core all this time, he was the type to honor previous commitments, and there had been no question of him not taking her to the party. So she'd been the one to back out, and sat at her frost-webbed window with a cup of weak tea, watching the dark, and wondering if she'd find the courage to take Bruce up on his invitation to join the boys' lives in some way, or if this, too, would be a path to forming herself in the new gaps Charlotte's absence had left, as opposed to the old ones. She'd been made of putty, with a talent only for occupying the hollows that had been bequeathed to her, and no idea what else to do.

Time would tell. She reached into one of the roomy pockets in her barn jacket; she'd brought apples. Birthday presents. She swung herself over the gate, lit on the hard, packed earth on the other side. She made a few clicking noises out the side of her mouth; in an instant the yearlings were nuzzling at her hands. Though she, and her parents, and Robbie, Bruce, and the boys, had survived, no aspect of their old family remained. They were a new family, born together with Ethan and Ben. Just as all the foals on the farm held one birthday in common, so all of them held an hour in common, after which they were new people with new lives. Each day from now on would be fraught with the music of accident, even of catastrophe; Knox was mortal, as was everything and everyone she'd ever loved. This was the music that had always been playing, its notes the only constant in all the world; she could finally make it out, humming in the dead grass and within every breath and step she took. The view, at least, was undiminished by the rhythm of it; she could see half the county from here, when she raised her head, and the house she'd grown up in, and the horses surrounding her and the way the land looked, as beautiful as ever. She scattered the rest of the apples on the ground, turned, and kept walking.

ACKNOWLEDGMENTS

THANK YOU to my parents, Blythe and Robert Clay, who have made every good thing possible, and who I'm just plain crazy about. Thanks to each member of my beloved family and in-law family for years of encouragement, interest, and support. Particular thanks are due to my brother Case and his wife, Lorin; to Lorraine Clay and Elizabeth Baldwin; to Sylvia and Joe Frelinghuysen; to Joy de Vink; and to Gioia and John Frelinghuysen. My gratitude to my husband, Nick, for the untold things he is and does for me every day, and to our beautiful daughters, Amelia and May, is boundless.

To Bill Clegg, my knight in shining armor, and to the gifted Jordan Pavlin for her unerring eye, careful hand, and innate kindness: I cannot thank either of you enough for your guidance, efforts, generosity, and patience, and feel so fortunate to know and work with both of you.

Thanks to Naomi Schub, Leslie Levine, Matt Hudson, Sue Betz, Kathleen Fridella, Peggy Samedi, Maggie Hinders, Carol Carson, Emmy Kenan, the MacDowell Colony, the people at Paragraph, and my teachers and friends from my time at Columbia for crucial help along the way.

Finally, thanks to Jenny Minton Quigley, without whom this book—and many other, much more important things—would not exist, and whose steadfast belief and friendship are among the great gifts of my life. Jenny, I love and will always be grateful to you.

Meet with Interesting People
Enjoy Stimulating Conversation
Discover Wonderful Books